Previous Books by Author

Remember the Words
Belonging After All

Justice Series

Justice in Omaha
Justice in Charleston
Justice in Hershey

e-Book

Did My Children Survive My Death? Don't Drink and Drive

JUSTICE IN SAN FRANCISCO

4TH IN JUSTICE SERIES

BARBARA E. SAEFKE

Order this book online at www.trafford.com
or email orders@trafford.com

Most Trafford titles are also available at major online book retailers.

Print information available on the last page.

ISBN: 978-1-4907-8936-1 (sc)
ISBN: 978-1-4907-8935-4 (hc)
ISBN: 978-1-4907-8939-2 (e)

Library of Congress Control Number: 2018947153

Trafford rev. 07/05/2018

www.trafford.com

North America & international
toll-free: 1 888 232 4444 (USA & Canada)
fax: 812 355 4082

An author reads and rereads their finished manuscript many times. With each reading of editing and correcting mysteriously appears another grammatical error of some kind or another. We then say, mostly out loud after the fifth time through, "How did I miss that?" With each reading, they are corrected. At some point, the author is so familiar with the story that these types of errors are missed, and as we read, our brains fill in the words that should be and not the ones written. So please be patient with us as we are not careless, as it would seem, but we may be too diligent and, hence, the errors. Please make the correction in your mind and keep reading.

CAST OF CHARACTERS

Jake and Peggy Farms	
Arnie and Adeline Cole	– Friends and longtime residents of Boone, Iowa
Roger Lange	– Former hardware store owner
Pam Farms	– Jake's mom
Lenny Farms	– Pam's ex-husband
Rick Farms	– Lenny's brother
Paula and Noah Bailey	– Peggy's parents
Penny Bailey	– Peggy's sister
Ross Wagner	– Penny's boyfriend
John Mason	– Jake's contact
Max Hunter	– John's best friend
Ella Hunter	– Max's wife
Nell Baxter	– John's lady friend
John Sr. and Michelle Mason	– John's parents
Mike Nash	– John's policeman friend and contact in San Francisco
Barry Ward, May Wells, Gabby Landers, Jane Miller, Jim Kennedy, and Louise Fox a.k.a. Foxy	– Baristas
Marie Ward	– Barry's mom
Myra	– Local bakery owner
Sue	– Manager at the library
Joyce Armstrong	– Lives in Omaha, runs the children's shelter, and helps the Justice Team
Brad Hensley	– Helps Joyce at the children's shelter in Omaha and the Justice Team
Paul and Anita Stewart, Baby Cassie	– John's friends from college who live in Boone, Iowa

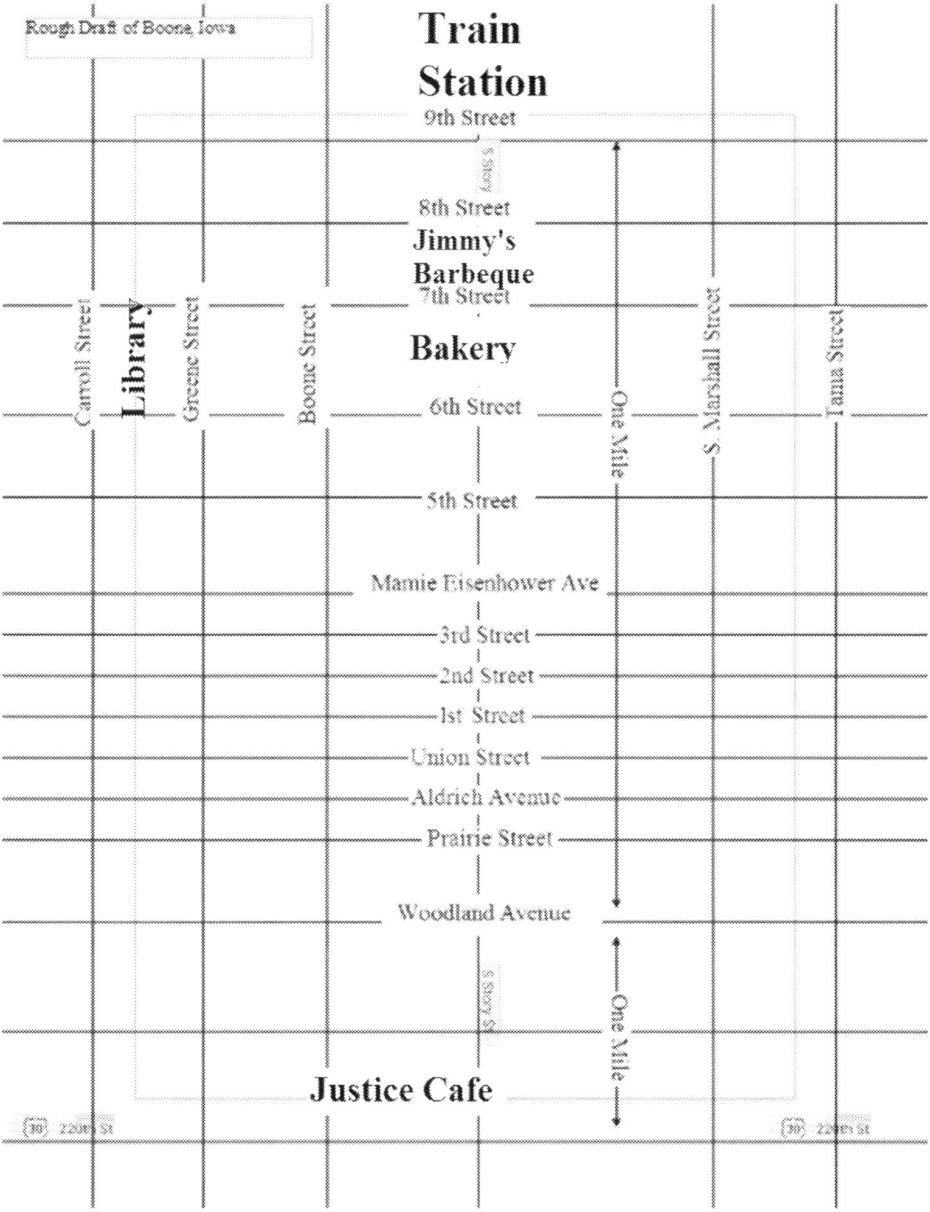

Rough Draft of Boone, Iowa

Train Station

9th Street

8th Street

Jimmy's Barbeque

7th Street

Bakery

6th Street

5th Street

Mamie Eisenhower Ave

3rd Street

2nd Street

1st Street

Union Street

Aldrich Avenue

Prairie Street

Woodland Avenue

Justice Cafe

Carroll Street

Library

Greene Street

Boone Street

One Mile

S. Marshall Street

Tama Street

One Mile

To The Fight For Justice

The fight for justice against corruption
is never easy. It never has been and
never will be. It exacts a toll on
ourselves, our families, our friends, and
especially our children. In the end, I
believe, as in my case, the price we pay
is well worth holding on to our dignity.

—Frank Serpico

CHAPTER ONE

John Mason was pacing in the Reno, Nevada airport. He was waiting for Jake and Peggy Farms' plane to land. He had all the research that he had done on his parents. He researched their names and the names John thought they'd changed them to. After several sessions with a hypnotist, John realized his dad was trying to tell him something. "If your mother and I were to change our names, they would be Heather Church and Preston Parker."

He had researched those names too. His dad was into computers and investments. His mother was very intelligent in both matters, but was only there as a resource for his father when he couldn't figure something out.

Otherwise, she took care of their only son, John Jr. Their son went to college at the University of Minnesota and met Max Hunter. They have remained friends and work at a printing company in Minneapolis.

Ever since someone claiming they were the San Francisco police told John that his parents died in a car accident, he didn't want to believe it. He still didn't believe it after the insurance paid him a settlement and he inherited his parent's hefty bank accounts. John refused to spend the money on himself, but he did spend it to get justice. He felt even though he didn't know what really happened to his parents, he could help others in finding justice for themselves.

That's when he heard of Jake, and since then, Jake has been helping him in doing just that—get justice. Jake had his own story in which he too wanted to help people. His parents left him and didn't tell Jake where they were, but even though he found his mother, he still wanted others to feel safe.

John looked at his watch, then looked at the flight arrival board. He noticed the Des Moines flight was delayed. *Crap.* He looked at his watch again. *Another thirty minutes. An eternity,* he thought.

Nell Baxter, his soon to be fiancée, helped him finish packing that morning, then made him lunch. He ate his soup but hardly touched his sandwich. Now the last thing he wanted to do was eat. He looked around and saw a Starbucks. He thought a cup of coffee would taste good. At least it was something to do as he waited.

While waiting in line, he thought of his parents and how much he missed them during the holidays, especially Christmas. The traditions they'd had for Christmas, he'd missed the most, decorating the tree after the ten-o-clock mass on Christmas Eve, drinking eggnog and eating his mother's Christmas cookies until the tree was all decorated.

On Christmas Eve, when it got dark, while most people were eating dinner, the three of them went Christmas caroling. His dad had a list of his clients, and they went to the ones who lived in the area. They went to the nursing home where his grandmother had spent several years of her life before she'd passed away. On the way home, they sang carols in the car with the windows down.

"Sir, can I help you?"

He looked up and noticed the line had moved, and it was his turn to order. "Oh yes, I would like a coffee with cream."

"Boring," said the guy behind him.

John laughed. "Trust me, I'm the most boring guy alive." He took his coffee and added his own cream, then walked back to the gate and sat down to wait.

His thoughts drifted back to Christmas Eve. When they got home from singing carols, they drank their hot chocolate, while John made hot ham and cheese sandwiches. Then it was time to sit and enjoy one another's company and head to church for mass.

John returned to the present when he saw people coming through the gate. He finished his coffee and threw the cup in the trash. He didn't describe himself to Jake and Peggy but told them he would recognize them. He hoped it was true. There was a lull, and no one was walking through to the waiting area.

Several minutes later, he saw Jake and Peggy. He waited until they walked past the chairs before he said their names.

They turned and looked at him. Peggy smiled. She recognized him from the café. "Hey, I know you."

Jake looked closer at John. "Yes, you were at the café. You took the tour."

"Yes, that was me."

"How did you know where we lived? And about the café?" Jake asked a little irritated.

"It was strictly a coincidence. My friends, whom you met, live in Boone, and I saw the grand opening in the *Boone News Republican.*"

"It *was* in the paper," said Peggy.

"I hope we aren't starting out upset with each other."

Jake smiled. "Not at all." He reached out, and they shook hands. "I'm just tired." He put his arm around Peggy. "We got up too early and didn't sleep much last night, and then our flight was delayed. Nothing a good night's sleep won't cure."

"Let's pick up your luggage and head to the rental cars."

The hotel was close to the airport. "This is probably going to be temporary, but I didn't want to drive too far the first night after traveling. I brought all the research I've done. Let's meet in my room in the morning around eight, and we can go over it. The whole thing needs a different perspective. I'll order breakfast—eggs, bacon, toast, and of course, a few pastries, and coffee."

"Make our coffee decaf."

"I will." Before John left Jake and Peggy's room, he said, "I'm so glad you're both here." He walked out and shut the door behind him.

ꕥ

Jake and Peggy were reading John's printouts. Peggy had her notebook and pen and was writing her own notes. The quiet was driving John crazy. They weren't talking, they weren't offering suggestions, and breakfast wasn't delivered yet. He could probably eat when the food did arrive, but what he wanted more than anything was his coffee.

John walked over to the dresser and decided to make a cup of coffee from the room coffee pot. He walked to the bathroom, filled his cup with water, went back, put the coffee filled filter in and poured the water into the pot, pushed the button, and put his cup underneath. He opened a cream and sugar packet, waited several minutes, and then dumped the packets into his cup.

He took a sip, noticed it wasn't that hot, so he gulped down the rest of the coffee. It wasn't that good either. *Now what?* he wondered. He watched Jake and Peggy. Peggy was writing a lot of notes. *Good,* he thought. I need all the help I can get.

John jumped when there was a loud knock at the door. He opened it, and the waiter brought in the food and set it down on the dresser. John gave him a tip and closed the door. He took the decaf pot and poured Jake and Peggy a cup of coffee. Then he poured himself one from the regular pot.

"Whenever you're ready, we can eat."

Jake set down the papers he was looking at and went over and filled his plate; Peggy did the same. John didn't think he was that hungry until the covers were taken off the food and the aroma of bacon filled the air.

They sat around the small table after Peggy removed all the research papers and put them on the bed.

"I want to read all the research before I can form an opinion. Then we can talk about what we do next."

"I feel the same way," said Peggy.

"Good. I know you'd like to be home for Christmas, so that gives us a little time. I'm hoping it won't take that long, but in case it does, are you willing to stay through Christmas, and if not, come back after Christmas?"

"I would be willing to do whatever it takes for however long it takes. Peggy and I discussed this at home, and we feel the most important thing right now is to find your parents." Jake took a sip of coffee. "When I graduated from high school, my parents disappeared, and when I couldn't find them, I moved to Boone, Iowa. I don't really know why I chose to live there. I thought about my parents a lot. When I was in Minneapolis, I met Peggy, and well, we've been together ever since. But, I wanted to find my parents, but after reading your research, I had it easy. I did find my mom, and she lives with us now. My dad was married to my mom and another lady. He chose the other lady to stay with.

"I guess what I'm trying to say is I know how it feels not to know where your parents are, and now I know how wonderful it is to have my mom in my life again. So yes, we will give you all the time it takes."

A tear rolled down John's cheek, and he quickly wiped it away. "Thanks." He busied himself with eating his breakfast.

They continued eating in silence, and when they were finished, John took away the dishes and set the tray outside in the hall. Jake and Peggy continued reading the research.

John decided to go for a walk and left them alone.

ꕥ

Pam, Jake's mom, drove over to Roger's for dinner. He was cooking meatloaf and wanted to spend all the time he could with her before he started massage school. Once classes started, he would spend a lot of time studying and doing homework. Pam was trying to think if there was something she could go to school for, or just get a hobby that she could do and keep Roger company while he studied. She'd have to think more about that.

Pam let herself in and walked to the kitchen. Roger was taking the meatloaf out of the oven. When it was safely on the top of the stove, he kissed Pam and wrapped his arms around her.

"How's my girl?"

Pam smiled. "I'm wonderful now that I'm here with you."

"You're too kind." He kissed her once more, then released her. "Let's eat, it's all ready."

Pam noticed the table was already set, so while Roger was dishing up the food, Pam poured the wine that was chilling in the fridge.

Roger said grace and let Pam take the first bite of the meatloaf.

"This is very good, Roger."

"Another recipe from Adeline. Now I know why Arnie and Adeline stayed married so long. They could fix any problem with food."

Pam wished that was true for everyone. She had been thinking of her ex-husband Lenny lately, and her wasted life being married to a man who was already married to someone else. The only positive thing to their relationship she could come up with was Jake, and she wondered why his father didn't want to see him.

While she was thinking of Lenny, she started thinking that Roger had another lady friend whom he was seeing. She knew it was crazy thinking, but she couldn't help herself after what happened to her. She didn't want to get hurt again, didn't want to ever be taken advantage of.

"You're quiet tonight. Is there something wrong?"

"Not really. Just a lot of negative thoughts going on in my head."

"I hope they're not about me."

"Yes, but I know they're not true."

Concerned, Roger set down his fork and gave Pam his full attention. "Tell me what's going on."

"I don't think I've ever told you my story. You've asked, but I kept putting it off. The reason was because I felt humiliated by my past. Jake is the only good thing that's ever happened to me. And of course, you."

"I want you to tell me what happened. Do you want to go in the living room where it's more comfortable?"

"Let's just stay here." She took a sip of wine for courage. "I got married when I was twenty, and we had Jake a year afterward. He was the best baby. My husband traveled for his job, so he wasn't home much. Things seemed fine, he kept traveling, and when Jake graduated from high school, I found out somehow that Lenny was married to someone else.

"I didn't want Jake to find out, so we moved without telling him. I wanted to get this straightened out. We stayed in a hotel for a couple of weeks, and when I thought he was going to go tell the other woman he was leaving her, he called two days later and said he was leaving me.

"I was stuck with the hotel bill and had to find a place to stay. I slept in my car, I got a job at a diner, and I was able to convince a landlord that I was good for the money even though I didn't have a down payment. He believed me. I realized that even with tips, I wouldn't be able to pay the first month's rent. I found another job during the day working in an office.

"I had to buy some clothes, which were the same pants and I just changed my blouse so it looked like I had changed outfits. I had a uniform at the diner. I went from the office, had a quick supper, then worked at the diner until midnight each day. I worked most weekends too. I waited tables, did dishes, and even cooked when the chef called in sick."

Roger had questions, but he didn't want to stop her.

"I had a little free time on the weekend when I didn't work. My plan was to save enough money so I could find Jake and tell him I was sorry for leaving him. I missed him so much. I didn't eat much because the less I ate, the more I could save.

"Jake got in touch with Lenny's brother, and he told Jake where I was. I was angry at first because I told him not to tell anyone, but when I saw Jake and Peggy in the dinner, my anger quickly left. They found me just in time for their wedding."

Roger took her hand. "I had no idea, Pam. Thank you for telling me. Now why are you having negative thoughts about me?"

"I'm thinking you have another relationship going on that I don't know about, that you are married and going to school is an excuse to go see your other wife or girlfriend. Like I said, it's all crazy thoughts."

"I have the same crazy thoughts, taking what Gail did to me and thinking you will do the same thing. We just have to trust each other. I know that's hard, considering our pasts, but trust me when I say I love only you, am seeing only you, and am kissing only you."

Pam smiled. "I know. Trust is so hard when you've been burned."

"It is. Are you ready for dessert?"

CHAPTER TWO

John thought of how easy it was to find Jake's mom and hoped his parents were just as easily found. He was actually sitting in a chair, and he didn't have the urge to pace. He felt peace, peace that things would work out, and to him, working out meant finding his parents before Christmas.

"I think I'm ready," said Peggy. "I have a few questions first."

"Ask away."

"Your parents' birth names are John Mason and Michelle Mason?"

"Yes."

"The names you think they changed them to are Preston Parker and Heather Church."

"Yes."

Peggy looked through several pages before she asked her next question. "San Francisco was where you lived with your parents, and you think they moved to Reno?"

"Yes, there is a reference to both persons living in Reno."

"What did your parents do before they left?"

"Dad worked with investments and computers. Mom helped when Dad couldn't figure out something."

"Where did he work? At home or an office?"

"He had an office a mile from home. Mom, very athletic, would walk there for lunch every day, and they would run for an hour. Then they would sit at the coffee shop by Dad's office for thirty minutes, have coffee and soup. Dad would go back to work, and Mom would walk back home."

"It was predictable. The same thing every day, five days a week."

"Yes."

Peggy wrote more notes on her tablet. She looked at John. "I think we need to start in San Francisco. I bet more than a few people knew their routine, the people at the coffee shop, the baristas making the coffee. If they had the same order over and over again, they would remember." She flipped her notes over. "But as long as we're here, we should check the address you have for Reno."

"Good idea, Peg." Jake wasn't used to not being in charge and waited for John to make the decision to get in the rental car and find the address. When the decision wasn't made, Jake said, "John, whenever Peg and I went on trips in the past, I usually took charge, but I feel you are in charge this time, so you make the decision what we do next."

"Please treat this like any trip you would go on and be in charge. If I don't agree with something, I'll say so. I'm just too caught up in the situation to think clearly."

"All right. Then let's get in the car and drive."

so cs

"Hey, Addy, are the bosses traveling again?"

"Yes, they are, so I'm the boss. You'd better get back to work."

Gabby laughed. "When are they coming back?"

"I think they wanted to be home for Christmas." Adeline thought about the reason they left this time—to find a friend's parents. She wondered if the trips in the past were to help people find their parents. She would have to ask next time she saw them. "If not, we'll have to think of how we want to handle being open on Christmas Eve and Christmas."

"We could do like we did for Thanksgiving—no coffee, no baristas. They bring in their own food, and we provide entertainment. But if Jake and Peggy aren't back by then, someone would have to be here and monitor the place."

"Arnie and I can do that. I'm sure I can get Roger and Pam to help out too."

"I'd even help if you let me come over for Christmas dinner."

Adeline knew Gabby didn't have a family, and if Jake and Peggy were gone, they wouldn't be there for dinner, and it would be just the two of them like it had been in the past. It was okay, they were used to it, but since Jake came along, it would be lonely without him and Peggy. Without consulting Arnie, she said, "Yes, we would love to have you. I'll invite Roger and Pam, and if the bosses are home, they'll come too."

Gabby gave Adeline a hug, which surprised them both. "That really means a lot to me. Thanks. I better get back to work now." Gabby turned around and walked to the coffee station. She wiped her eyes with her sleeves.

"What's up?" asked Jim.

"Allergies."

ꙮ

"Is this Adeline's dessert recipe?" asked Pam.

"No, it's store-bought. I took it out of the package and put it on a plate."

She took another forkful of the creamy cake. "Yum, this is good. We should probably go for a walk when we're done to wear off the calories."

"It's cold out there. Do you want to walk when it's so cold?" asked Roger.

"Yes. And no."

"I made a fire for us in the living room. I'll clear the dishes this time, and I'll join you in a minute."

Pam went to the living room and decided to look at the pictures on the mantle. She'd seen them before but didn't really pick them up and study them. The first one must have been his parents. Roger looked like his dad. She set that picture down and picked up another one. It was a picture of Roger with a woman. It was either his sister or Gail. She wasn't sure, and she really didn't care. Her negative thoughts were gone, and it was freeing.

Roger slid his arms around Pam, and the picture dropped on the mantle. She turned in his arms. "You scared me."

"Didn't mean to. Do you want to go for that walk?"

It was warm in his arms, and she could feel the heat coming from the fireplace. She was very comfortable and could easily lose herself in his arms. "I think we'd better walk."

Roger helped her with her coat, and he put on his. He opened the door for her. He held her hand as they walked down Story Street. Soon they'd passed the McDonald's and were almost to the Justice Café.

Roger held the door for her, and when they walked in, they noticed Adeline and Arnie talking to Gabby; they were the only ones there. "I can't believe it's so empty," said Pam.

Adeline waved them over to the table. "Sit, you two. We have a Christmas celebration to plan."

"You both are invited for Christmas dinner. Gabby is joining us."

"That's great," said Roger.

"What are you two doing out walking on a cold night like tonight?" asked Arnie "Unless the meatloaf didn't turn out and you are here for supper."

"Supper was great, and Roger even baked a cake." Roger laughed at Pam's comment. "If you call opening a package and putting it on a plate, baking."

"Oh horrors," said Arnie. "Adeline wouldn't get by with buying baked goods. They have to be homemade."

"You've eaten cookies out of the package before, Arnie."

"Yeah, but remember what happened after that?"

Adeline thought a minute. "No, I don't know what happened."

"I took your Buick away for a week."

She slapped him on the arm. "You did not." She shook her head. "What am I going to do with you?"

"Take me home and feed me."

"You'd think you ate all the time the way you talk about food, but you don't gain a pound."

"It's all that calorie-free cooking." He laughed and winked at his bride.

Gabby brought two chai teas over for Roger and Pam. "Enjoy." Roger pulled out his wallet and paid her.

"I can come for Christmas. Let me know what I can bring. I don't want you to do everything," said Pam.

"Bring Roger if you have to," said Arnie.

"I need to take Arnie home. He gets that way on an empty stomach."

"I'll take you home. You're not allowed to drive my truck."

The four of them took their coffee and left. Roger and Pam insisted on walking. Since Jake's house was closer, they walked there. Roger stayed until he finished his chai tea.

"Let's have dinner tomorrow too," said Roger. "Let's have dinner until Jake and Peggy get home. I would love to see you every night."

"Come here tomorrow. I'll cook."

"That's a deal." He kissed her and left.

꧁꧂

The address Jake drove to was an abandoned house that had the windows boarded with a big padlock on the front door. They sat in front of the house for a few minutes. "I want to go around back to make sure no one is there," said John.

Jake went with him, while Peggy stayed in the car. There was a padlock on the back door too. Jake pulled out a pick and tension wrench and went to work on opening the lock.

"What are you doing?" whispered John. "You can't open the lock. It's illegal,"

"I figure you can walk around the house and look, but you'll always wonder if your parents are in there. If you don't physically walk in and look, you'll never be at peace."

"So true," said John. It was more than true. He wanted so badly to find his parents that he had spent all his energy on them being at this address, this house.

The lock was opened, and Jake put it in his pocket. He opened the door and walked into the kitchen, with John following. It was clean, and the appliances were shiny. *Just like at home. Mom polished the stainless steel every day, it seemed.*

Jake opened the refrigerator and noticed the food still there. He took out the carton of milk and sniffed. "It's still good. Whoever was here before left not too long ago."

John had hope. Jake sensed what John was feeling. "But that doesn't mean it was your parents who were here."

"I know. I want them back in my life, and my mind is fogged about the facts and my dreams of spending Christmas with them."

"Let's check out the rest of the house."

Jake led the way. John looked under every piece of furniture, under every cushion. Jake looked for secret hiding places, since he himself has those same hiding places throughout his house. He knocked on walls, looked under sinks, and looked under rugs.

"I'm not finding anything," said John. He watched Jake knocking on the interior of the empty closet. "What are you doing?"

"Looking for hiding places."

"No one does that anymore, do they?"

"I do it. Ever since you started paying me, I've made hiding places to put the money."

John continued to watch in amazement as Jake carried a stool in the closet, got on, and on tiptoes, knocked on the top part of the closet. "Bingo!"

"Huh."

"I have to reach to get at it. Would you hold my legs so they don't move?"

John felt uncomfortable holding anyone's legs, but he did it. Jake took out his pick and pried off the hidden door and handed it to John. He threw it on the floor while still holding on to Jake.

"I'm going to get down." John let go as Jake stepped down from the stool. "Let's pull the bed over here, it's higher than this stool."

John obediently did what he was told. Jake climbed back on the bed, took a penlight out of his pocket and shined it in the hole. He didn't see anything but decided to feel around just in case. "Nothing yet, John." He slowly moved his hand over all the fake walls. When the got to the bottom wall, he felt something. He took it out and climbed down out of the closet.

John helped push the bed back, and Jake handed him what he'd found. "Do you recognize that?"

John turned pale and inched himself back and sat on the bed for support. "Yes," he whispered. "It's my dad's money clip. It has his initials, JM. He always had it in his pocket. I asked if I could have it, and he said no, that it was his. I never thought I'd be touching it."

Jake's phone beeped. There was a text from Peggy: *A gray car has passed the house three times since I've been sitting here. You'd better get out of there.*

"John, let's go." When John didn't move, Jake took his arm, pulled him off the bed and out the back door. He replaced the lock, and they ran to the car and drove off. John held tight to the money clip. He didn't want to lose it.

When they parked at the hotel, they looked around the parking lot to make sure no one had followed them. When they felt sure they were alone, Jake said, "It's lunchtime. I'll order the food, let's meet in John's room. His room is bigger than ours." He reached over and touched John's shoulder. "Let's go."

John mechanically got out of the car and followed Jake and Peggy to his room. Jake realized John wasn't going to get his key out, so he reached in John's back pocket, took his wallet and pulled out the card key and opened the door, and then John went in.

John sat heavily in the chair, still clutching the money clip. Jake found the food menu and ordered lunch. Peggy was writing on her notepad, adding to the notes she'd taken in the car. They just let John be until the food arrived.

Jake put the food on the table. "John, the food is here."

"Okay," he said in a weak voice. He stood and put the money clip in his pocket and sat back down. Jake put a plate of food in front of him, and John surprised them both by picking up his fork and eating.

"While you two were in the house, I went and talked to the neighbors on both sides. I noticed this car slowly going by when I left the first house, then saw it go by again while I was talking to the other neighbor.

"I found out from both neighbors, a couple in their sixties was living in the house. They rarely ever left. They had their groceries delivered to them, they didn't have a car. The only thing that they did with any regularity was eat their lunch on the front porch. Their house, they pointed out, sits back from theirs, and they could easily it see from their living room windows.

"Both neighbors were consistent with describing them. The man was tall, thin, and had curly hair. The woman was shorter, not thin or overweight, shoulder-length grayish hair, looked like she worked out."

"That's my parents. As you can see, I have my dad's hair. Now what do we do?"

"I got the license plate number on the car."

"Are you serious?" asked John.

CHAPTER THREE

"Max, this is John."

"John, I didn't expect to hear from you so soon. What's happening?"

"You'll never believe what happened just today."

"You'll have to tell me because with your workload and mine, I don't have time for guessing."

"This morning Jake picked the lock on the house I had an address for, for my parents. He found a secret compartment in the closet, and inside the secret compartment was my dad's money clip with his initials JM."

"Wow, you're making progress."

"That's not all. Peggy, his wife, was interviewing the neighbors on both sides of the house. The neighbors described my parents. The giveaway was the man had curly hair. *And* Peggy noticed a car driving by several times while we were there, and she got the license plate number."

"That is progress. Maybe you'll be home by Christmas after all."

"I don't want to get my hopes up too much. I need to call Nell and tell her what happened. Thanks for doing my work."

"Piece of cake. Don't worry about me, just find your parents."

John disconnected and called Nell. She couldn't believe the progress he'd had so far and was happy for him. "I love you, John. I'll set three extra places for Christmas."

ꕥ

The weather in Boone, Iowa, was sunny and sixty-five. Most of the leaves had fallen, and according to last year, it would've been winter-jacket weather. Adeline Cole was slowly walking up Story Street. She wanted to take in the fine weather they were having in case winter showed up early. She took a left on Sixth Street and over to Greene Street. She was meeting her friend Pam, who had taken over her job at the library when she retired.

She climbed the stairs to the Ericson Public Library, and once she was inside, she walked to the front desk. She looked around at the place where she'd worked for many years. She couldn't say that she missed working there but wondered why she didn't visit and take out books more often. But she was busy at the café. *Well,* she thought, *I could read at the café.* She'd give it a try. Actually, she decided she would check out a book now.

She wandered over to the literature section, then to fiction. She found an author she'd read before and looked to see if any books had the copyright for this year. That way she was sure not to take out one she'd read before since she didn't think she'd read a book since she retired last year.

"Hey, Pam," said Adeline as she approached the desk. "I'm going to start reading again. Can you check out my book?" She carefully took her library card out of her wallet and handed it to Pam.

"This looks like a good book. You'll have to tell me if you like it. I'd like to read more, but with working and seeing Roger at night, there's no time." Pam checked out the book and handed it back to her.

"I know what you mean about no time. I'm busier now than when I retired. Are you ready for lunch?"

"Yes, I've been waiting all morning for our date." Pam laughed. "Sue said I could have extra time for lunch."

"She's so sweet."

Pam took her purse from the bottom drawer. "Let's go, I'm hungry. I didn't eat my snack this morning because I didn't want to spoil my appetite. Even though it's a nice day, I'll drive. That way, we'll have more time to visit."

While they waited to be seated at the Tic Toc Italian Steakhouse on Keeler Street, they looked at the menu. When they were seated, they told the hostess what they wanted so they didn't waste any time. The more time they could sit after they ate without worrying about the food and the check, the more relaxed lunch would be.

"I miss the kids," said Adeline.

"I do too. When I know they are going somewhere, I feel like I can do anything now that they're out of the house, like have Roger over. But when they've been gone for two days, it's lonely, quiet."

"I don't know what I'd do if Arnie left for a few days. I'd go crazy is what I would do."

"I've been thinking of my ex-husband lately. Well, you know the story. I don't even know if I can call him an ex since I don't know if we were ever married." The waiter came with their salads and interrupted Pam's thoughts.

"What are you really thinking about that's got you so down in the dumps?" asked Adeline.

"I think he'll find me. He could find out the same way Jake found out, through Lenny's brother Rick or his cousin Larry."

They ate more of their salad and sipped their tea. "What if he does find you? What do you think he'll want?"

"That's just it—I don't know what he'll want. Maybe to get back together, maybe he only has one wife now and wants a second one. I was a sucker before, he probably thinks I'll be a sucker again."

"First, you have to stop thinking of yourself that way. It's not healthy."

"You're right, of course. I just feel like he's coming back, and it scares me. I told Roger about it, and if that's enough to worry about, we've both been worried about the other one seeing someone else in secret."

"I can understand why you would both feel that way. The way Gail left Roger for another man and Lenny having another wife, it's normal to feel that way."

"You're right. You're always right." Pam smiled.

Pam looked up when she heard laughter and saw it was Roger with a woman. They were being seated by the door so he didn't see her. The woman was tall, thin, had shoulder-length straight black hair. According to Pam, she had on a drop-dead gorgeous teal dress that worked well with her hair color.

They'd just talked about not having other people in their lives, and Roger claimed he wasn't seeing anyone. *I guess he lied.*

"Who is that woman?" asked Pam, not controlling her anger.

Adeline discretely looked toward Roger's table and saw the front of the woman's face. "It looks like Gail."

"Gail? Why would he be taking her to lunch? I thought they hated each other. It doesn't seem that way if they're laughing like that."

"Do you want me to go find out?"

"No!" Pam said a little too forcefully.

"Or sit there and assume all bad things. Get yourself worked up. Yell at Roger the next time you see him. Your relationship breaks up. You'll feel like hell for the rest of your life."

"Geez, Adeline!" whispered Pam. She grabbed Adeline's hand before she had a chance to stand. "*I'll* go over there and find out what's happening."

Adeline nodded. "Good girl. Stay calm."

Pam took a few deep breaths, stood, and walked toward Roger's table.

"Pam?"

Pam looked at Roger. "Oh, hi." She then got a good look at Gail. "Adeline and I are having lunch."

Roger stood next to her and put his arm around her. "This is Pam, Jake's mom. Pam this is Gail." He felt he didn't have to add any title, Pam knew who Gail was.

"Hi," said Pam. "It's nice to meet you."

"Yeah, same here," responded Gail, annoyed at the interruption.

Roger looked at Pam. "I'll see you tonight, although I don't know how hungry we'll be since we're eating a big lunch."

"I'll cook something light." She looked at Gail. "We can do other things, we don't have to eat."

Roger let out a nervous laugh. "See you around six." He dropped his arm and let her go back to her table.

"Who the hell is that?" asked Gail after Roger sat down. "We just got divorced, and you're seeing someone else."

"Well, you left me for someone else. You were seeing someone while we were still married. Why would you get so upset when we're divorced and now I'm seeing someone? Doesn't fair mean both sides are playing fair?"

"I wanted to see you today because I wanted to come back, start over. But I can see you've ruined any chances of that." She calmed herself. "I heard you sold the hardware store."

"Yes, I did. Something you never cared about."

"Only since you found more pleasure in a stupid tool store than you did with me. But now that it's sold, I would like to come back." She wanted his money, not him. "I can forget all about the other woman if you take me back."

"Just so you know, you ruined any chance of us getting back together when you walked out on me for another man—a younger, more handsome, caring man is the way you put it."

Gail could see he wouldn't take her back, so she decided to stop being so nice. She stood, took her purse off the table. "You'll never change. I don't know why I thought we could start over. You can keep seeing whoever you want. They'll find out soon enough that you don't know how to love, just how to take and take and take. Not only that, but you're also lousy in bed." She turned toward the door and almost ran out of the restaurant.

Adeline and Pam were watching and listening to the argument as were most people in the restaurant. Roger threw cash and his napkin on the table and left the restaurant just as quickly.

"I don't think you have to worry about Gail anymore. It was lucky you wandered over when you did. Seems Gail got a little upset."

"A little upset?" Pam smiled. "I feel I should go after Roger."

"Let him work it out. You'll see him tonight anyway. But instead of cooking light, he'll be awfully hungry by the time he gets to your house."

"Good point."

The two women stayed another thirty minutes and talked. Soon the subject changed from Roger to the café, to Jake and Peggy, to the wedding planning team. They both felt better after visiting over lunch.

"I'll keep you updated on Jake and Peggy, *and* Roger. I hope they make it home for Christmas."

"Either way, you and Roger are coming for Christmas dinner. Gabby is already coming."

"She's so sweet. Yes, I'll be there. Let's go. I'll give you a ride home. It looks like it could rain outside."

ᘓᘐ

They waited for morning before they drove to San Francisco. It was almost a four-hour drive, but with the stops, it took longer. They stopped twice just to get out of the car, stretch, get coffee, and have lunch. Jake was driving, and John was preoccupied with his thoughts. Peggy slept in the back seat. Her head was throbbing, but she didn't want to tell Jake. She didn't want him fussing over her. The motion of the car was making her head worse until she finally took some pain medication at the last rest stop. There were a few pills left from when she had surgery on her forehead, and she'd decided to pack them for the trip.

"How long before we're there?" asked John.

"Another hour. Peggy called ahead for a hotel room. We'll go there first and go over our plan. I know we talked about it already, but it never hurts to firm up the plans. Did your contact call you about who the car belonged to?"

"No. He said he was really busy but would run the license plate as soon as he got a free moment."

"I think the sooner we find out who the owner is, the sooner we can figure out more of the puzzle."

"I agree." John looked in the back seat and saw Peggy sleeping. "Is she okay?"

"No. But she won't tell me her head is hurting. When we get to the hotel, I'll insist she lie down or at least rest."

John still didn't know what went on in Hershey, just what the news reporters were saying, but he wouldn't ask. He just hoped Peggy was okay.

The hotel was quaint and tucked back from the highway. Peggy was groggy from the pain medication and welcomed a nice warm bed to lie down and sleep. Jake couldn't sleep. He was worried about Peggy, and there were too many unknowns about this mission. Not only that, but family was also involved for John. Jake could tell he was relying too much on Jake and Peggy finding his parents in time for Christmas. He would do his best but didn't want anyone disappointed.

He sat in the chair in the corner and looked at Peggy's notes and added notes of his own. He looked through the research again that John had given them and read it slower this time and added comments as he read. *Getting that license number is the key to it all,* thought Jake.

ꕥ

"Who the hell is at the Reno house?" asked Sam. "I drove by a couple of times and saw a car parked there. There's never a car there. It's a quiet neighborhood. Everyone parks in their own driveway, never on the street. Your car was the only car ever on the street."

"We don't know, we left there when you decided Preston and Heather needed to be moved, and now we're at the new location." He looked at his partner. "Were they at the house or just parked in the street?"

"Don't get smart with me. The other neighbors are old, they don't have family, they don't have friends, and no one ever visits them."

He didn't want to anger Sam anymore, so he kept quiet. He rolled his eyes at his partner instead. Sam ranted a little more, then disconnected.

"I wonder why he's so riled up. He's got so much money. Why doesn't he just walk away?"

"Some people just don't have the smarts, I guess."

His partner laughed. "Like us. We sit here day after day, and we never walk away."

"Well, we are smart because if we walked away, we'd never walk again."

ꕥ

Pam noticed Roger walking quickly toward the house with a determined look on his face. She wondered if he was still working through what happened at the restaurant. She opened the door before he had a chance to knock.

He walked right to her and kissed her. His kiss was rough and urgent. The sexual tension was immediate in her body, and she wrapped her arms around him, wanting him, desiring him. He backed away, leaving her lips, her body, on fire, aching with desire.

His own lips felt empty without hers on his, so he kissed her again recklessly, crushing his arms around her. His lips moved to her neck, to her cleavage. He moved two steps forward with her in his arms and shut the backdoor with his foot.

He held her up so her feet brushed along the floor as he walked to the bedroom, kissing her, aching for her. He set her down, unbuttoned her blouse, her jeans, took her clothes off, and let them fall to the floor. *You're beautiful!*

He took off his clothes and pulled Pam to him and kissed her with passion, desire, longing. His tongue explored her mouth, her neck, her shoulder. He eased her down on the bed and lay on top of her.

There was so much he wanted to say, but he said nothing and hoped this one act would tell the woman he truly loved just how much he loved her. He wanted to wait but realized the impossibility of it.

His kisses were hot on her breasts, her neck. She arched into him and held him tightly against her aching body. She couldn't remember the last time she'd made love, couldn't remember it ever being this wonderful. She knew there was no one else in their lives, just the two of them, together and in love.

Her skin felt velvety and moist below him as they molded into each other and moved in harmony. A cry of release worked its way through her body and escaped her lips when waves of ecstasy flowed through her. Then she gasped, and exhilaration filled her body, leaving it to wonder if she should scream again for the sheer delight of it or cry for the happiness to be so close to the man she loved.

They both found release.

He kissed her gently, with love. Kissed her nose, her chin, her eyes, and then he moved off her and lay beside her. "I love you."

She whispered the words back to him. "I love you too."

CHAPTER FOUR

"My contact still hasn't looked up the plate number. He went home sick yesterday and didn't feel good enough to go to work today. I'm not sure when he'll get back to the office."

"It's important we get it, but we've got other things we can explore while we wait. We need to go to the coffee shop they went to every morning and ask questions. There might be different employees there after all this time, but you never know," said Jake.

"We'll go to the neighborhood they lived in and talk to the neighbors," said Peggy. "Jake and I can go ask the neighbors. It might be too hard for you, if you know them, but they might open up to you more than they would to total strangers. You can always say no."

"I think it's a good idea. I never thought to do that before."

"Peg, how are you feeling? Did your headache go away?"

"I knew I couldn't keep that from you. It is better, but would you mind if we get back to the hotel early tonight, before dinner?"

"Sure, Peg. Do you want to stay here while John and I go to the coffee house?"

"That's the one place I want to go. I might get some ideas for the Justice Café." Peggy grabbed her notes and put them in her bag. "I'm ready."

"I think we should talk to the neighbors first, then go to where they had coffee." John ran his fingers through his frizzy hair. "I think you're doing it all wrong."

Jake and Peggy didn't say anything, just waited for John to change the plans. Jake remembered when he and Peggy were looking for his mom. He was irritable and wanted to find her that same day, no way could they find John's parents this soon, so he understood.

John walked to the window and looked out. It was rainy and cold, which explained the frizz in his curly hair. His hand was stroking his father's money clip in his pocket. *Where are you, Dad?* Several minutes passed. He turned, looked at Jake and Peggy.

"Your plan will probably work better. Sorry. I'm so worked up about this whole thing. We're actually getting some results already. Before I got to Reno, I figured we'd get nowhere. So now that I got a sign, I feel like we'll find them before Christmas. I need to hope that will happen."

Jake walked over to him and touched his shoulder. "It's all right. No need to apologize."

"I can't promise I won't mouth off again, but I'll try harder next time."

"To mouth off," joked Peggy. They all laughed. "John, just remember each step forward could mean a couple steps back, but Jake and I will not give up on you."

"Thanks, I needed to hear that." John took his coat out of the closet and handed Jake and Peggy theirs. "Okay, let's go to the café. I could use a strong cup of coffee."

ℵ ☙

Roger had his head propped on his hand, his free hand playing with Pam's hair. He traced the outline of her eyes, her nose, her lips, with a strand of her hair. A smile playing on her face. He let go of her hair and used his hand to touch her. The softness of her, the gentleness of her, took his breath away. He wanted to make love to her again, but he wanted her to initiate it. He didn't keep his word when he said he was going to wait before they had sex. He could justify it by saying it wasn't just sex, it was life-altering. Love-altering.

She opened her eyes and pulled him to her. "Hold me."

"Gladly."

She didn't initiate more lovemaking but just being this close to her was enough. Warm flesh on warm flesh. He wasn't sure exactly what Jake and Peggy were doing in Reno but hoped they wouldn't be home anytime soon.

"I'm sorry I didn't keep my word, Pam. I hope you still trust me. I don't know what came over me."

"You're forgiven."

"Thank you, because I don't know what I'd do if you were ever mad at me."

"You don't have to worry about that."

"If we don't make love again, can we eat? Did you have anything cooked for dinner?"

"Yes, but since you've already had dessert, I thought you spoiled your appetite for dinner, so I didn't mention eating."

"Just so you know, I never lose my appetite after dessert. It's only enhanced for more."

"Good because I decided to make a big dinner when I noticed you left the restaurant without eating."

"Yeah, about that . . ."

"You don't have to talk about it if you don't want to."

"I want to. Gail and I were having lunch because she wanted to come to the house to talk. I decided I didn't want her in my house, and seeing her in public would probably be better in case she got any ideas about taking more stuff out of the house. I'm missing a few things from when she came the last time. I thought she was taking her own stuff, but she took some of my mother's jewelry. I decided not to say anything because I didn't want to get her mad because when she's mad, she tends to yell a lot. The truth, I just wanted to get through it and leave it behind. I'll still remember my mom whether I have her jewelry or not."

"What did she want?"

"When you left the table, she got upset that I was seeing someone else after the divorce. I pointed out that she was the one who was unfaithful, but she didn't understand why I would date, mostly because she wanted to get back together with me."

"Unfortunately, I heard the whole conversation as did many of the customers," said Pam.

"Yeah, I figured. If they lived in Boone, they'd know it was Gail." He realized Pam had never seen her before. He let out a sigh. "You see me with a woman after our trust conversation and I bet you were ready to string me up."

"Adeline told me right away who she was, so I was feeling like crap for only a couple of minutes, and I felt extremely better when she walked out on you."

"I bet you did." Roger laughed. "So what's for dinner?"

"I have steaks marinating. I thought, before winter gets here, it would be nice to grill. I have potatoes and vegetables already done."

"Steak. I was going to order it for lunch. You read my mind."

They lingered a little longer in bed, then dressed. Roger lit the grill and sat on the deck thinking of Pam. Several minutes later, she interrupted his thoughts with the plate of marinated steaks. "You forgot something."

ဆ ဃ

They were at the coffee house John Sr. and his wife Michelle frequented, close to their home. John didn't remember ever going there, but when he came home to visit, getting coffee was not top priority.

It was crowded around the noon hour, but Jake thought if that's when they came every day, it would be a better possibility that someone would remember them.

"We should have a picture," said John. "There was one in the envelope with my research but I didn't think about bringing it with me. Do we need to go back to the hotel?"

Peggy took the envelope out of her bag and pulled out the picture. "Nope, don't think we need to go back."

John shook his head, thinking he'd never been able to do this alone. He would've given up by now, and he certainly never would've broken into that house. "Thanks, Peggy."

Jake watched the crowd, then watched the barista taking the drink and food orders. She knew what everyone wanted and knew them by name. Hopefully, he thought, she'd worked here for several years and would know John's parents. He would talk to her once there was a break in the flow of customers.

"John, have you always lived in San Francisco?"

"My folks lived in a small city close to San Francisco. Then after I was born, Dad got a big promotion and moved into the big city, as he would say."

"Since living in such a big city, what did you think of Boone, Iowa?" asked Peggy.

John laughed. "I liked Boone. Not a lot going on, but I don't need so much city life at my age. I like Boone a lot because my little Cassie lives there."

Peggy remembered Cassie from the grand opening of the Justice Café. "She sure is cute. Wait. Weren't you with someone? I don't remember her name."

"Yes, Nell. We are going to get married once I find my parents. I didn't want anything to stand in the way of our marriage. I told Nell everything, and we both decided I needed to do this."

"Getting married *and* having children too?" asked Jake.

"That's the plan. How about you two? You're younger than I am. Are you planning on a family?"

"We've been so busy we haven't talked about it," commented Peggy.

"Maybe we should talk about it."

"I didn't mean to start anything."

"I think we needed to be reminded. The Justice Café has kept us busy. When we get home, we're too tired to even cook."

Jake noticed the quiet and looked around. Most of the tables were empty, and the woman taking orders was now wiping tables. She stopped at their table and asked if she could throw away the napkins and empty cups.

"We can do it, but there is one thing you can do for us."

"Sure, I'm Abby, what can I help you with?"

Peggy handed Jake the picture, and he showed Abby.

"Do you recognize this couple? They came in here every day, ordered coffee, and lunch."

Abby studied the picture, then handed it back to Jake. "No, never seen them before." She walked away from the table and went through the door that said Employees Only. Several seconds later, she left with her backpack and coat draped over her shoulder.

"She knows something," said Jake. "If she's walking, I'll follow her. You two stay here." Jake walked quickly out the door and headed in the same direction as Abby. She was on her phone, walking quickly away from the coffee shop. Jake kept up, and since she was distracted on her phone, she didn't know he was following.

She turned the corner and kept walking. She disconnected the call and started running. Jake started running. Several blocks later, she ran up a flight of stairs to an apartment building. She scanned her cardkey and went in. Jake was steps behind her and through the door. He quickly went in the opposite direction as Abby, then circled back and followed her down the hall. He put his hood on and looked down the hall. She opened her apartment door and slammed the door behind her.

Jake took a pen out of his shirt pocket and wrote the apartment number on his hand. Before he shut the door to the street, he studied it, wondered if he could get it opened without anyone noticing while she was at work tomorrow. But he didn't know if she would be back to work after what happened. He left the building and joined John and Peggy back at the coffee house.

"She was obviously lying. I got her apartment number"

"How did you get that? All the buildings are secured," said John.

"As I followed her down the street, she called someone and was distracted and didn't notice anyone was following her because she never looked back. I was fairly close to her so when she entered the apartment building, I got in before the door closed behind her. She's on the main floor, and I followed her to her apartment. She never looked back.

"I can pick the apartment door easily, but I'm not sure about the outside door."

"I don't think my heart can take it if we break in again, especially a building where people go in and out all hours of the day."

"Peggy can come with me."

"I didn't say I didn't want to go." He let out a nervous laugh. "I just said my heart wouldn't take it. You'll just have to be prepared to scrape me off the floor."

"Whatever," said Peggy. "I don't think you'll faint."

"What's next?" asked John.

"I want to ask a few more people here and see if they react the same way, or we might get some information and won't have to break and enter." Jake stood and took his cup. "Anyone want a refill?"

"I'll take more coffee," said John.

"None for me, thanks."

Jake walked to the counter and asked for refills. "You were busy earlier, is it always like that?"

"Just on the weekdays. People stop by on their lunch, in a hurry to get back to work or to start their lunch and run errands."

"Maybe we'll come back on the weekend next time." Jake pulled out the picture and showed it to the woman who refilled his coffee. "Have you seen this couple here during lunch on the weekdays? I think they came every day during the week."

"Oh wow, they really look familiar. She pulled her glasses off her head and put them on. "Yes, I remember them. They were here every day, same time, and they always ordered the same thing. She would get a table, while he waited in line. Plain coffee, cream, and soup for both of them. But it's been a long time since they were here."

"Do you remember if they said why they wouldn't be back?"

"I don't remember. They just didn't show up, and I never saw them again."

"Did any of the baristas mention them?"

She thought about it for a few seconds. "Ah, I think Abby mentioned something about them. Then she wouldn't talk at all about them. Sometimes we talked about the regulars because we liked them, they were very nice, would leave a big tip. But after Abby's initial comment about them, she never said anything again. I tried to talk to her about them, but she told me to stop asking her."

Several people walked through the door. "Back to work. I hope I was helpful."

"Yes, you were a lot of help. Thanks."

ꕥ

Jim was making coffee for Adeline. She came in early, sat at a table up front, and took out her book from her library book bag.

"Here's your coffee. Have you read this before, or is this something new?"

"Actually, I read it in elementary school." Adeline laughed.

"Funny, Granny. I'd better get back to work. Enjoy your book."

Adeline lost herself in the story she was reading and didn't notice that Arnie came in. He ordered his coffee and sat by Adeline. "So this is where you are."

She looked up at him. "And?"

"I was looking for you at home, but apparently, you came here without telling me."

"There's a note on the counter where we always leave notes for each other."

Arnie laughed. "I looked everywhere but there."

"You getting forgetful, Arnie?"

"Yep, and I panicked when you weren't home. I'm glad I found you."

She leaned down and took another book out of her bag. "Here's a book for you, it's on home projects. You've been slacking on your home projects lately, I thought you'd want to get back into it. There's a project in here to make a Murphy bed."

"What do we need a Murphy bed for? We already have a perfectly good bed in our guest room. Noah thinks it's comfortable, so we shouldn't change it."

"Nice try. It's not for the guest room. It's for downstairs. I thought if we had a bed down there, we could have more guests."

"When you say more guests, are you talking about sleepovers?"

"Yes, sleepovers. If Jake and Peggy's friends, Joyce and Brad, visit again, Pam can sleep over here. Or Penny can stay here."

Arnie found the project in the book, studied it, and made a mental list of what he needed. "When do you want it by?"

"The sooner the better."

"I'm going to sit here with you, sip my coffee, and look at my new book."

"I knew you'd like it."

CHAPTER FIVE

"My contact is still out. I have his cell number, but if he's at home, he can't look up the plate number anyway."

Jake sensed he was down about not getting the information. "We've got a few things we can do without the plates. Let's get breakfast, then head over to the neighborhood and start asking questions."

"I think we should find out if Abby is at work today," suggested Peggy. "We can go during lunch again. If she shows for her shift, she won't see us in the crowd."

"I don't know if we'd get much information by looking in her apartment, but we'd get a phone number if we find her phone."

"How do you plan on getting her phone?"

"I think I could recognize her backpack again, and she kept her phone in the outside pocket. She keeps it behind the door that says Employees Only. If it's as busy tomorrow as it was today, it might be a safe bet I could go in there and get the phone."

"It's a big risk," said John. "What if you get caught?"

"I don't plan on getting caught. Peg, what colors did the baristas wear? I think if I had employee colors on, I wouldn't be noticed."

"Green shirts and brown pants."

"We need to go shopping. John, do you want to come with us or stay at the hotel?"

"I think I'll stay at the hotel, but could you get me some bottled water?"

"Sure. First, I'm going for a walk around the hotel. I need to think. Peg, we'll go shopping when I get back."

Jake walked down to the front desk and left through the front door. He walked on the sidewalks around the hotel.

If I get Abby's phone and get the number, how would I know who it belonged to? I can call the number, but I still wouldn't know whose it was, unless Abby has a name attached to the number, which she probably does. I could call on her phone, and then I would find out how the person answers the phone. We need to get to the bottom of this Abby thing. We'll eat breakfast in the morning, check out, and if we have to get out of town, we won't have to worry about the hotel.

If we need another day, we can always stay at a different hotel. As the last resort, we can try and get into Abby's apartment.

Jake walked around the hotel two more times. He wanted to go through his plan again and make sure he wasn't forgetting anything.

He let himself into the room. John was drinking a cup of coffee, and Peggy was going through the research documents again.

"Find anything more, Peggy?"

"Not really. Did you come up with anything?"

Jake told them what his plan was. John and Peggy gave him feedback, and then Jake and Peggy went shopping.

ꟷ

"I was too distracted thinking of you." He took the plate of steaks from her and set them on the side of the grill. "While we're waiting for the coals to get hot, we can do some serious kissing." He kissed her, and she laughed. "What's so funny?"

"It's a gas grill."

"Busted. But we can still kiss." This time he took her in his arms and kissed her slowly. "I'd better get the steaks grilled, or we could be here all night."

"You're welcome to stay, I just have to get to work in the morning."

"That's very tempting. I'll have to think about it."

They had a nice dinner. Roger ate all his steak and half of Pam's. Pam took him home after they ate. Roger would pick her up after work the next day, and they would go out to eat instead of cook.

Roger didn't want to outstay his welcome. Even though he knew Pam loved him, he still wondered if she did. He needed to get rid of those thoughts and start to trust his own decisions and trust that what Pam said was true. He would work on that.

He was going to start massage therapy classes soon, and he wanted to get his thinking straight. Distractions were what he needed to avoid in order to give his classes and his new career his full attention. He hoped too that Pam would help him with his homework.

ꙮ

Jake had on a green polo shirt, very similar to the baristas', and brown pants. Peggy stood in line and ordered coffee for them. John and Jake sat out of sight of the barista station. It was just as busy as the day before.

"You nervous?"

"Yes. Usually, I've made the plan at home before we even travel. This is spur of the moment, and I'm not sure of anything."

"You're doing great, kid."

Peggy came with the coffees and sat them on the table. "Abby's here."

"Did she recognize you?"

"Not with this blond wig."

"I'd better wander over and see if I can get behind that door."

As Jake walked toward the front, he picked up napkins on the floor and asked if he could take one couple's empty cups. He pretended to be working. He threw the cups and napkins in the trash receptacle and slipped through the door for Employees Only and closed it behind him.

He waited inside the door to make sure no one was going to follow him. When no one did, he looked for Abby's backpack. It was on the floor in the corner. He picked it up and searched in the front pocket. Her iPhone was there. He watched the baristas at the Justice Café enough to know where to find calls and recent calls. He found the recent calls, and there were two listed for yesterday, both the same name. Sam.

Since there was a name, a number wasn't visible. He tapped on contacts, typed in Sam, and the name and number appeared. He wrote the number and name on his hand and clicked call.

"What the hell are you calling me again for? You'd better have information for me this time. Who's showing the picture around? We'll have to move them again, probably somewhere outside of Reno. Don't call me again until you've got names." He waited. "Do you have names for me?"

Jake disconnected, put the phone back, and turned out the light. He cracked open the door and noticed there was still a line. He walked out of the room and blended in with the crowd, then walked out the door.

ꕥ

John had the car down the block ready to pull out when Jake got in the car. Peggy was in the back, looking out the window. "Here comes Jake."

He got in the car, and John pulled away from the curb. "Let's hit the freeway and find a gas station. I just want to get away from here." John was familiar with the area and drove to the freeway entrance. Five miles away, John exited and pulled into a Chevron gas station.

Jake told them what happened. "Sam was the guy she called. I clicked on his number, and fortunately for us, Sam answered the call and started talking as if it really were Abby on the line. He wanted to know who was showing the picture around and that he'd have to move them again, probably outside of Reno."

"Outside of Reno is a big area. It could be a hundred miles away in all directions for all we know," said John in frustration.

"I'm not discouraged yet. We just have to keep at it and follow our leads."

"What do we do with the number?"

"I'm not sure, but we have it."

"Is there a restaurant around here that you know of?"

"Just up the road." John put the car in gear and drove to the restaurant.

ꕥ

He disconnected the call. "That was Sam. He wants to move the Masons again. Someone is looking for them at the coffee house."

"I thought no one cared. Their son is in Minnesota working full time. Never comes to San Francisco. Seems to be okay with his parents being dead. I guess he's dating someone, and he occasionally takes a road trip with her."

"If it's not him looking, who is it?"

"Either way, I'm sick of sitting here day and night. At first I thought the pay was good but not anymore. I'd rather have a life."

ℰ ℬ

As they were eating, Peggy made reservations at another hotel. It was close to the coffee house. Jake decided they should stay in the area as long as Abby came back to work and they had Sam's phone number.

They would need disguises and have lunch during her shift. When she left, one of them would follow her. Or they might try and get into her building and look around in her apartment, possibly find out how Sam is involved in all this and why he even cares about John's parents.

Jake recounts what happened in case something was forgotten. "John Sr. and Michelle go to the same place every day, order the same thing. All of a sudden, they don't show up anymore. One barista is upset, Abby's not, claims she doesn't even remember them. Apparently, they never show up again.

"Their only son is home from college, and he tells his son that if he and Michelle ever wanted to change their names, it would be Preston and Heather. It seemed unusual, but no questions were asked. What was more unusual was that John Sr. was home from work."

"Wait!" said John. "Now that we're recounting everything, it was unusual that Mom was making lunch. When I'd call home, she would tell me she and Dad were going to the coffee house for lunch every day. It was busy, but they didn't care. It was a nice ritual that they had started. I went with them once when I was home. But that day, when I came home, I was expecting to go there with them. Then all the talk about changing names and Mom cooking lunch distracted me. I was confused, and no, I didn't ask any questions."

"So something happened during that week. According to Sam, he needed to move them again. They were at the address we went to, were moved, and now they'd have to be moved again. We need to figure out the date when they left or were taken from their home.

"We need more help. Someone is watching Abby, and someone is checking out your parent's neighborhood. I would rather not split up, and it would take too long to fill someone in on what we need."

"Joyce would come if we asked her," said Peggy.

"Who's Joyce?"

"She helps us when you send on us trips to get justice."

"Can she be trusted?"

"She was on the tour with you and your friends at the Justice Café. Joyce worked at the shelter in Omaha, and Brad was there getting information for a shelter he wanted to start in Florida." Peggy touched John's arm. "She can be trusted. So can Brad."

"How soon can they be here?"

"Depends if there are people at the shelter."

John poured coffee for himself and added cream, took a sip, pushed his pie away, and looked at Jake. "Call her. If you think we need more help, then I trust you to make the right decision."

"Give me the keys. I'll call her in the car where it's private."

Peggy took the keys, and as she walked to the car, she dialed Joyce's number. She crawled in the back. "Joyce, we need you to help us in San Francisco to get justice." Peggy filled her in and mentioned Brad would be needed too. Now she waited while Joyce talked to Brad and then to Julie, their office assistant. While she waited, she looked through her notes.

Joyce relayed the message to Brad. "A guy named Sam is responsible for taking the parents and relocating them. They really need to find Sam. We would interview neighbors, John Sr.'s coworkers, and more, if needed."

"Peggy, Brad can make it, and so can I. We've had a few volunteers working here for the last two weeks, and Julie said they can handle it if families stay at the shelter. Julie has been amazing. Okay, where do we go, and what do you want us to do first?"

Peggy told her the specifics about what they needed them to do, but they would have to make their own plane and hotel reservations. She gave them the Mason's old address. "Get a hotel as close as you can." Joyce was then filled in on more of what had happened so far. "So it might be dangerous, depending on where Sam is living or located. We can't be sure they don't have someone staking out the neighborhood. Get a rental car and we'll reimburse you for all your expenses. Be careful, Joyce."

"I will. We will. I will call when we get to the hotel."

CHAPTER SIX

The next day they were back at the coffee house. John and Jake had on black motorcycle leathers with a bandana wrapped around their forehead. Jake had black hair. Peggy wore a red wig with her leathers on. They didn't want to call attention to themselves, and yet they wanted to stand out. Jake thought the more they stood out as being different, the less they would call attention to themselves as being suspicious.

ꙮ

Abby was behind the counter. She kept looking at the door, and periodically, she looked at the customers having lunch and drinking their coffee. She didn't recognize anyone and wondered if the people who asked her about the Masons would come back. She didn't need any more trouble. Sam had left her when this whole crisis started, and she missed him.

Sam was mad when he talked to her before work today, and he accused her of calling him and hanging up. But she hadn't called. She checked her recent calls, and it had a four next to Sam's name. She thought she'd only called him twice, his call would make three, but how else could there be four calls? No one else could've used her phone, but now she started to worry about it, and she kept looking around to see if someone were watching her or looking suspicious.

Abby wished the bikers would leave. The customers were paying too much attention to them, and she wanted the place back to normal, so she could feel normal again, safe again. Any minute she was sure Sam would walk through the door and make her leave. The coffee house job was the only job she loved. She knew people's orders, knew people's troubles and joys. She felt like someone.

Abby was in love with Sam. They were getting married, but he started to be demanding, jittery, and after a while he couldn't be trusted. He lied about where he was at night, and there was a time he was gone for a week, and when he showed at her apartment, he said he had to go back home and take care of his mother.

Sam had told her when they first met that his mother had died five years ago. Abby called him on it, and then he felt he had to tell her what had happened the last week. Now Abby wished he'd never told her. He said the couple at the coffee shop was doing something illegal, and he was in law enforcement and had to put them in to a protection program. Abby thought he was a factory worker, but he told her he had to lie because he was in 'special projects.'

She jumped when someone came through the door. It wasn't Sam. The last time he'd left her apartment, he'd left behind a sealed document sized manila envelope. She never thought anything of it until now. Maybe she'll open it and see if it pertains to the Masons.

She walked to her boss. "Can I have the rest of the day off? I don't feel well."

He looked around the shop. "Sure. The rush is over. I hope you feel better."

"Yeah, sure. I hope to be here tomorrow."

ജ൫

"She's leaving," said John. "Now what?"

"Let's go. We'll talk in the car." They walked to the car in the opposite direction Abby was walking. They got in the car. "Tomorrow Peggy will go into the shop and order takeout for the three of us. We only want to make sure Abby is at work. If she is, then I think it's time to check her apartment."

"I'll be happy to get these clothes off," said John. "I can hardly breathe."

"Does your friend Nell know you wear leather?"

"No, she doesn't, and I'd like to keep it a secret."

"You're secret is safe with us," said Peggy.

ꕥ

Brad and Joyce stopped at a fast food restaurant and picked up food on the way to the hotel. They checked in and went to their room. Joyce read her notes while they ate their dinner. "Usually, we know what to expect and who we're looking for. This is truly a mystery. I hope we can find out something, a clue, anything."

"Me too," said Brad.

"I'm glad Peggy e-mailed me her notes, and we were able to print them out before we left. Let's start interviewing around ten in the morning. If people have gone to work, let's go back at seven. They should be done eating supper by then."

"Good idea. We can get breakfast then stake out the neighborhood and wait for ten o'clock."

"I forgot to call Peggy." Joyce took her phone off the desk and called. "Peggy, we're here." She told her their plan, and Peggy relayed the message to Jake and John.

"Get a good night's sleep and check in with me in the afternoon."

ꕥ

Abby found the envelope that Sam left in her apartment. It was sealed with packing tape. If she opened it and he came back to get it, he would know she opened it. She felt she already knew too much about the Masons, and if there was more information in the envelope, she could be considered an accessory, if something bad happened. But Sam told her he was protecting them, so nothing bad did or would happen to them. *Right?* She second guessed herself.

She put the envelope back where she found it, underneath the couch, and hoped she could forget the whole thing. The people asking her about the Masons is what scared her. She hadn't seen them yesterday and was glad they didn't come in. When Sam called, he was mad, but she didn't care. Her lease was up in two weeks. She'd move, change jobs, and get a new phone number so Sam couldn't find where she went.

Florida was a nice place to stay, she'd heard. No relatives or family in Florida. She'd never mentioned it to Sam that she'd like to move there someday. There was no way he could track her down. She'd take out cash and close her credit card.

She laughed to herself. *I've been hanging around Sam too long. Well, it's his fault he told me how to disappear so no one could find you.* There were a few more things she needed to do before she left. She'd been in love with Sam, but now she wasn't sure.

ꕤ

John called Max and let him know what was going on. "We might be breaking and entering again today. I'll do anything to find my parents, but I was so scared the last time we did it, and there wasn't anyone living there. Now, someone could come home at any time, and just my luck, they'd come home while we were there."

"I can come and visit you out there on weekends. Alcatraz is no longer open, you'll just have to tell me where they lock you up."

"I knew there was a reason I called you. Always the optimist."

"Just think of it as you're a lot further now with help than you were sitting home researching on the computer. If you have to break and enter, well, consider it as part of the process."

"I thought I was getting so much done, researching in the privacy and safety of my own home, but after just a few days, we've found out a lot." He played with the money clip. "I need to call Nell. I'll check in after I'm arrested." Max laughed and disconnected.

He dialed Nell's number. "Nell, I know you're at work."

"Not a problem. I need to hear your voice. How are things going?"

"Good so far. We had to have help from Jake and Peggy's friends. They're flying from Omaha. I wanted it to be a private search, just the three of us, but I'm glad now. The more eyes and ears we have out here, the better."

"I'm happy for you, John, and I miss you." There were a few seconds of silence. "Paul called and wanted us to visit again. I told him you were out of town, but he invited me to come."

"Are you going?"

"It wouldn't be the same without you, but I'd sure like to see that little baby again."

"If you go, give her a kiss for me."

"I will. Love you, John."

"Love you too." John disconnected.

There was a knock on his door. He looked through the peep hole, even though he knew it had to be either Jake or Peggy. He was confused as to who was outside his door. The woman had long black curly hair with a head band. She had on a leather Harley jacket. *That's Peggy. Or is it?*

"John, this is Peggy."

He opened the door. "Peggy, you changed your disguise. I didn't really recognize you."

She walked into his room. "I know. I didn't want to look like I did yesterday, in case, overnight, Abby got to thinking how familiar we looked. Oh, and we're ready to go. I hope you had a good night's sleep. It might be the only morning we have to sleep in."

"Yeah, I'm ready. Are you sure we have to look around Abby's apartment?"

"We'll see whether Abby came back to work today, and then Jake will decide."

John took his wallet off the bed and slipped it into his back pocket, took his phone and put it in his front pocket. He met Peggy in the hall.

"Jake is in the car." Peggy led the way down the hall, past the front desk, and out to the parking lot where Jake was waiting.

"John, are you ready for today?"

"Not if we search Abby's apartment, but for the rest, I'm up for."

"You can be the lookout, and Peggy and I can go in."

"Either way, I'll be a nervous wreck." He got in the front seat and buckled up.

Jake and Peggy buckled up as well, and Jake drove to the coffee house. Peggy had their coffee and food orders written down. He found a parking space two blocks away. "Okay, Peg, we wait here for you, then we'll drive to the apartment . . . I guess we make sure Abby's here first."

Peggy looked around for Abby while she waited in line. She'd order anyway whether she was there or not. "I love your jacket," said the guy in front of her.

"Thanks."

"You eating lunch alone?"

"No, I'm meeting my friends. I'm getting coffee and food for them."

"How can you eat on a motorcycle?"

"Ah . . . we're taking it home."

"So how can you carry food and coffee on a motorcycle?"

"Sidecar."

"Sweet. What kind do you have? Did you have the sidecar put on, or did you buy it like that?"

"Sir, do you want to order?" the barista asked the guy in front of Peggy.

Peggy pointed toward the counter, and he turned around and ordered.

"Will you be here tomorrow?"

"I come in every day," said Peggy.

"See you tomorrow. I'll go check out your sidecar."

Peggy shook her head. *I hope you're gone when I leave.*

Abby walked through the Employees Only door, tied on her apron, and went to the counter. "Can I help you?"

Peggy walked to the counter and handed Abby her list.

"How come you're late?" asked the guy working next to her.

"I overslept because the electricity went off." She looked at him. "Before you say anything, because I know it's one o'clock, I stayed up late, and when I don't work, I don't set the alarm, and I sleep until noon. My body thought it was Saturday, and I slept through the alarm." She looked at Peggy, took her money, and made change. "You can pick up your order at the end of the counter."

Peggy took her time putting the change back in her wallet. The boss came over to Abby and said, "Since you're late, can you stay longer? Until seven tonight?"

"Sure, I'll work." She'd be accommodating, she thought, so when she disappeared, at least they'd say good things about her.

Peggy got her order and headed to the car. "Hey, I don't see your sidecar."

Dang! "Did I say I rode it today?"

"Where is it?" he demanded.

"If I scream, my husband will come running and beat your sorry ass."

"Oh, aren't you tough."

Peggy took out her cell phone with her free hand and speed-dialed Jake. "Come get me. Now."

The guy laughed. "You are such a liar. No sidecar, no husband. You must come in here and order all that food to live out a fantasy that you have friends. Why don't you just give me three hundred dollars and I'll forget all your lies."

Jake walked between them and faced the guy. "I'm the husband, and she's not giving you any money. If you don't leave right now, I'm calling the cops."

"Well, Mr. Big Guy, why don't *you* give *me* the money?"

Jake took out his phone and dialed 911, but before he pushed the call button, the guy yelled, "Wait! I'm just joking around. I'll leave." He winked at Peggy. "See you tomorrow. Then I'll let you buy me coffee."

The guy staggered to his car and got in. Jake pushed the call button. "A guy just got into his car, and he was staggering and smelled like alcohol. He's at the coffee house." Jake gave the address and his plate number, then disconnected.

The guy started his car, put it in reverse, and rammed into the car behind him. They could hear the sirens in the distance. Peggy and Jake walked to their car and got in. John heard the sirens and saw the cop car down the street.

Jake pulled out onto the street. "What happened?" asked John. "Should I be worried?"

"No. It all started when Peggy bragged about her sidecar, and when she said she had a husband, the guy didn't believe her. I think he was either on drugs or drunk, so I called the cops so he wouldn't hurt anyone."

The squad car pulled in front of the coffee house and went up to the driver still trying to get his car out onto the street. He slammed his car again into the car behind him when the officer knocked on his window.

"Looks like he won't be bothering anyone for a while."

"Good. I mean, good that you two aren't running from the law."

"Not yet," said Peggy.

That comment didn't put John at ease, although he knew she was trying to lighten the mood. He wanted to just go home, but he didn't want to forget about finding his parents. He would stick it out no matter what happened. The memory of his parents eating

Christmas dinner at Nell's house kept him going. "Is there a report from your friends?"

"Not yet," said Jake. "They got a late start. Peg, what happened in the coffee house? Is Abby at work?"

"She came in late. I was the first one she waited on. I took my time putting my money away, and the boss asked her to work until seven tonight."

"Good. That gives us plenty of time."

"Plenty of time for what?"

"We can eat, then check out the apartment." They sat around the picnic table outside the hotel. They ate in silence. Jake was planning out the next move at the apartment. He'd be happier if he could get in the security door behind someone, like he did with Abby. He'd have to make sure John was up for the task, or he'd have Peggy step in, and John would be the lookout.

Hopefully, they'd get a lead on what to do next, and depending on what Brad and Joyce found out, they might find John's parents soon. He wasn't giving up. It was harder than finding his own mother, but for his own mother, the address was given to him, and she was really living there. Knowing the feelings he felt when finding her kept him going to find John's parents. Jake knew how wonderful it was to have his mom living with him. He wanted John to feel that way too.

John wondered if his friend was back to work today. If they could only get the license number, then figure out who Sam was, and then someone would tell them where his parents were. Or was that too easy? He didn't think so.

He ate his sandwich Peggy ordered from the cafe, not really tasting it while his thoughts raced. He missed Nell and wished she was here. The conversations they had after he told her his secrets were deep and fulfilling to John. No longer did he have to lie or be silent about the justice he wanted to bring to victims. Nell was supportive, encouraging. *She would be a good mother . . . Where did that come from?* wondered John.

Peggy finished eating and drinking her coffee. She remembered the day Jake found his mom, and what a happy day it was. She wanted John to be happy. He'd been so nervous ever since they met him at the airport. Peggy thought the unknown is often scary. John, she hoped, would find contentment in whatever happened.

If they didn't find the Masons, she wanted John to feel like he tried and gave it all he had so he could find that peace, and all the better if they were found. Whatever happened, she would give everything she had to the cause.

"John, what do you want to do? Come with me or be the lookout?"

"I'll go with you."

"I've decided to wait for someone to get into the security door and we would follow. I don't want to mess with the door. Once inside, we'd be hidden, and it would be easier to break into Abby's door. I didn't think there was a dead bolt. If there is, I don't think I'd know how to get in. We'll just have to wait and see." He looked at Peggy. "No, I don't want to wait and see. I'm going to make a phone call."

He dialed. "Arnie, did I get you at a bad time?"

"No, what do you need, kid?"

Jake explained what he was about to do.

"Do you have a pick and tension wrench?" Then he answered his own question. "Of course, you do." Arnie continued and told Jake step by step what he needed to do.

Jake asked a few questions until he understood exactly what had to be done. "Thanks, Arnie." He disconnected. "Let's go to the room. I'm going to practice."

It took Jake ten minutes to open the door without the key. He needed to get it open quicker than that. He didn't want to be in the hall that long tampering with the lock. He tried it again and again until he could do it in a couple of minutes. Then he picked John's lock on his door. "Okay, I think I can do it."

"Who is Arnie?" asked John. He didn't want to break Jake's concentration by asking questions while he was working on the locks.

"A good friend. He has taught me so much about construction, electricity, and plumbing."

"Does this guy pick locks for a living?"

Jake laughed. "Not Arnie. He's just a good guy who knows a lot about everything. Are you ready?"

Peggy was changing into her jeans and T-shirt while Jake was picking the locks. John started to sweat as they all walked to the car. He wiped his forehead with his arm, but that didn't help. When he was in the back seat, his hands started shaking, so he sat on them after he buckled his seatbelt.

Peggy drove and parked down the street from the apartment building. "We're going to sit on that cement wall by the entrance. We need to keep a conversation going so people don't think we're waiting to break in. We'll just make up stuff. Then when someone heads to the entrance, we follow."

"I'll try. I'm so nervous I don't even know if I can stand up long enough to walk over there."

"Take your time, John. You can always be the lookout."

"I don't think I'd be good at that either. I might just take the car and never come back."

Jake waited until John felt he could walk or make a decision to let Peggy go with Jake. John ran his fingers through his sweaty, frizzy hair. "I'm ready to go with Jake." He held on to the door and pulled himself out. His legs were a little shaky, but he stood and, to his surprise, was able to walk with Jake to the cement wall and sit.

"How's your son? I remember you said he wasn't doing very well in school."

John looked at him, confused, then remembered what Jake was doing. "Yes, little Randy is doing better now. His mother took him to live with her, and she works with him every day. Of course, she doesn't have a job, and now I'm paying child support."

"Child support! That's crazy. Did she pay you child support when you had Randy?"

"Nope."

They continued their conversation for another twenty minutes when a couple started walking up the stairs. Jake and John followed them into the building. The couple continued up another flight of stairs when they got inside. Jake and John walked down the hall and stopped in front of Abby's apartment. There was a bolt lock and a regular door lock.

Jake got busy with his tools, and before long, they were inside. John didn't even try to hide the fact that he was sweating and shaking. His mind willed him to do what he had to do.

"You look in the bedroom, John."

The place was clean, and there wasn't any clutter anywhere. No dirty dishes. Nothing sitting out. He opened the oven, the dishwasher, and all the cupboards. He opened the refrigerator. There was milk, a few cans of pop, and cheese sticks. In the freezer, there was ice cream and frozen pizza. He looked under the sink—nothing.

He moved to the living room. Nothing out of place there either. No computer, no magazines, no books. There were built in book cases with a few knickknacks of horses. He noticed a picture of a horse hanging above the couch. *She likes horses.* He took the cushion off the chair in front of the bookshelves and felt inside the chair—nothing.

The same was done with the couch—nothing, not even a crumb or a piece of fuzz. He looked around for more places to hide things. Although Jake was doubtful he was going to find anything, he still looked.

He walked down the hall and checked on John. For all Jake knew, he might've passed out. John was going through the drawers. "Most these drawers are empty. I looked in the closet, and there was nothing there. I even did the knock trick to see if there was a secret door. Nothing sounded any different. Did you find anything?"

"No. I don't think there's anything here, but my gut tells me there is." He looked at his phone to make sure Peggy didn't try to contact him. There weren't any messages. "You finish in here. I'll check the bathroom and look in the living room again.

The medicine cabinet had a bottle of aspirin and cotton swabs. The closet in the bathroom had extra toilet paper, Kleenex, paper towels, nothing in the tub or in the toilet tank. He walked back down the hall and stopped before he entered the living room. He looked at everything—the pictures, the bookshelves. John walked into the living room and watched Jake look behind the pictures.

Frustrated but didn't want to give up just yet, he stood back and looked at the room again. His eyes looked at the ceiling, the moldings, the hardwood floor, the throw rug. "Look at the rug. It's crooked. Everything in this apartment is neat, and nothing is out of place, except that rug. The corner of it is underneath the couch."

Jake got on his hands and knees, pulled the rug from underneath the couch, and part of a manila envelope came with it. He pulled the document-sized envelope out, set it on the couch, and put the rug back the way it was. The envelope was sealed with packing tape. He stood and walked toward John.

"We're taking this with us. I don't know what it is or if we'll need it, but either way, I'll put it back the next time Abby is at work."

Jake relocked the door, and then he used his picks to relock the bolt from the hall. No one was around, so it made it easy for Jake to work without anyone noticing them lingering in the hall. Jake put the envelope under his shirt, and he and John walked to the car.

"Take us to the hotel, Peg. Then let's check out and get a new place to stay." Even though they'd already done that before getting the number off Abby's phone, Jake felt if they moved around a lot, no one could follow them. Or that was the plan.

Nothing was said. They got to the hotel, packed, checked out, and Peggy drove to another hotel several miles away. They checked in and met in John's room where Jake planned on opening the envelope.

CHAPTER SEVEN

Brad knocked on the door of the people who lived next door to the Masons. He waited several minutes, and when no one answered, he moved on to the next house. Joyce was on the other side of the street. They made several copies of the Masons' picture from the e-mail Peggy sent before they left for Reno, so if anyone answered their door, they would show the picture.

"Hi." Joyce introduced herself. "I've been looking for your neighbors and was wondering if you knew what happened to them."

"I'm Gert. What neighbors?"

Joyce showed her the pictures. The elderly lady took the picture with her arthritis-stricken hand. "Come in, I need to get my glasses."

Joyce followed her in. The lady put on her glasses and studied the picture. "How long ago did they disappear? And where did they live?"

"At one time, they lived in the house across the street, the green one."

"I've been here a year, so I wouldn't know if anything happened. You might want to ask Pearl next door to me." She pointed with a crooked finger to the left. "She's lived here forever."

Joyce printed off business cards before they left home with her name and cell number. She thought, since she was interviewing people, she'd want them to call her if they remembered something after she left. "Here's my card. Call me if anything changes."

"Pearl loves mysteries. She *should* be retired so she could solve crimes. She's good at it. Too bad she thinks that at seventy-two, she should still be working."

"Thanks, Gert, for your help. Keep in touch."

Joyce skipped Pearl's house because she thought, if she works, she wouldn't be home, so she moved on to the next one—no answer. She continued down the block, but no one was home. She sent Brad a text. He responded immediately with *Let's go to the hotel and come back later when people are home from work.*

Joyce told Brad Gert's story on the way to the hotel. "Let's both go to Pearl's first tonight. If she's interested in solving mysteries, she might've been watching the neighborhood when they disappeared. Let's hope."

At the hotel, Joyce sent Peggy a text on their progress and wrote she would update them again tonight.

"As long as we have some free time, let's tour Alcatraz."

"Really," said Joyce. "I was hoping we could do the same thing."

He walked to her and put his arms around her. "We think alike, great minds and all that babble."

Joyce laughed. He kissed her. "It's nice to get away again. I think it's because I'm getting away with you. When we are home, or I'm in Omaha with you, we work at the shelter from morning until night whether there is someone there or not. We hardly get enough time to do this." He kissed her again.

"This *is* nice. Now that we got all the training set with the volunteering instructors and people enrolled, and even though it was time consuming it's been very rewarding.

"Remember the lady who, after one day of computer training, broke down and cried. She was so happy she learned something. Her husband forbid any electronic devices into the house, so she felt she could never find a job without computer skills. Now she can."

"It's amazing, isn't it?"

He kissed her again. "We'd better put on warmer clothes. It's chilly on the water."

They drove to Pier 33 and bought tickets.

The closer they got to the island, the more massive the lighthouse looked, and being on the water, they were happy with the warmer clothes.

When the boat anchored, they walked up the hill to the prison. They were handed a device with earplugs. "Put these on and make sure you hear me. My assistant will check with each of you to make sure yours works. Follow me.

"Alcatraz has an amazing history behind it, but it still had to be closed because of the high costs of running the island, much higher than the cost of other federal facilities. Food and water had to be shipped in, and the buildings on the island began to deteriorate from the salty sea air. There have been 1,576 men housed on the island over the nearly thirty years of operation."

They followed him into the prison. "Some of the most dangerous criminals were housed here: Scarface Capone, Robert Stroud, the Birdman of Alcatraz, to name a few."

As they toured the prison, the guide gave them more history and interesting facts about Alcatraz, which is nicknamed *The Rock.* The assistant collected their devices at the end of the tour. "In June, they will hold the Escape from Alcatraz Triathlon. It includes a swim for a mile and a half from Alcatraz, a hilly eighteen-mile bike ride through Presidio, and an eight-mile run on the trail through Baker Beach to the Sand Ladder. Get in shape and join us again in June."

"Have you done the triathlon?"

"No. But I'd certainly like to be in that good of shape to participate," said their guide. "Thanks for coming, and enjoy the rest of your day in San Francisco."

ഗ്ഗ

Jake took his pocket knife and cut the tape. He looked at John. "Do you want me to continue?"

"I feel more nervous now than when I was in Abby's apartment." He walked to the bathroom and took a towel off the rack and returned to the bed and sat. He mopped his brow with the towel and ran it through his hair. "Yes, let's open it. If we wait and it's nothing to do with my parents, I'll be disappointed we didn't move on in our plans."

Jake moved his knife along the sealed part of the envelope and opened it. He looked in first as if he expected something to jump out at him. He pulled out the inch-thick documents. "Let's go through these together." Jake looked around. There really wasn't a big enough space for the three of them.

"Let's go downstairs to the breakfast area. No one is usually there during the day."

Jake put the documents back in, and they took the stairs. Jake was right, no one was there. "When or if anyone sits down here, we stop what we're doing and go back to the room—that is, if it's something pertinent to the case."

Peggy and John nodded. Once downstairs, Jake again took the documents out, set them on the table. John and Peggy were on either side of him so they could see. Jake started out by reading the first one in a soft voice.

"Report 23: Sam Ward. I am investigating . . ." Jake looked at John. "Now we know it's pertinent to the case. So we don't waste time, let's get to a Kinko's and get this stuff copied, then bring the envelope back to Abby's. It's not seven yet, we'll have plenty of time. I just don't want her to look for it when she gets home and it's not there." Jake took the documents and envelope."

Peggy looked on her phone for the address of the nearest copy place. There were several closer than Kinko's, but they claimed they would do all the work and make copies for their customers. They needed the privacy where they could make their own copies so Jake drove further to have the privacy.

He put in his credit card and started copying. When that was done, he removed his credit card, took the copies and originals. He bought another envelope, but it was blue so they wouldn't get them mixed up. He also purchased packing tape, reclosed Abby's envelope, and got back in the car, and Jake drove to Abby's.

John stayed in the car this time while Jake went back into the apartment. Within five minutes, he was back outside in the car. "Envelope is back, the rug is back in the crooked position. Hopefully, all is well."

They were back at the downstairs table at the hotel, Jake reading the documents. There were pictures of the Masons in their yard, at the coffee house, walking in the park. There was a picture of people loading merchandise into the back of a van. Jake studied it. The next picture was the Masons walking by the truck. Since it was a closer shot, the merchandise was enlarged as well.

"This looks like drugs." Both Peggy and John confirmed that it did.

He set the picture down. "Okay, what if they saw the drug shipment? The person taking the pictures gave it to the boss, which,

I'm thinking, is Sam, instead of killing them." John winced, but Jake continued. "They relocated them, told them it was for their own good, probably had them believe they were the FBI, and they went willingly."

"I don't think my dad would've believed it so easily. In the picture, it looks like my parents were talking to each other and didn't notice the truck. I wonder if something else happened."

Jake continued reading until he came across another picture and handed it to John.

"It looks like they are in their backyard."

Peggy took the picture. "Who is that by the fence?" She handed it back.

John looked at it for several minutes. He took the other pictures and looked at them again. He pointed to the same man in each picture. "They were being watched. I'm starting to get confused by this whole thing."

"It will take us a couple of days to put a new plan together. As much as I would like to take a break, I'm going to keep reading," said Jake. "There's only a few documents left."

The last document had a picture of the house that Jake and John broke into. "Look at this house. This is the end of the documents. What happened after they left here? Sam and Abby must have broken off their relationship, or he just got too busy and didn't come around anymore. The trail stops at that house."

John took out his cell phone and dialed his contact. "Hey, it's John. How you feeling?"

"Not so good. The doc says I should stay home a few more days before going back to work." John's whole being took a dive. He wanted to move forward on this and find resolution. "You wanted a plate number. You still want it?"

"Yeah."

"I can call my partner and have him run it."

"I would owe you big time if you did that for me."

"Okay, I'll give him a call."

"Take care of yourself, and I hope you're back to work soon." John disconnected.

"He'll be out a few more days, but he's calling his partner so he can look it up."

"Perfect," said Peggy.

"Let's find a restaurant for dinner. By the time we're finished eating, hopefully, we'll get a report from Joyce and Brad."

ꕥ

Joyce and Brad got out of the car and stood on the sidewalk. They noticed Pearl looking at them from an upstairs window. "Pretend you don't see her," said Joyce. "If she's the neighbor spy, then we might have a chance in knowing what happened to the Masons."

Joyce knocked on Pearl's door, and when she was about to knock again, a spry elderly woman answered the door. "You must be the lady who talked to Gert. She called me when I got home and told me you would be stopping by. Come on in." She pointed to two chairs in her living room. "Make yourself at home. I'll make tea." Before they could object, she was down the hall heading for the kitchen.

The walls were a pale pink with a flower border. A triangle chest of drawers sat in the corner of the front wall, and the furniture had the same flowered fabric as the wallpaper border. A coffee table sat in front of the couch. There weren't any knickknacks, no pictures, no clutter. Joyce was tempted to open the drawers to see what kind of stuff she kept in there.

"I'll be there in a minute!" Pearl yelled from the kitchen.

To Joyce, that was permission to open a drawer—nothing inside. She opened another one—nothing. Brad walked over to her, took her arm, and led her to the couch. "Are you crazy?" he whispered.

She smiled at him. "No one that I know of doesn't own a small statue to put out or a collection of something," she whispered back.

"Everything is ready," said Pearl as she came into the room. She poured tea for Brad and Joyce, then herself. "I have sugar, honey, milk. You can add whatever you want."

Brad was not too thrilled about drinking tea, but he went through the motions, added a little honey, sugar, and milk, Sipped, put the cup back on the saucer, and tried not to frown from the awful taste.

"Now fill me in on what you want. I'll try and be as helpful as I can."

"When was the last time you saw the Masons? I heard they lived across the street, and then one day their house was for sale. No one saw them leave."

"They were nice people. They had a son who came home from college now and then." She took a sip of her tea, contemplating. "I do remember they just disappeared, but I don't know why."

"Did you notice anything suspicious going on over there before they were gone? Or anything suspicious after they left?" She thought of Pearl looking out her window and hoped she saw something.

"No, not really, but I work during the day, so I don't see much of what goes on. When I get home at night, I have my drapes closed, and I don't think to look out at my neighbors. That would be wrong to spy on people."

Brad wanted to say something, but he didn't. What he really wanted to do was leave. She was starting to make him uncomfortable.

"Oh, where do you work?"

Pearl's hand had a tremor, and her cup clanked down on the saucer. When she looked at Joyce, she looked guilty about something.

"I work at a factory downtown." She hoped they weren't familiar with the downtown area. "I've been there almost thirty years. The pay's good." *The pay is very good.* "Gives me something to do."

"What do you do there?"

"I answer the phone, set up meetings, appointments."

Joyce handed her a card. "Call me if you think of something." Joyce and Brad stood and walked to the door. Pearl continued sitting, looking at the card. "Thanks for the tea."

"Sure. Nice meeting you folks. I'll definitely call if I think of something." She let them leave on their own as she sat.

Joyce took Brad's hand when there were outside. "Follow my lead." They walked to the sidewalk. "Let's stand here for a while." They stood in front of the car and looked across the street at the Masons former house. "Turn around and kiss me, and see if you can see Pearl looking at us."

Brad wrapped his arms around Joyce and kissed her passionately. He kept his eyes on the house, but he couldn't see the upstairs windows. He kissed her forehead with his eyes half closed and saw Pearl looking out the front window. His lips found hers, and he mumbled, "She's looking at us. Let's go, she gives me the creeps."

They broke their embrace, got in the car, and drove off.

"If she's not into what happens in the neighborhood, why does she always stare out the window? She didn't know when we were coming, and she was looking out."

"Like I said, she gives me the creeps, and not many people do that."

"When we get back to the hotel, I'll call Peggy."

"I'll call Jake and give him my side of the story, and maybe with everything, they can figure Pearl out."

"I wonder if *anyone* can figure out that old bird."

"When we're done with our calls, let's get something to eat, then try and talk to more people. They should be home from work by now."

ꕤ

Jake conveyed what Brad had told him about their visit with Pearl, and then Peggy told Joyce's side of the story.

"I don't get why an elderly woman wouldn't have anything in her house—no pictures, no mementos, nothing in the drawer," said John. "Both my grandmas had stuff sitting out all over, pictures, books, magazines. My father's mother had her spoon collection displayed and her china."

"Do you remember Pearl from the neighborhood?"

"Not really," said John. "I knew there was a single elderly lady who lived there, but that's all I knew."

"I noticed Abby didn't have any knickknacks either—no clutter, no stuff, period," said Jake. "There might be a connection, or it's just an unlikely coincidence."

"Let's say they do know each other. Or they both might just know Sam. Sam likes women who don't come with baggage. Pearl might be a relative, Abby might be someone he fell in love with," said Peggy.

"Pearl could be his mother," said Jake. "He was living at home, noticed the Masons doing something or finding out something that he didn't like or felt threatened by, and helped them disappear, or made them disappear."

"The picture of the truck with drugs might be the reason. Mom and Dad were in the picture. Maybe they witnessed a drug heist, or they were thought to because they'd passed by. It seemed they were more interested in their own conversation than what was going on at the truck."

"Pearl works at a factory downtown," said Jake. He took out the picture of the scene with the truck. He pointed to the building in the background. "Maybe she works here, sets up drug runs, organizes everything. She recognized the Masons walking past. She was afraid if they reported what happened, she'd get caught, spend her golden years in jail. If Sam is related to her, possibly her son, the family would end up in jail."

"They had to get rid of them," said Peggy, "but they're not into murder."

"Thank God," said John.

Peggy continued. "Pearl stays home the next day and watches the Masons from her upstairs window. Michelle leaves and walks up the street. Maybe Pearl follows her and sees her going into the coffee house. She knows Michelle and didn't want to call attention to herself, so she tells her son instead of following her in."

"It's all speculation," said Jake as he looked at John. "We need to tie up a few loose ends first. Who is Sam? Who does the license plate belong to?"

"And what's up with Pearl?" said John.

"Good question," said Peggy.

ꕥ

Brad and Joyce knocked on a neighbor's door right next to the Masons, in line with Pearl's house. "I don't even want to look at her house, in case she's looking at us."

A boy in his teens answered the door. "What's up?"

"I wanted to ask some questions about our friends. They lived next door to you, the Masons. Did you know them?"

"Yeah, I knew them. I cut their grass. I went over there one day, and Michelle didn't come outside when I was done. She usually pays me right away. I noticed that night their lights weren't on. They'd never left home as far as I knew. The next day I went over there, and they were acting funny. Michelle paid me though, said I wouldn't have to do it again. I never asked why, and she never told me. She even paid me ten dollars more."

"Otherwise, did you notice anything funny besides the way they were acting?"

"One day, after school, I noticed a truck out front. It was dark. I stayed after to work on a science project that day."

"What kind of a truck was it?"

"It was a van truck or . . . a big white van."

"Did it have any lettering on it?"

"There was, but it was hard to read." He looked outside as he thought of the lettering. "It was as if it were worn off. Some letters were there, some weren't."

"Which ones could you read?"

"The first letter was a fancy S. The next ones were worn. The last two were NT. In the middle or on the side, it looked like a picture or something."

"A logo?"

"Maybe. That's all I really know. I sure do miss them. If you find them, tell them hi for me."

"We will," said Joyce. "You've been very helpful." She gave him her card.

ജ്ജ

Jake disconnected. "There's a truck that was in front of your folks' house. The kid next door said he made out some lettering on the side of the truck. The first letter was a fancy S, the last two were NT."

John slid the picture of the truck over to get a closer look at it. "Look at this. The same lettering is on this truck."

"Now it appears as if everything were connected somehow." Jake took a closer look at the picture, looked at everything—the truck, the people, the Masons, the building. He slid the picture back to John. "Look at the building, does it look familiar?"

He studied it for a few minutes. "Yes, that's the office of the self-storage facility just out of downtown. We went there once when we were moving from an apartment to the house."

"Do you have anything in storage there now?" asked Peggy.

"They turned us down. We didn't even get a chance to ask questions or to say what we wanted. The guy said the secretary had a day off and that he knew for a fact that all the storage spaces were taken. When we left, there were a few spaces with the doors open and they were all empty. There were about four of them. There was a truck there too. I can't identify it as the one in the picture though. We thought it strange that we were turned away and they did have storage there, or so we thought at the time. Maybe it was already rented out."

"Why do you think your parents were walking by there that day?"

"They liked to walk, walk everywhere. Dad would drive somewhere, and they'd get out and walk." John laughed. "I wished

I'd have inherited that energy. The only walking I do is when I pace the floor."

"Makes a person think better," said Peggy.

"Now what do we do?"

"I don't know for sure." He took Peggy's tablet, gave them a piece of paper and a pencil. "Write down what you think we need to do next. Then we'll brainstorm about our next move."

CHAPTER EIGHT

Brad and Joyce ordered room service the next morning. They were going to talk to a few more people, report in, then find out if they were still needed or if they could possibly help out in other ways.

"The first thing we do when we leave the hotel this morning is to drive down Lombard Street." She was reading from the brochure. "It has a sign posted 5 MPH. You'd better drive then because I've never went that slow in my life."

"I'll drive. We don't want to miss a curve and end up at the bottom."

Joyce's phone rang. She didn't recognize the number. "Hello. Oh, Pearl." She put the phone on speaker.

"I've been thinking about what you said yesterday, and I think I have more to add about the Masons."

"That's great," said Joyce. "We can stop by tonight after you get home from work."

"No, no, I don't think what I have to say can wait. I took the day off so you can come over any time you have free."

Joyce looked at Brad, then her watch. "We'll be there at eleven." Pearl hung up.

"She hung up without saying goodbye. Oh well, as long as we get information. I figured we do the drive first. Then we're heading to Ghirardelli Square."

"I sense a chocolate theme in Jake's endeavors. If I decide to go to this Chocolate Square and buy you chocolate, will you stay with me always and forever?"

"You not only have to buy me chocolate, but also keep it always in stock until death do us part."

"I think I can do that." He sipped his coffee. "Do we need to call Jake and check in about meeting with Pearl?"

"We can just call him when we leave her house and fill him in on what happened. I hope she has information that Jake can use. If I wanted to find my parents, which I don't, I would want all the information I could get."

"Let's make sure we leave with something John can use."

ജ ഗ

Brad knocked on Pearl's door. He wasn't looking forward to seeing her again, but he was doing it for John, not for himself, and when she started giving him the creeps again, he would remember who he was doing it for.

"Come in, come in." They followed her to the living room and sat in the same chairs. "I'll get tea." She headed down the hall to the kitchen.

"If I drink one more sip of that tea, I'll barf," said Brad.

"Just make it look like you're drinking it or enjoying it."

"Ha, not a chance that I'll look like I'm enjoying the tea. I'm going to make faces this time with every sip."

"Behave."

Brad had his eyes on the tray as she walked into the living room, his stomach churning at the thought of more tea. The tray was set on the coffee table. He saw the same teapot, the sugar, the honey, the cream. Joyce's tea was poured first, then Brad's. Pearl didn't pour herself tea, it was already poured. A warning sign shot through him.

He looked at Joyce, she was talking small talk with Pearl. He had to stop her from drinking the tea and, at the same time, take some of it with him so he could have it analyzed. His brains scrambled for a plan.

He didn't want to mask the taste this time. He wanted it pure. Joyce was busy holding her tea cup and talking about the San Francisco weather.

"Oh goodness," he uttered as his cup of tea spilled down his shirt.

Joyce took a long drink of her tea before she set it down to help Brad and a look of horror crossed Brad's face. "Let me get you another napkin." Pearl went walking back to the kitchen.

"Don't drink anymore of your tea," whispered Brad frantically. "I think it's poisoned. I don't think she had anything to tell us, she just wanted us over here. We need to get you to the hospital as soon as possible."

"I feel dizzy. What did you say?"

Brad took her tea and poured it back into the pot. Seconds later, Pearl came back with napkins and handed them to Brad. "Thank you, Pearl." He pretended to blot the tea from his shirt.

"Pearl, what did you, you, tell us?" slurred Joyce.

"Are you okay, Joyce?" He looked at Pearl. "I think we'd better go. She didn't sleep well last night. I think I just need to take her to the hotel and tuck her in."

"You can't leave without drinking your tea." She poured him another cup.

He had to think fast before it was too late for Joyce. "Could you write down your phone number for me so I can call you for another visit?"

"Oh sure, I'll go get something to write it down with," she said while still watching him pretending to take a drink of tea. She smiled as she left.

He poured his tea into the pot and heard her footsteps coming back down the hall. She sat down and gave him her contact information. "Thanks, Pearl. I really need . . . to get . . . to . . . leave . . . you . . . be . . ." He stumbled trying to help Joyce up. He noticed Pearl's plastered smile on her face. He got Joyce into the car and raced down the block. While he was driving, he called 911, got directions for the nearest hospital, and increased the speed.

Pearl looked out the window when they left. *The way he's speeding, he'll crash the car, and they'll both die, and no one will suspect the poison.*

ꙮ

"She drank some bad tea."

Joyce was taken to a room on a stretcher. They pumped her stomach and gave her charcoal. While waiting in the lounge, Brad called Jake.

"Pearl called us and said she had information for us. We were there an hour ago. Short story, Pearl poisoned Joyce. She would've poisoned me too, but I figured it out before I drank it. I'm still waiting for the doctor to come out and tell me how she's doing."

"What hospital are you at? We'll be there as soon as we can."

"Jake, stay where you are. Keep looking and figuring out what needs to be done. Just give me a little direction on what to do. Should I report Pearl? The sooner I do it, the less likely she'll have a chance to get rid of the poison."

"She might be connected to Sam, and from reading the notes, he might be a bad cop. Pearl might be his mother. We're just not one hundred percent sure. If he is a cop, he might tip off Pearl and get her out of town before he sends a squad car over there to arrest her."

"For now, I just want Joyce to be okay. Oh, hang on, the doctor is here."

"She's doing fine," said the doctor. "We got her stomach pumped in time, and she's resting. We'll keep her overnight under observation. You can go back and see her."

"Thanks, Doctor . . . Jake, Joyce is fine. Nothing was said about the poison."

"I'm glad she's fine, Brad. I'll get back to you in an hour and let you know what to do next. Remember, if at any time you want to go home, let me know. You've already helped so much."

"We're here for you, Jake. Just let me know what to do. I'm heading back to stay with Joyce and wait for your call."

Jake disconnected. "Bad news." He decided to start with the end of the story. "Joyce was poisoned by Pearl, the lady who lives across the street from where your folks lived."

Startled, Peggy asked, "Is she okay?"

"Brad got her to the hospital in time."

John was pale as he sat there comprehending the information he just received—Pearl, the lady he was told was a good neighbor. "*Pearl* did the poisoning?" asked John in disbelief. "I never meant for anyone to get hurt. I'm calling off the search, and we all go home where it's safe."

"That would be a good idea, but I don't think they'll stop just because we all went home. They've probably figured out by now who you are, John, and I'm assuming they know you live in Minneapolis. They can easily trace Peg and me, especially if Sam is in law enforcement, and from reading the documents we found in Abby's apartment, it sounds as if Sam is in some branch of authority.

"What we need to decide is if Brad should tell the doctor that Joyce was poisoned. The doctor, I would think, would have the responsibility to call the police. Brad would be questioned, he'd give Pearl's name, and if things went according to protocol, Pearl would be questioned.

"If Sam is on the police force, once he heard Pearl's name, he'd question her himself, find out what she did was needed to protect their operation, and Sam would destroy the police report, and come after Brad and Joyce."

"What happens if Brad doesn't report it?" asked Peggy.

"We have more time to put the pieces together, link Sam and Pearl together, find the Masons." He touched John's arm. "It's your call, but before you answer, if you do call off the search, I'll send Brad, Joyce, and Peggy home, and I'll stay here and continue to search for your parents. We are too close to just drop it and go home."

Jake moved his hand and rested it on the table. He hoped John would stay and help. If John's parents were found, it would be nice if the first person they saw was their son. But he didn't want to force him to do anything. Finding his own mother was easy compared to this. In finding the Masons, crimes were involved, and now there was attempted murder. He looked at Peggy, and she was studying John.

She looked tired. Sleep hadn't come easily after her abduction in Hershey, but she hadn't had a nightmare in several weeks. He sensed a good nap would restore her energy. It was a few days since he checked in with anyone at home and decided that after John made his decision, he would check in with his mom and tell her he loved her and was glad she was back in his life.

"I really want to continue the search, but as soon as someone else gets hurt, I'm calling it off," said John, looking at Jake.

"I can't promise you anything, but right now, we have to decide whether Brad tells anyone about the poisoning. I say no for now. He gets Joyce out of the hospital as soon as she's discharged and we have them stay with us."

"That's a good idea. They shouldn't be anywhere in the area," agreed Peggy.

Jake picked up his phone and called Brad. "Brad, how's Joyce?"

"She's sleeping. Her color is back, and it's so . . . good to . . ." He couldn't hold back the tears.

"I'm glad to hear she's better." Jake thought of something that he hadn't thought of when discussing the plan with John and Peggy. "Can she be moved?"

"They want to keep her overnight." Then the realization hit Brad. "Let me try and wake her. I'll call you back."

"Joyce, wake up." He shook her gently. "Joyce, can you hear me?"

She stirred, moved her legs, and opened her eyes. "Brad. What happened?"

"Remember the tea? It was poisoned. You're in the hospital, but I think we should leave before Pearl sends someone looking for us. She thought I drank the tea too. She might be checking the hospitals to see if we're here. You had your last name on that card so it would be easy for her to call the hospitals in the area and ask for your room number."

She looked down to see if she had a gown on or was still in her clothes. "Good, I still have on my clothes. Is my bag here?"

"It's by my chair."

"Help me up and we'll see if I can walk."

He uncovered her, put on her shoes, and helped her swing her feet over the side of the bed. When the dizziness lifted, he helped her up and held her until she was steady on her feet. Her bag went over her shoulder and she was left to stand by herself.

"I don't think we're going to get by with just walking out and taking the elevator. He looked in the closet, found a gown, put it on her, and hiked up her jeans so they didn't show. "Put on another gown like it was a robe. Let's walk up and down the hall a couple of times. They'll think it's therapeutic or whatever you want to call it."

Joyce hung on to Brad's arm for support and walked slowly down the hall. They noticed a stairwell at the end of the hall.

"Ms. Armstrong. How are you feeling?" Brad and Joyce turned around. "You gave us quite a scare."

"I'm feeling much better. I think walking helps."

"Don't tire yourself out, maybe one more lap, and you should rest."

"I'll make sure of it," said Brad.

"I'm going to take a quick break. Then I'll check on you." The nurse walked to the desk then to the back room.

Brad looked around. The desk was too far away for anyone to notice them, and no one else was in the hall. They turned around and headed to the stairwell. Brad pushed through the door, and Joyce followed. "I'll need to hang on to you walking down the stairs."

"Oh crap!"

"What's wrong, Brad?"

"I was going to call Jake when you woke up. Too late now. Let's keep going." Brad helped her down each step. They were on the third floor, so it took a while to get to the first floor. Joyce went into the restroom and took off her hospital gowns and met Brad in the hall. They walked out the main entrance to their car. Brad drove to the hotel. They packed, left the keycards on the dresser, and put the *Do Not Disturb* sign on the door. Brad would call the hotel desk the next day and check out.

They pulled into the gas station several miles from where they were. Brad looked at his watch and couldn't believe so much time had passed since Joyce woke up. He hoped Jake wasn't upset with him.

"Jake, sorry I didn't call before. Once Joyce woke up, everything just happened so fast. We left the hospital, got our stuff from the hotel, and now we're sitting at a gas station."

"We were worried about you." Jake gave Peggy and John a thumbs-up. "We are probably close to where you are. I think we should all be in one place." Jake gave him the hotel address and John's room number. He instructed them to clean out the rental car of all their stuff and bring it to John's room.

CHAPTER NINE

"Pam, have you heard from the kids?" asked Adeline while they were meeting again for lunch.

"Yes, Jake called. He seemed different. He was telling me how much he loved me, glad that he found me, and so happy that I lived with him and Peggy."

"Is he okay?"

"I think so, but I do wonder what has happened while looking for his friend's parents."

Adeline was going to tell her that Jake called Arnie and asked how to pick a bolt lock but decided not to worry Pam with that information. "I'm sure everything is fine. Arnie does that to me sometimes, tells me how much he loves me, gets a little cuddly about it, and then he's good for a year." They laughed. "How's Roger?"

Pam blushed. "A little cuddly." Adeline smiled. "He's a very nice guy. Things heated up when he came over for dinner after I saw him with Gail at the restaurant."

"It's about time. Roger is a good man, and he needs a good woman like you, Pam. He's had too much heartache over the years, and from what you told me, your life hasn't been easy either. You both know what you don't want your relationship to be like, so you're that much further ahead. You're good for each other."

"Thanks, Adeline. I think so too."

ഇര

Sam took the elevator to the third floor and walked to Joyce's room. She was gone, but he knew she was there, the sheets were pulled back on the bed. He walked to the desk and asked where she was.

"Oh, her husband and she were walking the halls so Joyce could get her strength back. I told her not to get tired out." She looked at her watch. "That was an hour ago."

"She's not in her room."

"She might be in the bathroom. I'll go take a look." Sam followed her. The nurse knocked on the bathroom door in Joyce's room. She knocked again, then opened the door—empty. "I don't know where she is."

Sam hurried down the hall to the elevator. He slid behind the wheel of his car and called Pearl. "She's not here."

"Did they move her?"

"No, she's gone, which means he's gone too."

"That can't be. I was told they were keeping her overnight and that her husband was staying in the room."

"How did you get so much information?"

"I told the nurse I was her mother."

"Aren't you clever? Well, they're not here. I'll run a check on hotels when I get back to the precinct. They have to be staying in the area." He disconnected, disgusted with incompetents who couldn't do their job. *I should've just asked Abby to marry me and left the state. I wouldn't be in this trouble if I had.*

At his desk at the precinct, he ran a check on Joyce Armstrong, then just Armstrong—nothing. Was Joyce even married? He Googled her name, and many hits came up about a children's shelter and her assistant Brad Hensley. He ran his name, and sure enough, he got a hit on a hotel in the area.

He took the squad car over to the hotel and went to the front desk, showed his badge, and asked for Hensley's room number.

"What's this about?" asked the clerk.

"He's wanted for questioning. I need the room number." The clerk wrote in on a piece of paper and handed it to the officer. The room is just down the hall on the right.

"In case they're out, I'll need you to open the door."

"Ah, I don't think I should do that."

Sam took out his badge again. "You'll do as instructed." They walked down the hall, and Sam knocked—no answer. The clerk swiped the master cardkey and opened the door. Sam walked in, but the clerk went back to the desk. He didn't want to know why the police was so interested in getting into the room.

Shit! They're gone.

He avoided the front desk, went out the side door, and drove back to the precinct. He got to his desk and made a call on his cell phone.

"Are they still in the house?" he asked, referring to the Masons.

"Yeah, no one has left."

"Are you sure? People seem to be disappearing lately."

"We saw them in the yard a few hours ago. They just sat in the lawn chairs looking out over the lake. We went over and sat with them so they didn't get any ideas."

"If you value your life, make sure they don't leave. Get them back inside and lock them in. No more privileges."

ƐƆƇƐ

They parked in the back lot, took everything from the car, and walked to John's room and knocked. Jake, John, and Peggy were all packed. In case Brad and Joyce were followed, they went out the front of the hotel, put all the luggage in the trunk, and the five of them got into the rental SUV.

Jake drove through the neighborhood and kept looking out his rearview mirror. After twenty minutes, he was sure no one was following. He drove to Reno, assuming it wasn't safe in San Francisco anymore. They got a suite so they'd all stay in the same room. Jake was feeling bad that Joyce was poisoned, and he didn't want anything to happen to anyone else.

Joyce was tired when they got to the hotel, and Brad told her to get a good night's sleep. He would join her after talking to Jake. Peggy went with Joyce to her room.

"How are you feeling? I was so worried about you."

"I felt like I had the flu. Luckily, they gave me something to stop the diarrhea before I messed up my clothes. Otherwise, I wouldn't have been able to leave the hospital. I'm still not sure why they didn't get me into a hospital gown, but it worked out that they didn't. I certainly didn't think Pearl would serve us poisoned tea. I really thought she would have information for us. Luckily, Brad disliked the tea so much from the first visit that when Pearl brought it on a tray and set it down on the coffee table, he noticed her cup was already full. He thought it was odd since she had a teapot on the tray and filled our cups from it, but not hers."

"It was fortunate Brad was so alert. I know I already said it, but I'm glad you are okay." Peggy hugged her. "You'd better get some rest. I'm not sure what will happen tomorrow. If you two want to go back home, that's fine too. Just let us know, and we'll fly you back."

"I won't leave now, not after I've been poisoned. I'm in it for the duration. Good night, Peggy."

Peggy walked to the sitting area where the guys were talking about what they were planning for tomorrow. Although she was interested in what was happening tomorrow, she thought it was a good idea to just let the men talk. She said goodnight and went to bed.

ℵ ℵ

Room service was ordered, so they could stay in the room and formulate their plan. The brainstorming they'd done before Joyce and Brad joined them was also taken into consideration, although they had a lot more information now.

Joyce was still tired. She was sitting on the couch with her robe on over her pajamas. She hoped, after several cups of coffee, she'd be fully awake and be able to help. She also hoped she'd never be poisoned again. She vowed to never, ever, drink tea from this day forward.

"Whose phone is on the table in the kitchen area?" John got up and retrieved it. "It's been noisy this morning."

"That's mine," said Joyce.

John handed it to her, and she checked her messages while the phone was on speaker. "Ms. Armstrong, you need to come back to the hospital so we can check you out to make sure you are doing okay. Please call us immediately." A number was left for her to call.

The next message: "This is Sam from the police department. You've violated protocol by leaving the hospital while an investigation is under way. Evidence points to you being poisoned, we are looking into that, but you need to return to the hospital for questioning."

"That's the lamest excuse I've ever heard," said Brad. "We did not report it as a crime. I just said I thought it was bad tea. Like I said last night, my shirt is covered with the poisoned tea, but I didn't turn that in either. I don't know if they could get a toxic report from my shirt, but I'm keeping it just in case we need to go after Pearl. And speaking of her, how would Sam, who is probably the Sam in question, know that she was poisoned? Of all the people who come into the hospital, why was Joyce singled out? Unless, of course, Pearl and Sam talked."

"I wouldn't call the hospital nor return there," said Jake. "Power off your phone. Knowing Sam, he might be tracing it, which leads me to believe we should leave once again and find a new hotel."

Joyce powered off her phone.

"Let's eat first, then check out. We need to talk to the kid who lives next door to where the Masons lived. He saw the truck, and maybe he saw something else, and with the right questions, he'd remember."

Jake found the name and number of the neighbors and called. "Is your son home?"

"Who's calling?" asked his mother.

"This is a friend of the Masons."

"Oh, the Masons, Collin loved the Masons. I'll get him, just a minute."

"Hello."

Jake introduced himself and asked if he wanted to help in finding the Masons. He did. Jake told him how he could help, and he was in one hundred percent.

ꟸ

A woman was jogging down the street and ran up the front walk. Collin was waiting for her, and they took off running in the opposite direction. They continued to run through the park and through the neighborhood to the south. The woman was getting tired, and she wanted to rest. They found a park and sat on the bench.

"Collin, tell me everything you know about the day the truck showed up at the Masons," said Peggy, trying to catch her breath.

"After your husband called, I wrote everything down." He pulled the paper out of his pocket. "Yikes, it's all wet." He carefully opened it, and he had times and places listed. "I walked to Genny's, my girlfriend's house. She lives behind Pearl. I didn't cut through Pearl's yard though. I walked around the block. She was telling me how nosy Pearl was, always looking out her window. She figured when she wasn't looking out her back window, she was looking out her front window.

"I was at Genny's for a couple of hours, and I saw a man and Pearl in her backyard. Genny started spying on Pearl just for spite. They were arguing. Genny thought the guy was Pearl's son. She wasn't sure, just assuming. He left after a few minutes. I noticed it was time for me to get home, so I walked back around the block.

"We were going to eat in an hour, so I stayed on our front porch. It was a nice day, and I like to be outside. The truck pulled up in front of the Masons house. The only thing I could think of was they were going to move. It was that kind of truck, or maybe because the lettering on the side was Serpent Storage." He looked at Peggy. "I didn't remember all that when Joyce was at my house asking questions."

"That's a big help, Collin."

"I noticed nothing went into the truck or came out of the truck for ten minutes. Then a man was in the lead, the Masons behind him, and another man behind the Masons. I thought for a minute their hands were tied, but I figured I was just seeing things. I'm not so sure anymore that I *was* imagining it. I think their hands *were* tied. So now that I've thought all that through and put some pieces together, I don't know what to make of the whole situation."

"My husband Jake and a few friends are at Serpent Storage now."

"If they ask questions, I don't think they'll get any answers, especially if they kidnapped the Masons. They need to break in the office and take all their paperwork and burn down the building." He laughed. "I watch too much television."

Peggy wasn't so sure he was that far off. That was everything that Jake was planning, except burning down the building.

"You've been a great help, and if we find them, you'll be the first to know. I have another favor to ask. Keep tabs on Pearl. She tried to poison my friend Joyce and her friend Brad. Luckily, Joyce made it to the hospital in time."

"Genny says truth is stranger than fiction. Can I tell her what's going on? She can watch Pearl from the back."

"If you think you can trust her, and you know for sure she won't tell anyone else, you can tell her. I'll trust you to make the right decision."

"Maybe I'll just tell her to watch Pearl and report to me anything suspicious. She knows I like a good mystery. I'll jog back home. You getting a ride?"

"Yes, and thanks again, Collin, for your help." He jogged off, and Peggy walked toward the car. Joyce was driving another rental car they had picked up that morning. They used Peggy's name and hoped Sam didn't recognize the name in case he decided to investigate. Peggy got in and buckled up.

"How'd it go?" asked Joyce.

"It all seems to have happened at the storage place. Collin *thought* he saw the Masons' hands tied when they were escorted to the truck, but after talking to him, *he's sure* they were tied. Now it's kidnapping, poisoning, and accessory, added to Pearl's charges, and who knows what else she's guilty of."

"I was thinking if there is one bad cop on the force, there has to be another one. I just don't know who it would be," said Joyce. "Unless it's Sam's partner. That might make it easier to find out who he is."

"Have you heard from Brad?"

"No. I left my phone at the last hotel room just in case there is some way to trace it even when it's turned off. It was just a flip phone. I want one of them new high-tech phones, and now I have a good reason to get one."

Peggy checked *her* phone—nothing. The next thing they had to do was find a hotel and make sure they weren't being followed.

ഇ൦൬

There were several Serpent Storage trucks parked in front of a row of garages. The office was in the back and couldn't be seen from the road. You had to drive all the way in and around the garages to see the office. Jake knew that from their website. He wanted to get to the office without driving in where he could be spotted. Instead, they drove around the business several times and hoped there would be a way they could walk in after dark.

It was too risky in daylight to go to the office, but they wanted to scope out the area when it was light out so they wouldn't miss anything. They made their plan while they drove around one more time.

John and Jake would walk through the back woods, while Brad was in the car watching the area. They would try and find information on the Masons. Hopefully, the information they found would continue from where Sam's info ended from the envelope they found in Abby's apartment. Now they would wait until dark.

CHAPTER TEN

Sam needed a cup of coffee, and he knew a barista who could make it just right for him. He and his partner pulled up in front of the coffee house and parked in the no parking zone. That's what having a cop car was all about—have special parking privileges. He didn't really care. When he had his car, he would park there too and dared anyone to give him a ticket.

Abby saw Sam and his partner walk through the door. The place was busy, so she didn't think he saw her. "I need a bathroom break," said Abby to her coworker.

"Yeah, sure, leave me, why don't you?"

"That's my plan. Oh, and tell the cops that you haven't seen me all day."

Sam and his partner walked toward the counter, and the people waiting stepped out of their way and let them go first. "Where's Abby?" asked Sam. "I need a double espresso, and only she knows how to make it just right."

"I haven't seen Abby all day. I can make the espresso." He looked at the partner. "What would you like to order?"

"I want a mocha with no whipped cream."

"Wait just a minute," said Sam. "She hasn't been here all day? This is the day she works. This is the shift she works. Why didn't she come in today?" He moved his face right in front of the barista. "Are you lying?"

He looked right back at him. "No, I'm not lying." He entered the drinks into the computer and told them the total. He had a cousin who was a cop, and he was just as arrogant. No way was he going to buckle under to that jerk standing in front of him.

Sam wasn't going to pay, but his partner quickly pulled out his wallet and paid for both drinks. He was frustrated with Sam the last few days, but Sam wasn't sharing what was wrong. *Who cares? My shift is over in an hour, and then I have a week off.*

Ten minutes after the cops left, Abby came back to the counter. "Thanks for doing that for me."

"Why does a cop know your name?"

"It's a long story. Just forget it ever happened." It was getting closer to the day she would move out of her apartment and never come back to the area. She didn't care if Sam wondered where she was; she wanted to get away from him. *I might just open that envelope too before I leave.*

ᘐ

"What's with you these days?" asked Sam's partner.

"Why do you care? You're going on vacation."

"So you're holding that against me."

"I am. Things are falling apart, and you're heading to Boston."

"My kid lives there. I haven't seen him in a while. I got a new grandkid now. I want to see him. They're having a family reunion that I've missed the last couple of years."

"Well, you go then, I'll take care of everything as usual," said Sam, his voice dripping with sarcasm.

"I thought your mother took care of that couple who came snooping around. They should be dead by now."

"Whatever happened, neither one died. I think they snooped around the other neighbors too. Mom doesn't even want to get out of the house and come back to work. We've got shipments she needs to organize and plan."

The money from the drugs bought his plane ticket, and his wife was so happy they were finally getting out East to visit. He cared less what Sam was getting himself into. He especially didn't care about Sam's mom. She was a bitch and a busybody, and she was skimming some of the money that belonged to him. They could all rot while he was gone. He slammed the door when he left the squad car and walked to his locker. He changed clothes, and his vacation had officially started.

ꕤ

Brad dropped off Jake and John, and he parked out on the road. If anyone drove in, he would see them immediately. He didn't want his flashers on because he didn't want anyone stopping to help him. He thought of getting out to get some fresh air but didn't want to call attention to himself. As far as he knew, everyone who had met him so far on this trip was in on the scam. The nurses, the doctors, the hotel clerks—everyone was suspicious to Brad.

He wanted to call Joyce and hear her voice, but she didn't have a phone, and he didn't want to be distracted while on the lookout. He hoped Jake and John were successful.

"I hope you don't have to pick any more locks," said John. "I feel like we're the bad guys."

"If I do it again, let's hope it's to get your parents out of wherever they are.

ꕤ

"What do you think is wrong?" asked Michelle.

"Who knows? We were sitting outside minding our own business, and those two men who keep watching us came running over and told us to get inside and stay inside. I'll go crazy in this place. We're just lucky that Lake Reno is out there to look at. It's calming to have a lake nearby."

"I miss John," said Michelle. "I don't care who is listening. I haven't seen any cameras or wires like in the other places. Maybe they couldn't afford it anymore. I'm getting out this time, John. I'm getting the first plane to Minneapolis, and I'm going to make it right with our son.

"I want the same thing, honey. He's probably married by now."

"We could be grandparents and don't even know it. If we stay here, we'll never get to see them either. I thought they'd have just killed us by now. I felt lucky they didn't, and we never made waves or tried to escape, but the lake brings back so many memories, memories of taking John fishing, waterskiing, swimming."

She looked at her husband with a seriousness he'd never seen before, "Let's plan a breakout. Let's do it in two days. That should give us enough time to plan, like we have anything else to do but plan."

"Yes, that's perfect," he agreed.

ꕥ

Jake and John were looking through the files in the office. The flashlights gave off enough light, but it was hard to look through the file cabinets with only one free hand. He put the flashlight in his mouth and freed up his other hand. They looked under what they thought was the most obvious, M for Mason, but there were actual files of renters there.

Twenty minutes had passed, and so far, there was nothing out of the ordinary. John was ready to give up, to pursue other angles, but when he looked at Jake, he saw persistence in his eyes. If Jake, someone who'd never met John's parents, was going to keep looking, even though he himself gave up the search, then John too would continue searching.

You've come too far to give up now, said the voice in his head. *Keep looking, you'll find what you need.* John had renewed energy.

"Hey, look at this," said Jake. He was sitting at the desk and spread out documents and was taking pictures of each page. "This might be what we need. It looks like a police report. It might be Sam who wrote it up, and mysteriously lost the paperwork at the office, and brought it here to file. Its looks like the original. It's been signed with blue ink.

"It's been signed but unreadable. Doctors don't even write that badly."

John was looking over Jake's shoulder. "If he became a doctor, he could skip the handwriting class. He's aced that."

Jake looked up and focused on John. "I didn't know you could be funny." Jake laughed.

"I'm a real comedian. Just trying to get through this bad situation. What does that stuff say?"

"I'm not really sure, but after each picture I take, I'm e-mailing it to Peg, and she'll print it out on our printer at the hotel. When we leave here, we'll head to the hotel, and we'll have a reading assignment before we know what to do next." He looked up. "Keep looking, just in case there is something else here."

John decided to look elsewhere besides the cabinets. There was a lost and found box on the counter. He looked through that, then started opening drawers located underneath the counter. He saw unopened boxes of pens, staples, paperclips, file folders. He froze, took a few minutes to think clearly, put his hands on the counter for support. Jake was next to him, put his arms around him.

"Sit down, John. What did you find?"

ꟷ

Peggy printed out copies so she and Joyce could read the documents, then let the guys read when they got back.

"I hope they're still at this address. The first place we went to, Jake found John's father's money clip. That place must've been the second location they were moved to," said Peggy. "There is this one at the end here, which, if it's only three places they've been moved to, they must be here. Seems they kept them in Reno for some reason."

"Not that San Francisco isn't big enough," said Joyce, "to hide someone."

"We probably won't be able to walk in and walk out with the Masons. There might be guards that we'd have to deal with first. I'd like to make sure everyone involved is caught and brought to justice. Jake is better at figuring that out than I am. Now we sit and wait."

Joyce was feeling better, she'd had a short nap and felt revitalized. She hoped Brad was safe. He was tired and stressed and hoped he didn't fall asleep in the car while he waited for Jake and John. That would be disastrous if someone came to the storage place and they walked in on them rummaging through the office.

She hoped they were all safe and on their way home. She heard the cardkey click in the door, and she ran to the door and held it open. Brad had dark circles under his eyes, and he looked haggard but oh so beautiful to Joyce. She took him in her arms and gave him the same comfort he had given her.

"Let's sit down on the couch," suggested Joyce.

John went straight to the bathroom. He needed to wash his face with cold water, needed to calm down. Needed to scream. He thought of getting into the shower and crying his heart out. But he didn't want to waste more time if Jake decided to move on the information they'd found. Just a few minutes he thought, that's all he needed. He undressed, got in the shower, and turned the water to hot.

The hot water pelted down on his weary body and lightly burned his skin. The sobs came out of his ravaged heart, and his tears were lost in the water washing over him. When his body ached from the release, his sobs turned to crying. When he could no longer cry, and his sadness turned into renewed energy, he turned off the water, toweled off, and got dressed. The bathroom mirror was full of steam, but he really didn't care what he looked like. How he felt was the only thing that was important to him.

He felt like no one could discourage him anymore. He would find his parents no matter what, and if he died trying, he would have died happy. He opened the bathroom door, and the steam poured out. They were waiting for him in the sitting area. They finished reading the documents and were drinking coffee.

No one asked how he was doing, even though they had all heard him. They felt bad for him, but when he came into the room, they could tell by his demeanor that he had healed some and was ready for action.

"Pour yourself some coffee and join us, John."

John poured his coffee and added cream, then sat. "You probably already decided what to do next, and I hope it involves going to one of the addresses. I didn't read the documents, but I noticed two addresses."

"These documents pick up where the ones in Abby's apartment left off. I'm not sure why Sam wanted to keep written records. It's easier to prove guilt with records."

John put his hand in his pocket and pulled out what he found at the storage office. He opened his hand so everyone could see. "I found my parents wedding rings in the lost and found box. At first, I didn't recognize them, thought they were just rings. While I was looking in drawers, I had a gut feeling to look again, not about the rings, but to just look again. I picked up everything and looked at it. When I picked up the rings, I looked carefully at each one.

"My parents had an engraving on the inside of their rings: *I love you more today!* I looked on the inside, and it was there on both sets. Sam might have known those rings were very important to my parents, so he took them. I don't know why he would keep them lying around like that, but I don't care."

Peggy walked over and gave John a hug. "We're getting closer. Thank goodness Sam has been so careless in keeping evidence. We'll get them back, John."

John was feeling good before when he found the rings, but with Peggy's reassurance, he felt renewed they would find his parents. He smiled to himself and put the rings back in his pocket next to the money clip.

Jake looked at his watch. "It's late now, but I think we need to drive by this address so when we go back in the morning, we'll have an idea on how the place is laid out, if there are any guards, and how many, and how many of us we'll need for the rescue." He looked at John. "If there is a rescue to be made . . . I don't think we should get our hopes up too high, but I don't want sloppy work either." He scrubbed his hands over his face. "Sorry, none of you ever do sloppy work. I'm tired. I know you all do your best, and it shows.

"John, you and Brad come with me and we'll case the area."

ꕥ

"What the hell." Sam was with a temporary partner while his was on vacation. "I finally found out the name of the person Joyce is working with, traced them to this hotel, and now they're gone. They had to have checked out minutes before we got here. The coffee pot was still warm."

"Why are we chasing these guys? How many of them are there?"

"Two that I know of. They kidnapped two people, and now they're on the run." He didn't have to know the kidnapping didn't just take place or that he was the one who did the kidnapping. "We are tracking them down so we can find out where this couple is before they kill them. One thing we got going for us is that one of the guys of this kidnapping team tried to poison his wife or girlfriend. I think he lied at the hospital that he was the husband and he made up a big story about how she accidentally got poisoned.

"He took her out of the hospital that same day when she was instructed to stay overnight. For all we know, he killed her off already."

"They're killing off people in their own group?"

"Yes," he lied.

"It's getting more and more complicated," said the partner.

"We'll catch them, and when we do, remember they'll say anything to get off. They'll even accuse the police of the kidnapping and the poisoning. They can't be trusted."

"I've dealt with people like that before. I know how they lie and cheat just to avoid jail time. What do we do next?"

"For now, I have to follow up on a break-in at Serpent Storage." Sam didn't want to say he thought it was related to the people they wanted to find because he didn't want anyone to link the crimes with the storage place. If the business was investigated, the police would surely find drugs in one of the storage units. The money coming in was more important to Pearl and Sam than even family.

He pulled around to the office. "Hey," Sam said to his partner, "you stay in the car. This won't take long."

He pulled out his key and unlocked the door. He was told someone broke into the office, but upon investigation of the door, it must have been by someone who already had the key. There was no sign of a break-in.

The guy who called Sam was hired six months ago and wanted the woman's and man's wedding rings. He was going to ask his girlfriend to marry him. Funds were tight, he had eyed the rings in the lost and found before and came to the conclusion no one had claimed them for so long, it didn't matter anymore, and besides, he had a use for them.

When he got there to retrieve the rings and take his woman out to dinner, the rings were gone. He was so angry he called his girlfriend and called off the dinner. He said he had to work late and asked if they could reschedule. They rescheduled for the next night, but he still wouldn't have the rings. Hopefully, Sam would know where they were. The only reason he called was he thought the rings were stolen.

Sam took everything out of the lost and found box. It wasn't that big, so it didn't take long to look through everything. Then he looked inside the gloves and mittens—nothing. Who knows, they could've been taken out of the box and accidentally fell in the waste basket. He didn't really care anymore; there were bigger things to take care of.

Before he left, he found where he kept the documents and made sure they were still there. *Still there.* The robbery has nothing to do with the Masons. *I'm getting sick of this whole thing. I think I'll go pay Mom a visit.*

ꕥ

"Did you find what you were looking for?"

"Nope. This is embarrassing, but my Mom called while I was in the office, and she wants me to stop over for a minute. She didn't say what she wanted. She hasn't been feeling good lately."

"Fine with me."

No one talked on the way to Pearl's. Sam was trying to put everything together. Why were people looking for the Masons? *One of the men is probably their son. Nothing ever works out the way I want it to.*

Sam pulled into his mother's driveway, put the car in park, and walked to the backdoor. The door was opened before he went up the four stairs. "Get in here."

"What's wrong, Mom?"

"I saw someone at Collin's house whom I'd never seen before. She had long hair and was wearing a jogging suit. She didn't even knock at the door, and he came out, and they jogged away down the street."

"He just has a girlfriend. I wouldn't worry about it." He looked in the fridge for something to eat and pulled out a piece of lunch meat and cheese. "Oh, by the way, someone took the wedding rings at the office."

"I told you to bury them or throw them away. Putting them in the lost and found was stupid. Do you think this Joyce person took them?"

"I don't know, but first thing in the morning, I'm going to tell those two thugs watching the beach house to kill the Masons. We should've done that right from the start. I'm tired of the whole thing." He put the last of the lunch meat in his mouth. "I better go, my new partner is in the car." He hugged his mom goodbye.

CHAPTER ELEVEN

"Arnie, this is Jake. How are things at the café?"

"Things are good. It's surprising how well things run with Adeline in charge." Arnie laughed. Adeline was sitting next to him at the kitchen table. They'd just eaten a late supper. "What can I help you with?"

"Mostly I wanted to check in with you to make sure everything was all right. I don't know when we'll be home."

"Christmas Eve is in a few days. Do you think you'll be home by then? If not, we'll just take back your presents."

"Hush, Arnie," said Adeline. He laughed.

"I don't know, that's the problem. We've made progress, but I don't know if we'll be ready to come home." Jake desperately wanted to be home for Christmas. He felt he was neglecting the café. Peggy wanted to decorate the café for Christmas before they left but didn't have time to do it, and he really hadn't done that much shopping for Christmas. Peggy and Pam went one evening, he just hoped Peg got all the presents in that one trip.

"I can pick you up at the airport if you need me to."

"That would be perfect. Oh, and I might need to break into a car. Do you know how to do that?"

"I know of a couple of ways. You got something to write this down with?"

"Yeah, I'm ready."

Arnie told him exactly what to do, and then he gave him step-by-step instructions on the second way to do it.

"I have another question. You might not know how to do this, but how do you make a fake driver's license?"

Arnie laughed. "You underestimate me, kid. Write this down too. You have to have a good printer." He told him step-by-step instructions. "Do you understand?"

"Yes, thanks Arnie, much appreciated, and thank Adeline for running the café while we're gone. When I get back, I expect a full report on how you know how to do all this illegal stuff, or never mind, I don't really want to know." Jake disconnected.

"I'm glad you didn't tell Jake we spent last weekend putting up decorations at the café. It will be a nice surprise when they get home." She took a sip of her water. "Oh, and how the heck do you know how to break into a car?"

"Remember, my dear Adeline, I had to break into your car twice after you left the keys in the ignition and the spare keys were in your purse on the front seat."

"Oh, I remember now. I love you, Arnie, you're always helping me out." She thought for a minute. "But how do you know how to get it started without a key?"

"That's my little secret."

"And more importantly, how do you know how to make a fake ID?"

Arnie winked at her. "Some things are not to be shared with one's wife."

She looked him straight in the eyes. "Are you really Arnie Cole? Or are you an impostor?"

Instead of answering, he kissed her. "Not going to work, sweetie, but I'll forget it for now."

She kissed him back.

ꟾ

"In the morning, I'm walking out the front door, and I'm going to keep walking or running whatever it takes to get out of here," said Michelle.

"I'll be right behind you." He didn't think it was a good idea, but he would support his wife because he too wanted so badly to see his son. She got him thinking about grandchildren when they had talked of escaping earlier. *Is he married? Does he really have children? Is he still in Minneapolis?* The only way he would get his questions answered is to run and never look back.

The place they were staying at now was much better than the last places they'd stayed. Lake Reno was beautiful, calming, and tended to take away stress and problems of the heart. But the problem was when you went inside and closed the door on it, reality set in.

He *was* ready to break out and find freedom. No longer did he want his groceries delivered, and if he wanted a haircut, he didn't have to wait for weeks for someone to come in and cut it. He'd let his hair grow long because of that and never requested another haircut. Both he and his wife had long ponytails down their backs, his gray, hers white.

They were thin but in good shape. They exercised every day because they wanted to keep up their strength. There was no television, and they had only a CD player with two CDs that were worn and skipped when they played them.

Yes, he was ready. He envisioned his body filling with air, fresh air, fresh freedom air. He went to his wife and held her. "I'm ready, babe!"

ᘓᘐ

"I'm not looking forward to killing those two. How about we split up the duties, you know, share the responsibility?"

"Yeah, that's fine. Even though I hate this job, I'll sort of miss it. I'll have to get reacquainted with my wife and my kids. I'll have to find something to do with all my extra time. I'm retiring after this. I've saved all the money. My wife and I decided to just put my paycheck into the bank. Well, she thinks I get a paycheck."

"Good thing you do the taxes, or she'd be reporting your income to the IRS." He looked out the front window. "Same with me. I do the taxes, the wife works, but she needs my money too. She has expensive tastes."

They continued on about their lives until after midnight, then decided to take turns sleeping. They wanted to be alert in the morning.

ꕥ

Jake was going over the information they learned from driving by the new address they obtained from Serpent Storage. "The guards are outside the house on the opposite side of the street. They were very observant when we drove by, craning their necks to get a better look at us. So I only drove by once. We went to the main building and asked if there were any cabins we could tour. There were, so we went on a tour. I asked if all the cabins were the same, and she said they were. I took pictures of everything, checked the locks on the windows and the doors.

"I told her I really liked the end cabin and asked when they'd be moving out. She said that three months were paid in advance and they'd only been there about a week."

He took the pictures from Peggy. "Look at these and memorize them. The more we know about the cabin and the area, the better prepared we'll be. I don't know if the doors on the cabin are locked from the inside or the outside. We can always break a window in the back."

There were minutes of silence while the three men studied the pictures. Questions were asked, and when they felt comfortable about the surroundings, the cabin, their plan, Jake told them to get a good night's sleep.

"Up at four thirty," said Jake.

There were no groans, no excuses for the early hour. They were quiet, left with their own thoughts. Jake hoped it would work out, John was excited about seeing his parents, and Peggy knew it would all work out. Brad and Joyce wanted this mission to be a happy ending from all the roadblocks they'd already endured. But they all had one objective in common: the desire to bring the Masons home for Christmas.

John needed to walk, but he didn't want to leave the hotel. He didn't even want to leave the room. He thought of Joyce being poisoned, and he thought Sam would stop at nothing to keep them from finding out about their drug ring and kidnapping.

Instead, he went to the lobby and called Nell. "Nell. I know it's late. Thanks for answering your phone."

"Are you okay, John? You haven't checked in for a couple of days. I didn't want to call you thinking you had other things to think about. You sound so tired."

"Jake's friend was poisoned. They're serious, Nell."

"Are you coming home?" She didn't want to tell him to come home, she knew this was his quest, and she wasn't going to discourage him by laying demands on him, but someone being poisoned scared her.

"No. We are going to rescue my parents in the morning. Before you get too excited, there are two men on the street watching the place. We have to deal with them first. I'm sure they have guns."

"John! Be careful."

"We plan on it. I'd better go. I need to call Max too. I love you."

"Call me as soon as you can tomorrow. I love you too."

He dialed Max's number. "Hey, Max. You're up late, good." John told him what he told Nell. Max verbalized his concerns more than Nell, and he wanted John to get the police involved so he would stay safe. John agreed with his plan, his ideas, his theories, but in the end, there was only one way to do it. The Justice Team would rescue John's parents.

ꟈ

Jake instructed them to get a good night's sleep, but he and Peggy did anything but sleep. They devised their plan, made revisions, tweaked this, added that, omitted something else, until Jake felt it was the best possible plan. It was two o'clock when they shut out the light and got under the covers. But they still talked, still planned.

They had their alarm set for three thirty. They would shower then go to the corner gas station and get coffee for everyone. He was familiar with everyone's quirks and knew who wanted cream and sugar, decaf for him and Peggy, although it was tempting to get caffeine.

While they were there, they got breakfast sandwiches for everyone. Peggy thought they'd be better than doughnuts. They were back at the room at four thirty. Everyone was sitting in the same place they were the night before, all wearing black.

"Coffee!"

"I thought you only got that excited with me," said Brad.

"Priorities, priorities," said Joyce. They laughed.

"Food too. You don't really know me all that well, and yet you bought my favorite sandwich," said John. "Thanks."

Jake was glad everyone was in a good mood because what they had to do was anything but easy. While they drank their coffee and ate, Jake and Peggy went over their plan with everyone from the time they left the hotel until the time they drove off with the Masons.

When there was something that needed clarifying, they would go over it several times until there were no more questions as to what was to happen.

CHAPTER TWELVE

Their luggage was loaded into the car Peggy and Joyce were driving. The men drove in a different rental car to Zephyr Cove and parked a considerable distance away. John took several deep breaths. They all knew the Masons might not be there, even though the guards were. It could be a setup, but no one voiced their doubt. John was ready for anything—everything.

Peggy and Joyce drove by the cabin and the car across the street. Peggy circled around and parked half a block behind the car. She turned off the lights but left the car running. The cabin was now on their left. They checked the clock on the dash, and in twenty minutes, they would act. While they waited, they talked about nothing in particular, pretended to be drinking alcohol straight from the bottle.

It was a vodka bottle with water in it. When Joyce had downed the last drop, she tossed the bottle out the window. It rattled along the sidewalk. Both Peggy and Joyce laughed.

ΩCS

"What the hell are they doing back there? And why did they have to pick this street. Our luck, they'll keep drinking until they pass out.

Of all the days to have an audience when we were instructed to kill the Masons." He looked at his partner. "Do you have your silencer?"

"Yep, right here," his partner said and patted his pocket.

"I don't think they're leaving anytime soon. This just keeps getting better and better," he said sarcastically. "As soon as they leave I'm going back there and picking up that bottle. I don't want to have anything cluttering up the street. Sam gets word and he'll think we've been drinking.

ꕥ

"They're talking, so that means they're awake," said Peggy.

Joyce checked the clock—ten more minutes. She took another empty vodka bottle and threw it on the sidewalk, and it crashed into pieces on the cement.

"This is fun," said Joyce. "It could be helpful to relieve stress. Too bad it's just a recorder and I'm only pretending to throw stuff out the window.

ꕥ

The three men were careful as they walked to the Masons, hiding in the shadows of the cabins and trees. The one thing they didn't count on was that the sky would be clear, and the stars would be shining brightly, with the full moon reflecting off Lake Tahoe. It was a beautiful scene, but no one noticed.

It took them longer than twenty minutes, but Jake knew the plan would either fail or be a success, whether the timing was right or not. He heard the commotion coming from the street.

Peggy and Joyce walked up to the car, Peggy on the driver's side, Joyce on the passenger side. The windows were lowered.

"Get out of here. You're both stinking drunk."

"Hey, big boy," said Joyce. "Why don't you come out and play?"

He looked at this partner and shrugged. "We can always kill the Masons after we've had a little fun—a little sex, kill someone, then go home to our families and pretend nothing happened."

"That sounds like a great idea since we've been in this freaking car forever." He looked at both women. "A little young, but who cares? The outcome is the same."

They got out of their car, and Peggy lured the driver over to the passenger side.

ꝏ

"It's such a beautiful scene off the lake," said Michelle. "A perfect day to break out of this place." She was confident they would get away.

"Hey, Michelle," called John Sr. from the front room. She joined him in front of the window. "Look across the street."

Two women were talking to the lookout men. "It seems angels were sent to help us. Let's get out of here."

Their plan was to walk out the back door, circle around to the woods, and run like hell until they found a place to hide. With no money or ID, they didn't know how they would get far, but they didn't care. They wanted—needed—to taste freedom, and today was the day they would taste it.

John Sr. tried to open the backdoor. It was locked from the outside. After they were told to go inside and not ever go out again, the door must've been locked. Michelle's spirits fell, and if she let herself do what her body was telling her, she would've thrown herself on the floor and had a good cry. But her spirit, although broken, was telling her to run no matter the obstacle.

She just assumed the door would be open since they were being watched. She refused to chide herself for not thinking of it sooner.

They heard something from the outside of the door. They ran to the front window, and the two guys were still out front. "Who the hell is out there? Maybe it's a raccoon." Then went back to the door, and it swung open. The first person they saw was their son.

"John," whispered Michelle as tears rolled down her face.

"Hurry!" said John.

ꝏ

The Masons were helped into the already running SUV where Peggy and Joyce had left it across the street. When everyone was inside, Jake pulled away from the curb. They looked out the window at two screaming men who were handcuffed to the car's door handle.

Jake smiled and silently thanked his wife and Joyce for a job well done. They passed the woods and were heading out the driveway to the main road when Peggy and Joyce pulled in behind them. The next stop was the airport.

John took an envelope from the mesh compartment on the seat in front of him. His mother was next to him. He put his arm around her and hugged her. "Mom, I missed you so much."

Michelle couldn't speak, she was so overwhelmed with emotion. She hugged her only son. His chest was heaving against her. He was silently crying. She held him as close as she could while still in their seatbelts.

They sat back, and then John leaned forward and reached out his hand to his dad. He took it. "Dad" was all he could say, then leaned back. He laid his head on the headrest and closed his eyes. He wanted to call Nell and Max and tell them. What he really wanted to do was lower his window and shout at anyone who would listen that he found his parents. His eyes were wet, and he was happy.

The thoughts on everyone's mind was that it was going to be a joyous Christmas, not only for the Masons, but also for the Justice Team.

❧

"Drink your tea," said Pearl.

"Did you poison my tea too?" asked Sam.

She laughed. "I wouldn't poison my son." She poured more tea for herself. "I hope you destroyed that paperwork you had on the Masons. If it got in the wrong hands, we'd be fried."

"Don't worry about it. It's in the office somewhere, and if I don't know where it is, no one else will find it either." He didn't want to mention there were still documents at Abby's apartment. But if Abby opened that, she's too dumb to know what to do with it. He was safe. The Masons were probably dead by now, and since no one knew they existed, no one would miss them after they were dead.

He would retire next year, take vacations with all the money he'd saved, and live the good life. His mom could do whatever she wanted. She could even retire at her age.

His cell phone rang. "Sam, the cops are here. They have a court order to look in all the garages."

"Shit! I'll be right there."

"I wouldn't show my face if I were you," said the officer on the phone.

"I'll tell them it's a mistake, and they'll move on to something more important."

"They're looking for you for questioning. They didn't say why. Got to go."

"What's that all about?" asked Pearl when he disconnected.

"Nothing." His phone rang again.

His temporary partner Ron said, "Sam. You know that kidnapping you were telling me about? Well, the police have the two men who were watching the cabin in custody. They're singing like canaries. Got to go."

He *wanted* his mother to poison him now. The pain might be the same, but it wouldn't last long. *How did everything go to hell so fast?*

ꙮ

Ron was at the station looking at the documents that were hand-delivered to the front-desk clerk. Everything was documented about the kidnapping. Sam was in deep trouble, but so was his partner. In two hours, the police would be at the partner's family reunion out east, arresting him for several felonies. Then there was the woman who called in on a hotel lobby phone and asked where she should FedEx documents to Sam's boss. Yesterday Lieutenant McCoy looked at the documents, and this morning Ron had reviewed them: more pictures from the drug heist and from when the Masons were first kidnapped from their own home.

The police traced the call from the woman about the FedEx, but when they got to the hotel, no one had checked in in the last seventy-two hours, but the clerk remembered a woman, or a girl he thought, who came in and asked if she could use the lobby phone.

Now they should have Sam at the precinct for questioning, if he was at his mother's house. His phone rang. "Sam is in interrogation room C. Do you want to observe and you can tell me afterward if his story matches the one he told you when you rode with him? We've got the partner sitting in a jail cell in Boston."

"There were two guys at the crime scene," he told Ron, "handcuffed to their car. They are confessing everything, but it doesn't make sense. They want a lighter sentence, so I think they're making up things. Not sure if there is a lighter sentence for kidnapping." He laughed. "Get down here, the interview is about to start."

Sam turned in his badge and gun at his mother's house to the arresting officers. Pearl said she'd get the best lawyer and have him out in no time. She needed the best lawyer for her son and also herself. She didn't have a chance if they found Sam guilty.

ꕥ

Brad leaned forward from his small seat from the back of the SUV and gently tapped John on his shoulder. "John, open the envelope, we're almost at the airport."

John opened the envelope and handed his parents their IDs. The IDs had their real names on them. He wanted to give them back their identity and not the names of their past hell. Michelle held it tightly in her hands. John Sr. didn't know what to do with it. It had been quite some time since he had a wallet.

John reached into the envelope and pulled out a wallet and handed it to his dad. He immediately put his ID in the window pocket. He took his wife's ID and put it in the slot behind his.

Jake pulled into the rental car lot at the airport, and as they were getting their luggage out of the back, Jake went to the office to get his receipt.

They waited almost forty-five minutes for Peggy and Joyce. They all wanted to get on the shuttle together.

Jake hugged Peggy, then Joyce.

"Excellent work. I'm not even going to ask how you did it."

"Team work," said Joyce.

"Let's get the shuttle to the airport."

The shuttle was outside, and the driver was loading their luggage. The shuttle was just big enough for seven people, so the driver didn't have to wait for other passengers.

John was proud to introduce his parents to everyone.

"I just want to know who handcuffed those two men. If we had time, I would've gotten out and kicked the bastards."

"Mom, you've changed."

"She's not the nice lady that I married. She's gotten feisty, but I still love her."

Jake interrupted. "We'll have to get tickets when we get to the airport. Being this close to Christmas, it might be difficult. Three of you flying to Minneapolis, two to Omaha, and two to Iowa. John, you get your tickets first. The rest of us aren't leaving until you fly out. I don't think we have to worry about anyone coming to the airport looking for us because they should all be arrested by now, but I don't want to come this far to have something happen. We're still here to protect you."

"We really appreciate all you've done for us," said John Sr. "We were going to leave this morning and just run until we dropped from exhaustion. I wasn't wild about the plan, but Michelle was determined to leave, and I would support her no matter what."

"It's still hard to believe we're free. We're in a vehicle, and our hands aren't tied, and we don't have a hood over our heads, so we can't see anything." She took her son's hand. "John, are you married, have children?"

"No to both. I told Nell I wanted to find you before I asked her to get married. It wouldn't be fair if I were obsessed with finding you. I couldn't give my full attention to the marriage. Oh, she said she'll set a place for you for Christmas dinner. She was that positive that you were coming home. She's the best, Mom. We want babies too."

The shuttle pulled up to the airport entrance. They took the tram to the main terminal, and the Masons walked up to the ticket counter. Twenty minutes later, they were back sharing their travel information.

"There's a flight out in three hours, but we'll have different seats. We don't care, we just want to leave this place," said John Sr.

Jake opened his luggage and pulled out two winter coats for Michelle and John Sr., then Jake and Peggy and Joyce and Brad went to separate ticket counters to purchase their tickets. Jake and Peggy were flying out in four hours and Joyce and Brad, in two. The first thing they did was look for a place to eat. When they were seated at Timber Ridge, they ordered wine and burgers.

"You'll have to promise me that the first chance we get, we'll have grilled steak," said Michelle.

"I can't promise grilled since we have about six inches of snow on the ground and the temperature is below zero. I think in the coat pockets are hats and mittens."

"I don't even care if it's cold, I'm free. I'm with my husband and son. That's all that matters right now."

John dug in his pocket and handed his parents their wedding rings. Michelle put her hand to her mouth. "I thought they were destroyed." She put hers on, it was loose, but she didn't care. John Sr. glanced at the engraving, then put his on. John handed his dad the money clip.

"You found it!" Tears came freely. He took it. "It was a long shot, but you found it." He gave it back to his son. "This is yours. You risked your life for me."

John took it and put it back in his pocket.

"I want to know all the details right from the start—how long have you been looking, how did you find the money clip, the wedding rings, everything. Don't leave anything out." He looked at the clock on the wall. "We've got plenty of time."

Jake nodded at John, so John told his parents the story. He started with the hypnotist, explained the insurance money he got from their supposed death and how he used it to get justice and explained the Justice Team. "We had an address to one of the places you stayed, so we went there first. The windows were boarded, and the place was closed up, but Jake picked the lock. We'd looked everywhere, but Jake found a secret place and found your money clip."

John continued the story until the end.

There were questions from John's parents, which were answered. Joyce told the part about the poison tea. Peggy mentioned the jogging date with their old neighbor Collin. "He saw you taken away with your hands tied and described the truck you were thrown into. We were able to link the information with Serpent Storage. Then it seemed everything fell into place, even that you were ready to go when we got there."

"You and your mother are very close and had that sixth sense about each other. You could figure out what the other was thinking and doing," said John Sr. "I used to think it was silly, but it just saved our life."

Michelle asked each person what they did for a living and asked some questions. She especially liked what Joyce and Brad were doing with the shelter. She definitely wanted to see the shelter in Omaha and the Justice Café in Boone.

"Looks like we'll be taking a few trips in the future," said John Sr.

"You'll need money, so I'll transfer back what's left of your insurance money."

"No, you keep it and continue to do what you've been doing with it. It's yours." Michelle looked at her husband, and he nodded. "We had several accounts overseas from our investments. We didn't get around to putting it in the will. It's one hundred million dollars." She looked at everyone. "I'm going to make a donation to the shelter and to the Justice Team."

"You don't have to do that, Mom."

"She's gotten stubborn over the years, I don't think you have a say in it."

John laughed. "Somebody pinch me, I still can't believe this is all real."

"One more question. You are all strangers. Why did you want to help John find us?"

Brad looked at his watch and realized they should be boarding their plane. Brad stood. "You'll have to answer that question for us, Jake. We're going home."

Joyce and Brad gave hugs to everyone. "Let us know when you come to Omaha. I can't wait to see you again," said Joyce. Brad took their bags and headed to the gate.

The past crisis was just that, put in the past, as they talked about the present—Nell, Christmas, Max. Jake remembered finding his mom before their wedding and couldn't wait to see her. Peggy noticed how happily the three of them were talking, updating each other, bonding.

So much time was lost, thought John, but in a flash, the gap was closed. They could move on to the future. There was a wedding to plan, trips to schedule, babies to care for. Their first Christmas, they wouldn't take anything for granted. No one had presents for one another, although John thought Nell might have taken care of that.

Had he called Nell? He couldn't remember. Did he call Max? "Excuse me while I call Nell. I don't even know if I talked to her yet. I'm losing it." Michelle put her hand on her son's. He grabbed it with his other hand. Several seconds passed while he took in the emotion of his mother's hand, the realness of it, the tenderness of her touch.

"Are you going to call already?" asked his dad.

"Funny, Dad." He dialed Nell's number. "Nell, good news. Oh yeah, sit down. Keep those extra plates on the table. We're coming home, honey." He called Max. "Hey, Max. My parents are with me at the airport in Reno. We'll be home before noon."

"You need a ride?"

"Yes. I'll call you when we land. Thanks." With no one else to call, he put his phone away. "Max is picking us up. Nell already has the table set for four." He looked at his watch. "We'd better head to the gate. I don't want to spend another minute in this place."

More hugs were given, and the Masons left holding hands.

Jake and Peggy had another hour to wait. They went to their gate and sat down. Jake called his mom. "Mom! We're coming home."

"I'm so happy you'll be home for Christmas. Did you find John's parents?"

"Yes, they just left for home. Are you available to pick us up at the airport?"

"I just happened to ask for the day off, so I'm free all day."

"Perfect. Thanks, Mom. I love you, and I can't wait to see you."

CHAPTER THIRTEEN

Jake and Peggy unpacked when they got home and were going to take a nap but decided to go to the café and see if anything was needed. Several students had put together tables, and they had their computers set up, working on a class project. Books were opened on students' laps for reference.

They noticed the decorations: lights streaming down the walls, greenery and lights in all the windows, balloons with ribbons tied around them hanging from the ceiling. They looked up to the loft: Greenery with red berries were twisted around the railing and continued down the bannister.

Jake took Peggy's hand and led her up the stairs. The loft had the same decorations as the main level. They walked down the stairs and looked in the theme rooms. The first two didn't have any decorations. The next room, however, overwhelmed them with the beauty of it. A large tree was standing in the corner, decorated with red bulbs, red lights, and ornaments in the shape of coffee cups, to-go cups, mini coffee cans, everything coffee.

Lights were streaming down the walls, and in the windows were Christmas bulbs hanging down with glittery lights flashing on the pane. The green marble tabletops blended in well with the decorations.

On the opposite wall of the tree were stockings with the names of each employee hanging from a plastic sheet of a fake fireplace.

Just when they were about to leave, Peggy looked up and pointed. More balloons wrapped in ribbon and sprayed with fake snow were hanging from the ceiling at different levels.

"Oh, Jake, I think we should transfer ownership of the café to all the baristas, Adeline, and Arnie. They don't really need us."

"They need us," said Jake, but he was feeling the same way. "Now *you* need to be positive. We opened this place to let people know we had real jobs. We've given many people an opportunity to use their creativity to do all this, so let's be happy about that."

"Good idea. We've got so many things to be happy about. I wonder how John is doing. We'll have to call him on Christmas. We'll call Joyce and Brad too."

They walked out into the main area to the counter. The coffee area was also decorated in the same theme.

"Hey, boss, it's about time you got home," said Jim.

"We decided to make it home for Christmas."

"I didn't want to miss Adeline's cooking," said Peggy. "Jim, the decorations are incredible. Thank you so much."

"Jane organized the decorating committee. She works nights as you know, and before she worked her eight hours, she came by with her little boy Timmy. She sat and drew everything that needed to be done, asked Adeline if there was enough money in the budget for what she wanted to do. Adeline said there would be, so Jane got busy shopping, and when one of us wasn't busy, we helped. Arnie and Roger brought in their manly ladders and put up the balloons.

"Hey, Arnie, are the bosses invited to your big bash?"

Arnie poked his head out of the walk-in fridge. "I think my wife invited everyone in Boone, Iowa, to the party, and there is no more room for anyone else." He walked out to the counter. "It's good to see you kids made it back home. Of course, you're invited." He looked at Jim. "Can you make me that holly berry latte?"

"Sure, coming right up. I'll make three of them, two will be decaf."

"Thanks, Jim," said Peggy.

The three of them sat in the corner away from the students. "How was your trip? Did you find John's parents?"

"Yes, we did. Thanks for your expert advice. We were able to make IDs so they could fly home. Otherwise, it would've been a long road trip back."

"Whenever you need to know something, I'm your man."

Jake told Arnie the Masons were happy to be going home but left out the details of their kidnapping, that Joyce was poisoned, and the handcuffing of two grown men to a car. Just the pleasant details of the reunion were conveyed. Jim set their drinks on the table.

"Has Arnie told you about the party at the café, Christmas Day?"

"Fill us in," said Jake.

"Same as Thanksgiving. No baristas here, no coffee served, but Adeline is bringing her Christmas dinner and guests here. The premise is to bring your own food, we'll provide the shelter and the entertainment."

"Sounds like fun," said Peggy. "I feel bad for not being here, and when I come back, I feel even worse no one needs me."

"Ah, boss! We need you, Peggy."

Peggy laughed. "Thanks, Jim. Right answer." Jim walked back to the counter.

Arnie talked about the party coming up the next day and that Adeline has been cooking for days, but she's loving every minute of it.

"What were you doing in the fridge?" asked Jake.

"Making sure everything works properly."

Jim yelled over from the counter. "His wife kicked him out of the house so she could get something done."

Arnie laughed. "And that's the truth." He leaned closer to Jake and Peggy. "I've been worried about Adeline. She's spent so much money on gifts this year. She bought everyone who works at the café a present. Then she paid to have it all wrapped. But what really bothers me is that she said Jake gave her the money. I'm not sure why she'd tell a story like that."

"Because it's true. I asked her to pick up the presents I had ordered before I left, and I would give her the money. She was glad to do it, but I made her promise she would pay to have the presents wrapped. She promised, I gave her the money, and hopefully, she got everything on the list."

"By the looks of our spare bedroom, she got that and more." He sipped his coffee. "I'm not sure why I thought she was pulling my leg with that story, but I *should* know better. She's never lied to me during our marriage, and that's been a heck of a long time." Arnie was glad he asked and glad Jake gave his wife the money. Not that he minded, it just seemed like such a far-fetched story.

"Let's stop over after we finish here," said Peggy. "Maybe we can help or at least say hello. I miss her."

ꕤ

Pearl was a witness to her son's arrest. He had to turn in his badge. That hurt her worse than when he handed over his gun. He'd wanted to be a policeman when he was in grade school. His dream came true with hard work and determination. He was a good cop, still was, in her mind. Why was selling drugs wrong? After all, they only sold to adults. What they did with the drugs after that wasn't their problem.

She was packing, taking time off from the commotion and the upset that was going on right now. Her suitcase was closed and set by the door. She'd forgotten all about finding her son a lawyer. She figured the department would get him a good one. Her taxi was coming in thirty minutes. She hadn't seen her sister for some time. She'd head to Texas and stay with her. There was no warning that she was coming, let alone staying for a week, but Pearl didn't work that way. She was impulsive and expected everyone else to adjust to what she wanted.

Pearl had a daughter, she was older than Sam, but she moved out of the house as soon as she could, and Pearl never heard from her again. Her loss, she would tell herself over and over. *I wonder what she'd think if she knew her brother was just arrested.* She always told Pearl Sam was the favored child. Pearl always disagreed.

How could he be the favored child when she got everything she wanted—clothes on her back, shoes on her feet? And so what if Sam got designer clothes and she didn't? So what if he got a bigger allowance and only did half the work? She put it out of her mind when there was a knock at the door.

"I am so ready for this vacation!" she told herself.

She opened the door thinking it was the cab driver. "Here's my suitcase . . ."

"You have the right to remain silent . . ."

"What? Get those handcuffs away from me! I haven't done anything wrong."

The Miranda rights were finished. "You're under arrest for attempted murder on Joyce Armstrong, for dealing drugs, for being accessory to kidnapping . . . Should I continue with the charges, or will you come willingly with us to the station? We also have a search warrant. If we find the poison you used, it will add nails to your coffin."

"Impossible. You can't prove anything. Women don't get the death penalty, only men do."

She was handcuffed. "I'm not sure where you got your information, but that doesn't mean you can go around doing bad things to people, and besides, the guy who was with her had the tea all over his shirt. He gave it to us to run a toxicology report. They both gave their statements after we picked up your son."

One of the officers poked his head out of the kitchen and held up the box of poison, so only his partner could see and nodded.

"Let's go, Pearl." The officer noticed her suitcase. "You'll have to postpone your vacation—indefinitely."

She wasn't going to go kicking and screaming like her son did, although she felt like it. She resisted getting into the back seat of the squad car, but once there, she yelled of the injustices being done: arresting innocent people, innocent people trying to do good for the community. But no one was listening, no one cared. They had the facts, and nothing she said would make them believe any differently.

ℵ ℵ

"We were outside the cabin because we'd gone to a party and just hung out and talked before we had to go home to our wives."

"How did you get handcuffed to the car?"

"Two women were drunk, and they parked behind us. They were drinking and threw their bottles out the window. One smashed and broke. You can go check for yourself. The broken glass should be all over the sidewalk."

"They threw the bottle out the window and it broke? I don't believe your story because I was at the scene and we combed the area, the sidewalk, the street, where their car supposedly was and where we found you. There was no glass anywhere."

"It's true, I'm not lying. You can ask my partner the same thing."

"Yep, already checked. He said the same thing, but you two had plenty of time to think up a story before we got there."

"The ones that handcuffed us are the ones who kidnapped the Masons, and now they're getting away."

"I never mentioned a kidnapping or the Masons' name. How did you know all that?"

"I need a lawyer."

ᘓᘐ

Arnie led the way into his house. "Smells great in here. Adeline! We've got company." No answer. He walked to the living room and saw her sleeping in the recliner. She was covered up with her two quilts and looked so peaceful. Arnie checked to see if she were breathing. When he was happy with the results, he walked back to the kitchen.

"Sit down, I'll pour the wine."

"It's so good to be back home," said Peggy.

The wine was poured, and Arnie sat at the table. "I guess this toast is to John and his parents." They clinked their glasses and drank.

Jake took out his phone. "If you don't mind, I'm going to give John a call. I'm sure everything is all right, but I want to make sure."

"Hey, John, this is Jake. How is everything going?"

"Just great. I don't think I've ever been so happy. Nell is here, and we're just sitting around and talking. We decided to take it easy today and hopefully get in on some Christmas Eve events tomorrow." He looked at Nell. "Nell went shopping while I was gone and bought clothes and toiletries for Mom and Dad. That's why we thought we'd take today off and rest. No need to go out."

"That's great, John. If you need anything more, let me know."

"Oh, my contact called and gave me information on that license plate. It belonged to Pearl. We can't prove she was driving it, it could've been Sam driving. Either way, the old girl won't need her car anymore."

"So true," said Jake and laughed. "I'll let you go. Have a Merry Christmas, and say hi to your mom and dad for us." Jake disconnected. "Everything is fine. John is very happy." Jake thought of the substantial amount of money John paid them. Jake didn't want to take it, but he did and used it for the hotels and rental cars. He gave Joyce and Brad over half of what was left after expenses for the shelter.

No amount of money could pay for the joy of finding his mother, and he was sure the same was true for John. "I'm going to call Mom and have her come over. She said she had the day off."

Ten minutes later, Pam knocked on the door, then let herself in. She saw the wine on the counter, took the wine glass Arnie had gotten down for Adeline, and sat at the table and poured her wine, then topped off everyone's glass.

"What do we have here?" asked Adeline, coming in from the living room. "I must have been resting,"

"Resting? Out like a light would be more accurate."

She got a wine glass out of the cupboard, grabbed another bottle out of the fridge, and set both on the table. "I've got food if anyone is hungry."

"I'm very hungry," said Peggy. "Let me help you." Peggy walked over to the fridge.

"There's food in the downstairs fridge. I've got meatballs, pickle wraps, those little weenies, and tons of Christmas cookies."

"Yum." In just minutes, they were putting food in the oven to heat it up.

"While we wait for that, we'll drink wine," said Adeline.

There was a knock at the door, and in walked Roger, Noah and Paula right behind him. Peggy ran to her mother and gave her a hug. "I'm so glad to see you." She hugged her dad. "I'm glad to see you too."

"What brought all this on? And whatever it is, we'll do it again," said Noah.

"I'm just glad to see you. Come on in. We're having wine while the food is warming in the oven."

Arnie got to his feet and hugged them both and moved out of the way so they could slide around the table.

"You're staying with us, aren't you?" Even though Adeline knew the guest room had presents in it, she was always ready to have the Baileys stay whenever they came to Boone.

"We already got a hotel and had a nap before we came here," said Paula. "We love staying here, but we thought it would be better. We'll still be here all the time, just not to sleep."

Arnie was happy when Noah came to town. They remembered some of the same things from the past and usually got into good discussions on current events. They both had a good sense of humor.

They ate, conversed, drank wine, and planned their Christmas dinner that was to be held at the café. At one point, the women helped Adeline stuff envelopes for the baristas. Everyone got the same thing so they didn't have to worry about matching up names. There were also envelopes that needed to be stuffed for some of the regular customers. With those, they had to make sure the name on the envelope and the name of the gift certificate matched.

When that was done, they followed her to the basement, and she showed what she'd already made and asked for suggestions.

"Suggestions? You've got everything, and I mean, you've made everything," said Paula. "You must be exhausted."

"I took a little catnap while Arnie was at the café earlier. I'm just glad it's all done. Arnie talked me into getting the pies at the bakery."

"Next time, let me know what I can make. I worked in a diner, so I'm good at improvising," said Pam. "Do you have sweet potatoes on the list? You probably can't make that ahead."

"No. Not made and not on the list."

"I found out Roger likes them, so let me bring that. I have a great recipe. You won't know if you're eating sweet potatoes or pecan pie."

"I don't like them at all," said Paula, "but for something that tastes like pecan pie, count me in."

CHAPTER FOURTEEN

"Mom, you don't have to cook breakfast." John slept in and hadn't slept in this late in the morning since he'd left home for college. Now that his parents were with him, he didn't have a care in the world. "I can cook."

"I'm cooking, now sit down and get out of my way."

John laughed. "Geez, you sound good." He stayed where he was.

"Remember what we had for breakfast every Christmas Eve?"

John Sr. came into the kitchen. "I remember." He walked over and kissed his wife, then hugged his son. "Waffles."

John filled in the rest. "With blueberries, whipped cream, bacon, and eggs, and coffee cake for dessert." He turned on the oven light and saw the coffee cake. "Where did you get the recipe and all the stuff? I don't think I had that much food in the house."

"You two went to bed at eleven, and I thought we should keep with tradition, so I asked Nell to take me shopping. She paid for everything, so I need to pay her back. She's coming for breakfast or now brunch."

John smiled. *It keeps getting better and better.* There was a knock at the door, and they heard Nell's footsteps coming down the hall. She was carrying presents. "Where should I put these?"

"Put them under the tree," said Michelle.

Both John and John Sr. said, "What tree?"

Nell headed to the back of the house, and the two men followed her. John couldn't believe what he saw: a tree with gold and red decorations. The paper on Nell's presents were done in the same red and gold wrapping.

"Hey, where did that come from?"

"We passed a Christmas tree lot on the way to the grocery store, and on the way back, we had the guy tie it to the roof of my car, and lucky for us, your neighbor was out with his dog, and he helped us bring it inside. We stopped and bought decorations too. We'd been up most the night anyway, so we decided to set it up and decorate it."

"This is the best Christmas ever," stated John.

An hour later, brunch was served, and they talked about past Christmases. Nell talked about her family, most of which John did not know. He realized he was so caught up in his issues that he didn't even think to ask Nell about her family. Michelle made more coffee and helped Nell clear away the dishes.

They decided to go to mass before they'd opened their presents. The tradition had changed somewhat, but the most important thing was they were together. They made New Year's resolutions, and John and Nell set a wedding date. There was no formal or informal asking for Nell's hand in marriage, but Nell was okay with that. Talking about the wedding made her happy, and if she didn't get a ring until that very special day, she would be all right with that too.

John Sr. shared that he and Michelle were going house shopping after the holidays, and the first thing their son asked was if they were looking in Minneapolis. They vowed they would never go back to San Francisco to live or to visit. Yes, they were looking in Minneapolis. Although the winter so far did not please either one of the Masons, they wanted to be close to their son and his new wife.

Michelle was very pleased her future daughter-in-law was going to be Nell. They'd become fast friends, and she was moved that Nell took the time to buy her and her husband clothes. She also thought many times since they arrived in Minneapolis about the four strangers who rescued them.

When they'd met with strangers in the past, they were there to harm them or to kidnap them or to threaten them. Her views had changed when she realized not all people are mean and cruel. Some are considerate, loving, and selfless.

Yes, she was going to love their new life. Christmas was the perfect point to start again, and they would cherish every moment of every day. They would be grateful for their son and never miss an opportunity to tell him they loved him.

They entered the Basilica of St. Mary in Downtown Minneapolis and moved into a pew halfway to the altar. They knelt and thanked God for one another. The beauty of the stained-glass windows conveyed Bible characters with a sense of spiritual, mental, physical, and emotional healing—a release from the outside world.

When entering St. Mary's, you enter a whole new world—a shelter, a haven, a respite from your worries and troubles. It's you in a community that shares the same eagerness to hear His word and to keep the Christmas message in perspective.

For the Masons and Nell, it *was* a new beginning with family, family that didn't make the decision to separate from one another but someone else had. From this day on, they would make up for lost time, make Minneapolis their community.

Michelle and John Sr. had big plans to start over. They also had guidelines or boundaries they would follow. They would never let anything like that happen again to them, and they would also help others who were being bullied or blackmailed or treated poorly. John would have to explain to them how this Justice Team worked. They wanted to be a part of it. If not physically, then they wanted to find people who needed help and to make sure that they got justice.

The choir started singing "Silent Night." Michelle didn't want to sing along, she wanted to just take in the words and the music, and soon her eyes were wet. She took her husband's hand and her son's and moved them to her lap. She hung on to them as if they were saving her from falling. Surely she would wake in the morning, in the same cabin, in the same city, day after day, until she died of a broken heart. And if that were true, she would enjoy this dream, this night, this moment.

John Sr. pulled his hand away and put his arm around her shoulders and whispered in her ear, "This is really happening, and I guarantee it only gets better."

She put her head on his shoulder, still holding her son's hand. *Yes, it would only get better. We already experienced the worst.*

Their posture was straighter, their mood restored, and their hearts were lighter as they walked down the stairs to go to their car after mass. Carolers were standing on the side of the Basilica. Michelle was freezing, she wasn't used to the cold weather, but she wanted to stay, to listen to the beautiful singing. This time she participated in the singing, and as she sang along, she felt a warmth tingling through her body. Soon she didn't even notice the cold, but she did notice the heavy snowflakes falling, covering everything with white.

They wanted to stay forever and sing, but after another song, the carolers stopped singing and walked away to go home to their own families. So they did the same. On the way home, they stopped and looked at Christmas lights. An hour later, they were home drinking hot chocolate and sitting in front of the Christmas tree.

"Let's toast to family." They raised their cups, then drank. "Your mother and I didn't buy any presents, as you know, but looking at those presents already under the tree, somebody better open them."

John got on his knees and slid the presents out for Nell to distribute them. Michelle and John Sr. had two each. "Ordinarily, I would complain because we don't have presents to give, but it's been a long time since I hoped for presents."

Michelle ripped into the paper and opened the box. "Oh my, it's beautiful!" She pulled out a green sweater with white trim and a pair of green pants. "My new favorite color. It looks like it would fit too."

She opened her other present with the same enthusiasm. When the cover came off the box, she gasped. Nell had blown up a photo of the three of them when John was in college, with FAMILY on the frame. "This is so nice. Nell, did you do this?"

"Yes. I had lots of time while John was away. I was getting bored. Okay, it's my turn to open my gifts," said Nell. She opened the biggest box first. There were tickets to an after-Christmas special concert with Doc Severinsen at Orchestra Hall. She fanned them out. "There's four tickets."

"The power of positive thinking," said John. "We'll all go."

ꕥ

Jake and Peggy were passing out presents at the café earlier on Christmas Eve. One present was a square box containing a travel mug with Justice Café on the side and the barista's name underneath. The second was an envelope. They each were given five shares in the company.

Barry Ward, who was working until noon, walked over to Jake and thanked him, then asked if he could talk to him in private.

"Yes, let's go in one of the conference rooms." Jake led him to the one that was decorated, and they sat at one of the small tables. "What's on your mind?"

"I don't really know how to say this. You know I'm from San Francisco, right?"

"Yes, Barry, I knew that."

"I was going to Skype with my mom tonight. She called me yesterday with news, but she said it was a mistake and that she'd be home ready to get my call."

Jake didn't feel good about this. His stomach churned with every word.

"She called me this morning and said now it wasn't a mistake, and no one will be home when we were going to Skype."

Jake didn't interrupt. He wasn't sure he wanted to hear what Barry had to say, and even though his gut instinct told him this was serious, and probably related to what happened to the Masons, Jake thought it was just too coincidental to be true.

"My dad is in jail. He was accused of awful things. I don't believe that they are true, but I want time off to go home."

"Yes, go home. That's not a problem. You're a good worker and always fill in when we need you. Now it's someone else's turn to help you out."

"Oh, there's more." He looked at his hands on the table. "My grandma Pearl is in jail too."

As soon as Barry mentioned Pearl, Jake knew it was not a coincidence anymore, it was real. He felt awful realizing it was related to the case the Justice Team was working on. "I'm so sorry." And he was. He knew the charges they were facing, and the sad part of this whole thing, Jake felt, was the greed that was displayed by his dad and grandmother, not taking into consideration their families.

"Stay as long as you want. You have my phone number, call me anytime, and keep me updated on your family. When would you fly home?"

"In the morning. I'll finish my shift today, go home, pack, and hopefully get a good night's sleep."

"If you need a ride to the airport, let me know."

"Foxy said she'd bring me. She has to go anyway to pick up her brother."

"Okay, then everything is set. Thanks for confiding in me, Barry."

"Thanks." His shoulders were bent forward when he walked out the door to go back to work, never noticing the beauty of the room, only thinking of his family.

Jake sat and stared at the tree, the lights pulled him in, and he thought of the Masons—a happy ending. What Barry will go through will be anything but happy. He'll find out that his father and grandmother are frauds, and they will stay in jail, most likely for the rest of their lives. Peggy was better at praying than he was. He decided to go tell her what happened. He walked back to the main café area. Peggy was laughing with Foxy. Barry was cleaning the tables, keeping busy.

"Peg, do you have a minute?"

"Yeah, sure. Merry Christmas, Foxy." Peggy followed Jake to the same table and sat. Peggy sat where Barry was just sitting.

"Peg. This is the most impossible situation ever and yet . . ." He took her hand.

"You're scaring me, Jake. Just tell me."

He decided just telling her *would* be the right way to proceed. "Barry has to go home to San Francisco. His mom called and told him his dad and grandma Pearl are in jail."

Peggy gasped and grabbed his other hand. "Oh no. That poor kid. When is he leaving?"

"Tomorrow. Foxy is giving him a ride to the airport."

"What an awful way to spend Christmas! I could probably think of a hundred what-ifs, but the bottom line is they're both guilty, and Joyce being poisoned was huge, so I didn't care after that whose grandma she was. But I care for Barry."

"Send up some of your prayers for Barry and his mom."

"I will," said Peggy. "Should we tell anyone else? Do we need to tell anyone else?"

"I might give John a call. But I'll wait until after the holidays. The other baristas need to know he'll be going home for the holidays, but we don't need to tell them the situation."

"I wanted to call Joyce and see how she was doing. Can I use your phone? I forgot mine at home." He handed Peg his phone. "Hey, Joyce, how are you feeling? How's Brad?"

"I've got news for you. Brad was so scared I was going to die, he proposed this morning while we were still in bed. He said he couldn't live without me. We had champagne, eggs, and bacon for breakfast. It's so wonderful, Peggy, as you know."

"Congratulations, Joyce. Tell Brad the same from both of us."

"I don't know when we'll get married, but for now, nothing matters except that we're together."

"Again, Congratulations. I'm so happy for you. Merry Christmas." They disconnected. "Joyce and Brad are engaged. Brad did a lot of thinking while Joyce was in the hospital. He decided he couldn't live without her."

Usually, Jake thought that was just girl mushy stuff but knew the seriousness of the thought behind the act and was happy for them. "They belong together, and it's obvious they love each other."

ജ്ജ

Roger and Pam had a romantic dinner at Roger's house before they went to the Coles for Christmas Eve. Noah and Paula had an early dinner with Adeline and Arnie. Ross and Penny were at Jake and Peggy's for supper. Penny had last-minute presents she needed wrapped, and Peggy helped her before they ate.

Paula put the red tablecloth on Adeline's dining room table after dinner and helped with some last-minute decorating, while Arnie and Noah set up chairs in the living room. They had a spacious room ever since Arnie took down a wall and opened up the space. As far as Adeline was concerned, it only proved to be a good idea when the mess was cleaned up after Arnie had worked on it for three weeks.

The Christmas tree was in the far corner, decorated with red lights, red bulbs, and white poinsettias. An angel dressed in white silk, holding a fake candle, graced the top of the tree. The presents were already underneath.

Arnie had hung red and white lights around the windows. On the end tables were a collection of snowmen. There was a red and green plaid cloth on the coffee table with a stack of Christmas coasters.

The years after their parents died, Adeline and Arnie would spend Christmas Eve and Christmas Day alone, and they were content with that. However, since they met Jake and his family, Peggy and her family, they were happy to have a full house for the holidays.

Roger saw Noah and Arnie sitting in the recliners in the living room. "Looks like everything is done. I got here just in time," said Roger. He sat on the couch. "It looks nice in here. I wasn't putting up a tree this year. I just wasn't in the spirit of the season. Then Pam comes over and puts up the tree, and I got in the mood real fast."

"I didn't see that you brought any presents with you. That was the rule—bring presents for the host and hostess."

"I brought myself."

"What a prize you are!" Arnie laughed. "Hey, Noah, have you heard of re-gifting? Well, I'm re-gifting Roger to you." The three of them laughed.

"Hope you're handy around the house," he said to Roger, and he knew he was since he'd owned a hardware store. "Paula got this notion last week she wanted the carpet ripped out so she could have wood floors. So I'm sure Pam will want to redecorate once she moves in."

"I'll help you out," said Arnie. "I'd even travel to Minnesota. Adeline has been talking about traveling. Minnesota might not be on her list of must-see places, but it's a trip, right?"

"That would be great. When do you want to come?"

"When the temperature is in the seventies, and I mean seventy above." They laughed again. "But we'll be ready whenever Paula wants to start the project."

Jake and Ross joined them. "Sounds like the party is in here," said Ross, walking in. "It's a little warmer in Iowa. It's a nice break. Not so much snow either."

"Don't know why anyone would live in Minnesota in the winter," said Arnie.

"People do go South for the winter, I'm just not one of the lucky ones," said Ross. "I wonder if Penny would move to Florida after we get married."

"No, she won't move," said Noah. "My baby girl stays close to me—close meaning within two hundred miles."

"I'll have to check where it's warmer within that many miles."

"Move to Boone," said Arnie.

Paula came in with a tray of wine glasses, Peggy and Penny had the wine bottles, Adeline and Pam had appetizers, even though they knew everyone had eaten dinner. The coffee table was filled with food and drink. The wine was poured and passed out. When their favorite foods were on their plates, they sat down in the chairs around the room. Penny walked back to the kitchen and brought in her presents and put them under the tree.

Arnie talked about traveling to Minnesota. Adeline readily agreed. Penny mentioned they hadn't set a date yet for the wedding. Ross wanted to finish school first, which was another year. Pam talked about the library. Roger got up enough nerve to tell his friends that he had enrolled in massage therapy school and was starting classes in the spring.

Arnie joked with him but in the end, thought it was a good idea since he could use a good massage after all the chores Adeline gives him to do.

Penny was anxious to open presents and whispered to Peggy, "When do we open presents?"

Peggy shrugged and looked under the tree. There were quite a few presents, and she was anxious to open them too. When they were younger, Paula would give in and let them open one present at noon on Christmas Eve, and then they were good until evening when they opened the rest.

Paula was watching her daughters eye the presents, and she smiled. Nothing had changed. They were still kids at heart and loved to open presents.

"Should we open presents?" asked Paula. Both daughters beamed. "My kids can't wait much longer."

"We usually open them on Christmas Day," said Arnie.

"Party at Peggy's house. Get your presents, and we'll open them over there," said Penny.

Everyone laughed.

"Go ahead and pass them out," said Adeline.

When all the presents were passed out, Roger picked up a small box with his name on it. He turned to face Jake. "Jake." He said his name so seriously that people stopped talking and listened. "I would like your permission to marry your mother."

Pam put her hand to her mouth, she was so surprised. Time stood still while Roger was waiting for an answer. Jake looked at his mother. He knew she was happy with Roger. Roger treated her right, and he knew he would take care of her.

"Yes." Jake waited a couple more seconds, then said, "You have my permission."

He handed the box to Pam to unwrap. She fumbled with the wrapping, and the box dropped in her lap. "Oh!" She picked it up and carefully unwrapped it. Roger took it from her and opened the box. He took the ring, "Will you marry me?"

"Yes, yes, I'll marry you."

Roger put the ring on her finger. It was a gold band with a single inlaid diamond. She sat in his lap and kissed him. When she realized what she had done, she quickly sat in her own chair. Everyone clapped.

Jake hugged and congratulated her. She walked around the room showing off her ring and got hugs from everyone. Knowing Peggy's sister just got engaged, she said, "Penny, I have plenty of questions for you about getting married. Maybe we can talk tomorrow at the café."

Penny was so pleased that Pam wanted to talk to her, she couldn't answer. She looked at her sister hoping she would answer for her, but she found her voice and answered, "Yes, I would love to talk about it."

"Thanks, it means a lot to me."

Penny felt so good after that that she no longer had the need or the want to open presents. She just smiled. Paula watched her youngest daughter and knew all Penny wanted was to be included and needed. She'd had a date in high school she was so excited about, but the boy stood her up, and ever since then, she never felt wanted or needed. Ross came along and changed that somewhat, but she could sense her insecurity in certain situations. She silently thanked Pam for putting the smile on her daughter's face.

"Just don't tell Penny the bad things about the groom-to-be," said Roger. "I don't have time to look at any catalogs or pick out a tux or approve invitations."

"Not a problem," said Pam.

"You and Penny should leave all the arrangements to the wedding team," suggested Adeline. "We do everything for you, except walk down the aisle." That brought more laughter.

"If it gets me off the hook with being involved in all the planning, I say hire them and don't look back," said Roger.

"If you can put up with pink tennis shoes, you can put up with anything." Arnie remembered when the women were in Des Moines and bought the shoes, forming their new wedding planning team.

"That, I can tolerate," said Roger.

"I'm hiring right now," said Penny.

"Yes! Another road trip to Minneapolis," said Adeline.

When Pam gave in and hired the wedding team too, they continued opening presents.

Roger opened Pam's gift. It was assorted gift cards to restaurants in the area of the massage school. She thought he wouldn't have time to cook, and he could stop and eat before class. He thought they should drive around campus tomorrow before Christmas dinner and locate the restaurants.

Peggy opened her present from Jake. It was an iPod with a docking station.

"An iPod—I'll have to read up on how it works."

"You said you wanted to take up jogging, so you can have all your music on here and listen to it while you're running."

"If you need help setting it up, let me know," said Penny. "I have one just like it.""

"How did you have time to shop?"

Jake looked at Adeline. "I have my resources."

Jake opened his present. It was an iPod. "What?"

Adeline laughed. "I went to the store and told them I wanted two iPods and two of all the accessories. Peggy told me she wanted you to jog with her."

"I guess now I have no excuses."

Adeline opened her present. "Arnie, how wonderful!" It was a Scrabble Fiftieth Anniversary Collector's Edition.

"We used to play all the time until the board fell apart. So every night, after supper, we're going to bond over a game of Scrabble."

"I love you, Arnie."

Arnie opened his present. Adeline had given him a coffee cup, just like the baristas. "Since you get five cups a day, you can save the earth by using your own cup." She handed him another present. "This is for you too."

He opened it carefully. He beamed when he opened the box. "Tools! My favorite gift."

"They are small enough to keep in a shirt pocket or back pocket. Lately, you haven't had a screwdriver around to fix anything.

"That's on purpose, my dear Adeline." He put the Velcro case in his top pocket. "No fixing anything today. I got the rest of the week off." He winked at his wife. "Thanks, honey."

Noah presented Paula with her gift. She was hard to buy for, but one thing he did know about her, she was always going somewhere or doing something. Paula opened her present and beamed at the sight of the box. Noah knew at that moment he'd made the right choice.

"It's a Garmin! Now I'll never get lost."

"And I'll never again get that phone call when you ask me how to get home and yet you have no idea where you are." Everyone laughed.

Paula handed Noah his present. He had started to take an interest in doing home projects ever since he met Arnie. She decided she'd give him a few suggestions.

"Hey, Arnie, look at this." He walked over to Arnie and showed him the layout of a deck. Arnie studied it carefully.

"Looks easy, even for a beginner."

Realizing there was more in the box, he took out another piece of paper. This one had a landscaping design for their backyard. Even though Noah loved to garden, and the front yard was beautiful, he never quite got to the backyard.

"Wow, this is great. Look, Arnie." He pulled a gift card out of the box, and it was from the local hardware store. The dollar amount would cover both projects, which was quite a bit of money. He walked over to Paula, pulled her in his arms, and kissed her. "Thank you so much."

"Hey, stop that stuff while we're watching," said Roger. "Now are you going to pass those layouts around? Because I want to see the one of the deck."

Arnie passed them to Roger, and he studied it as Arnie had, only he had an idea to build his own deck. "Pass that gift card around too," demanded Roger.

Noah took the card and put it in his wallet, then stuck it back in his pocket. "Nope, that card is all mine."

Ross and Penny decided not to give each other presents, with Ross paying for school and more money being spent for their wedding, but Penny did have a present for Ross.

She got him a new backpack. His old one was ripped, and he kept losing his pencils.

When the presents were opened, the food eaten, they left, one by one to go back to their homes or hotel rooms. Jake thought they should jog home, but he was reminded there weren't any songs yet to listen to.

Peggy asked Penny and Ross to come over so she could set up the music for them. She was excited to hang out with her sister and brother-in-law.

Roger took Pam to his house. They hadn't made love since the time at Jake's. They both decided to wait this time, although it was harder since they'd already had a sweet taste of each other. They stayed up and talked after midnight, then went to their separate bedrooms.

For the first time Pam took note of Roger's decorating or Gail's, the colors in each room, the furniture, the carpeting, the rugs, the kitchen appliances. She didn't dislike anything but thought it would be a good idea if they started fresh. Even a new coat of paint would make the place look different. *Or a new house altogether.*

Noah and Paula put on their pajamas and went to bed early. They knew a lot had to be done tomorrow. The food had to be transported from Adeline's in the morning to the café and then they could finally see the decorations they kept hearing about.

Arnie got the crazy notion to try out their new Scrabble board. He and Adeline played four games and went to bed exhausted after their long day.

CHAPTER FIFTEEN

Lenny Farms spent Christmas Eve alone and was sure he would spend Christmas Day alone as well. His wife kicked him out. Although she said she needed time to think while he wasn't there, he knew she'd never want him back.

He wasn't supporting his family, and his memory wasn't as good as it once was when he had to keep all the facts straight of which woman lived where, the lies about where he worked, and the lies about where he kept his money, so she'd have to support the family for now.

That last story never seemed to work, especially after five years and he hadn't contributed a cent for the mortgage or expenses.

Some women were more understanding, they just loved him and didn't care if he ever worked or provided for them. But now he was getting tired and just wanted one woman to spend the rest of his life with. Pam was the one he decided to go back to because Pam was the only one who had given him a child—Jake, he thought his son's name was, but then his memory had failed him lately.

He thought she worked at a diner in a small town in Missouri, and he'd actually went there and asked when her shift started, and he was told she didn't work there anymore. He went there every day for a week at different times just to make sure they hadn't lied to him, but she was never there.

So what if he'd left her stranded in a hotel room and convinced her to leave home and not tell their son. He could think of a hundred things that he'd done to her over the years they were married, but he was one hundred percent sure she had forgiven him by now and was just as interested in finding him as he was in finding her.

He would show up at his brother Rick's house and find out if he knew where she was.

ꟼOCƷ

With music on their iPods, they got up early, dressed warm, and ventured outside. They didn't run because of the ice on the sidewalks. They held hands and walked in the street where the snow was worn away. They headed down Story Street, turned on Third, then made the full block by coming up Greene Street and over on Sixth.

Pam was in the kitchen making coffee when they came home. Roger was sitting at the table. "Out jogging?"

"Well, we walked fast. It's a start. We had good music, thanks to Penny."

Jake's phone rang, and he took it off the counter. "Hello."

"This is Barry Ward. I haven't left for the airport yet, but my mom called. She said she couldn't afford a lawyer, and if one got appointed to my dad, she didn't think he'd try very hard to prove dad's innocence."

Jake took Peggy's hand and led her to the bedroom, shut the door. "What would you like me to do?" He put him on speaker.

"I was wondering . . . Do you know a good lawyer?" Jake and Peggy looked at each other. The situation couldn't have gotten any worse. Jake knew his dad was guilty, had the proof, and presented the proof to the authorities. It was definitely a conflict of interest. He would have to get back to Barry, call John, and see if he has an answer.

"Barry, I will look into it and get back to you."

"Okay. You can call back at this same number. I got to go, Foxy is here. And thanks."

"What do we do, Peg? We know the other side of the story, but my heart breaks for Barry." He pondered the situation. "I just thought of something. Why was Sam seeing Abby when he was married and had a son? Things aren't looking good for Barry if he finds out everything about his dad."

"Some people aren't good at commitments. I know it's Christmas, but I think we need to call John in on this."

Jake dialed John's number. "John, Merry Christmas. How are your parents adjusting?"

"Very well, and Merry Christmas to you."

"I have an employee who needed to go home for Christmas at the last minute. He said his dad and grandma are in jail and he needs to go home."

"Would that home be in San Francisco?"

"Yes. He just called and asked me if I knew a good lawyer to prove his dad's innocence."

Sharp, rapid pains shot through John. His knees were about to give out, so he sat heavily in the chair. Sweat covered his body. He looked at his parents sitting in the living room, and the last thing he wanted to hear was the people involved in their abduction needed lawyers to find them innocent.

Jake waited patiently for John to answer or to yell or to protest. Several minutes passed and he didn't get any of that. "John, are you there?" He didn't ask if he were okay because he was probably anything but okay.

"Yes, I'm here. I just want to scream at the injustice of it. I don't want that poor kid to suffer either when he finds out the truth. I do know a lawyer, he's fair, and I won't prep him with any information first. He lives in San Francisco. Give me a minute while I find his number."

Five minutes later, John picked up his phone. "His name is Dennis Coyle." He gave Jake the number. "Tell him I referred him and give him Barry's number. I don't think we have to say anything, the facts speak for themselves."

"Thanks, John. Tell your folks hi from Peggy and me."

Jake dialed Coyle's number. Surprisingly, he answered. Jake told him the information and gave him Barry's cell number. He said he'd call right away and set something up with his dad in jail for today too and to say hi to John.

"I still feel bad for Barry," said Peggy. "So many innocent lives affected by this. People who don't care about family or friends, just themselves and dollar signs. Poor kid is going to be heartbroken, and it being Christmas, when people should be happy, doesn't help."

"I know. I wonder what hours he works the next week. We need to find someone to fill in for him. I wonder if Foxy knows the story. I don't want to tell anyone about his dad, only he should tell his coworkers if he wants to."

They walked back to the kitchen, filled their cups, and sat down. "I'm starved," said Peggy. "I think we should have something to eat, even though we'll be eating at noon. And besides, it's only eight o'clock."

"I'll help," said Pam.

ꕥ

Barry was about to board the plane when his phone rang. It was the lawyer, and he'd already set up a meeting with his dad for later that day. Coyle also explained if he didn't want him on the case to say so now so he could cancel the appointment with the prison. He would go to his girlfriend's house instead.

"I want you on the case, but we can't afford you."

"I do pro bono cases all the time. I'll call you after I see your dad." He disconnected. He'd never done a pro bono case but thought if the request was from John, he'd do it. *John must think the guy's innocent, or he never would have recommended me.*

Coyle had won all his cases. He believed in his clients, and if there was doubt on Coyle's part, or if the evidence presented itself to his client's guilt, he would recuse himself from the case. He checked his watch—three more hours. He decided to call his girlfriend now to let her know he had to come later, he had a case. She would understand, she always did. He not only didn't think he deserved her, but he also knew without a doubt he didn't deserve her. She was too good, too kind. But when they were together, he made it up to her. Tonight he would ask her to marry him, and he hoped she would say yes.

ꕥ

Pam and Roger went back to Roger's house, and Jake and Peggy were getting ready for Christmas dinner when his phone rang. "Boss, I got a call from the lawyer. Thanks. He's seeing my dad today at the prison. I got to go, we're on the tarmac in San Francisco. Thanks again."

Jake hoped Barry would be okay. He couldn't think of an outcome that would be favorable to the family. His phone rang again.

"Jake, this is Brad."

"Hi, Merry Christmas."

"Yes, so far, so good, not so sure about tomorrow though."

"What's wrong?"

"The San Francisco police have more questions for us, and they want us to come to the station. I told them absolutely not. He wanted us to meet off-site so we'd be safe."

That doesn't sound right. "What's the name of the officer who called?"

"I wrote it down—Jeremy Nelson. He said he was an officer at the precinct in San Francisco. I'm supposed to call him back later today."

"I'll get back to you before then."

"Peg!" he yelled out." She came from the bedroom in her new Christmas red dress. "Wow! Peg. I feel like I need to put on a suit."

"You look good just the way you are." She easily went into his arms. "I think this is the best Christmas ever."

He held her at arm's length. "I think there is something still going on in San Francisco. Brad got a call from Jeremy Nelson. He claims to be an officer there and wants Brad and Joyce to come in for more questioning."

"Let's go turn on the computer and find out what we can about this guy." They'd moved the computer to their bedroom from the living room. There was extra space, and it freed up space in the living room when they entertained.

As Peggy was searching, Jake changed into dress clothes. He even put on a tie. No way was he going to look like a bum when his wife was so dressed up. He stood behind her and pulled her hair away from her face, kissed her neck.

"Hey, pal, we've got work to do." Jake was content with just playing with her straight dark brown hair. "Look."

Jake bent over to see the screen. It was a picture of Nelson with his uniform on. There was a write-up about how he saved a child's life who was drowning in a neighborhood pool. Jake took the clothes off the chair in the corner and pulled it next to Peggy. They both read every word of the article.

Peggy brought up another site. In this article, he was shot in the line of duty.

"Looks like he's legit."

"I know I say be positive, but now we have to question everything we're reading and keep digging." They looked at several more sites.

"Wait! Go back to that last one." He stared at the picture for several minutes. "Can you make it bigger?" When the picture was bigger, he could clearly see the Serpent Storage truck in the background. "Look, Peg. Let's look on the police website."

He wasn't an officer, he was a lieutenant. Five years ago, Sam Ward and his partner worked under him. Now Sam worked under Lieutenant McCoy, the lieutenant Abby and Jake sent incriminating evidence to. "I think Brad and Joyce should go, but I will go with them, and hopefully, no one gets hurt this time."

"I'm going too. But we have to be careful we don't run into Barry. Not that we would, but what were the odds Sam is Barry's father?"

"Anything is possible, that's for sure," said Jake. "I'll call Brad. Then let's go eat dinner."

Jake asked Brad if he and Joyce could afford to take more time off. "We've had to turn people away from the shelter, so we really can't get away, but if they need us to come in, then we should."

"I'm not so sure it's on the up and up. Peg and I would go with you to make sure you're safe." He thought of something. "Did you see Nelson when you were questioned?"

"We never went into the station. We gave our statements by phone. We had to ID ourselves by voicing our personal information over the phone, with social number, driver's license ID, address, phone number. I gave the shirt to the doctor. It must've taken a few days for him to decide what to do with it. But no, we never went to the station."

"Perfect. Peg and I will go in your place, and you can stay where you're needed, at the shelter. Call him back and get details. Tell him you can come in two days."

"I'm feeling better about staying home, but not better about you two putting yourselves in danger. Do you think John would go with you?"

"I'll tell him and try to persuade him to stay home. Leave me a message when everything is set up."

Jake decided to wait until tomorrow to call John. He didn't want to spoil his Christmas, although he didn't think anything could spoil John's day.

ꟸ

The tables in the main section of the café were full. People were talking, drinking their own beverages, eating their own food, conversing with one another. Jake and Peggy stopped at all the tables and wished them a Merry Christmas, and asked if they needed anything, and reminded them the carolers were coming soon.

Hand in hand, they walked up to the loft and said hello to the young couple sitting by the window. They were eating turkey sandwiches, and the pumpkin pie was already cut on their plates. "Merry Christmas," said Jake, thanked them for coming. Still hand in hand, they walked down and joined their family and friends in one of the theme rooms that was decorated for Christmas.

Peggy didn't notice the first time she was in the room, but this time Perry Mason had a Santa suit taped on. It fit in perfectly with the decorations. *Clever,* she thought. Jake and Peggy were the last ones to arrive. On the side tables there was non-alcoholic wine, champagne, eggnog, and appetizers.

Peggy looked around and found her parents sitting with the Coles and joined them.

"Where's Penny?"

"She and Ross slept in. They were up late last night."

"Yeah, I was too!" She giggled.

"Paula, look outside," said Noah. White fluffy flakes were slowly falling from the sky, clinging to the lone oak tree in the back of the café. People stopped what they were doing and looked through the red lights that outlined the windows. The quietness, the calmness, drew them in. It was two worlds. The one they were looking out at was white, calm, and serene. The one they were in was warm, filled with Christmas colors with the smell of good food.

The sound of carolers was getting closer as they walked down the hall singing toward the festivities. The snow was forgotten, and their heads turned toward the sound of "Silent Night." Mesmerized by the choir's red velvet dresses of the women and green sweaters of the men, they remembered a baby in the manger being born into the world.

The carolers walked throughout the café singing carols, then settled into the main area to take requests.

The women had the food Adeline prepared, ready to serve. Pastor Stone from the First Baptist Church was there and said grace before they ate. The pastor was new to the area and was excited he and his family were invited to spend Christmas at the café. Their family was in California, and they didn't have the money this year to see them, so when Jake called and invited them, his wife had tears in her eyes, and their two boys jumped up and down with excitement. After he prayed, he joined his family at the front table.

"Hey, Peggy. Merry Christmas," said Penny. She gave her sister a hug. "Oh, nice dress." Penny was wearing a green dress. "You never wear dresses. Are you sick?"

"I just wanted this year to be special."

"We're getting in the food line. We woke up thirty minutes ago, and I need food."

ᘐᘓ

Dennis Coyle was waiting in the visitor section sitting in front of the glass window, waiting for Sam Ward. He didn't know what to expect. Because of the holiday, no one was available to give him information. Some notes were made from the arrest report, and information he'd gotten from several news reports on the Internet didn't look to be in Ward's favor.

His son Barry wanted to be there for the questioning, but he told him to stay at home with his mother, and he would call when he was done talking to his father. The door opened on the inmate side, and Sam was escorted to the window in front of Coyle. He lifted the phone but didn't say anything.

Coyle introduced himself. "Your son arranged to have me represent you. Fill me in on what's going on."

He sat smugly in his chair. "I'm innocent. That's all you need to know."

"Not really, I need to know everything because if this goes to trial, I don't want any surprises."

"No surprises. I was wrongly locked up."

"Then I need to know what you were wrongly accused of." Ward didn't answer. "Okay, if not for me, then be a little cooperative for your son."

Sam didn't really care about his son. He was an accident, his whole marriage was an accident. The marriage was boring. He was restless. He got sick of barely making it from paycheck to paycheck. His mom worked at the storage place, and she thought there were drugs being stored in some of the garages. She called her son, the cop, to investigate.

Sam found drugs and reported back to his mother. If they came up with the right plan, they could cash in on the profits. Pearl told the drug dealers to get out and that her son was going to report the incident. They got mad and told her to watch her back. That's when she told them her plan. They could store the drugs, but there had to be a cut to her and her son. They agreed, and before long, because of his status with the police department, Sam was in charge.

Cash came in every day, and he no longer had to worry about bills and food. His wife wondered how he could afford a new car, but he brushed her off, saying she needed to mind her own business. Her car barely transported her back and forth to work. She'd had the same car for the last sixteen years. Sam had planned to buy her one, but then he got one instead.

He was at the coffee house getting his morning cup of coffee, and he met Abby. He decided it was a nice way to start the day, so he made the coffee stop a morning ritual. Soon he was asking her out, and then they'd bought an apartment together. He claimed his job had him putting in long hours, so he wouldn't be there very much, but he'd pay half the rent.

"I need something from you, a statement. Anything," said Coyle.

"My innocence speaks for itself."

"Okay, let me review what I just found out on the Internet. You're dealing drugs. You've stolen drugs and money from the evidence room at the precinct. You kidnapped two people. You're an accessory to attempted murder."

"I didn't steal anything out of evidence. My partner did that."

"And he's locked up. I heard he's telling everything."

"He's stupid. No one is going to believe him."

"I got news for you. All twelve jurors won't think he's stupid when he's on the stand at your trial. And if over half believe what he says, you'll be locked up for the rest of your life."

Sam knew that wasn't true. His friend Nelson was working on killing the witnesses. The people who rescued the Masons wouldn't show up here again, he was certain of that. So that left no one to guarantee him jail time. No witnesses. No statements from the supposed victims of the kidnapping or the poisoning.

"Tell my son to keep out of this, and as far as I'm concerned, you're off the case."

"Your son is trying to help you."

"Tell him not to. I don't need him or his mother."

"Do you realize it's Christmas? It's a time for family. It sounds like you despise your family."

"Whatever. I got my mother. She'll head over there and make it look like she's interested in her grandson."

"Another news flash—your mother was arrested, and she's spending Christmas in jail."

"You're lying!" he yelled. "My mother is not in jail. You're making it up."

The guard came out, pulled him out of his chair, and took him back to his cell.

"That went well," said Coyle out loud. He called Barry when he got in his car. "This is Coyle. Your dad was uncooperative. He didn't give me any information to use so I could prove his innocence. If he doesn't talk to me the next time I'm here, I'm not taking the case."

He couldn't believe his dad wasn't talking. He always had an opinion about everything. "I'll talk to my mom and see what we can do."

Poor kid. I don't think his dad will listen to anyone, especially family.

"I'll keep you updated."

CHAPTER SIXTEEN

Eugene's son dropped him off at the café, a place he frequented, especially since Mable was also going to be there today. Her daughter dropped her off. Eugene and Mable also lived next door to each other. They enjoyed their time together at the café. Today they decided to spend the afternoon with each other. Eugene brought hot coffee in his thermos, and Mable brought turkey lunch meat sandwiches.

When Jake and Peggy noticed them while making their rounds to welcome their guests, they stopped at their table and invited them back to celebrate with them. Eugene and Mable packed their coffee and sandwiches and followed them to the celebration.

Mable took Eugene's arms. "Oh goodness! It's beautiful in here."

"Let me take your things. I'll put them on the open table over there," said Jake as he pointed to the table. "Go get some food and enjoy yourselves."

Mable was walking better, but she didn't think she would be able to balance her food and walk too. She kept holding Eugene's arm. She noticed Adeline, the lady at the library, by the food.

"Hey, Adeline."

"Is that you, Mable? Look at you. You look so pretty in your Christmas sweater."

Mable looked down and beamed. "Thanks."

"Help yourself to the food, there's plenty." Adeline noticed Mable didn't have her walker and she was a little unsteady on her feel. "Why don't I help you to your seat, and then I'll get your food for you."

Relief washed over Mable. "Thanks, I'll take you up on your offer."

An hour later, Eugene and Mable were still talking and drinking Eugene's coffee.

"Look at that tree," said Eugene. "I didn't put up a tree this year. Mostly I didn't want to have to take it down."

"I got a tree. When it's time to take it down, my daughter comes over, puts a bag over it, and transports it downstairs. Next year, she'll bring it up and it's all decorated. I just have to straighten out a few things."

"You are so smart, Mable." He looked in her pale blue eyes and wondered what it would be like to wake up to her energy, her good nature every day. At his age, he needed humor in his life. This might just be the season to change all that. "What you doing for New Year's?"

"I haven't thought about that," said Mable. After a few seconds of silence, she said, "You're invited to my house. Just walk over. If we fall asleep in the recliners before midnight, it's no big deal," said Mable.

Eugene laughed. "It's a date."

The snow turned from peaceful and serene to treacherous and dangerous on the roads. Luckily, the people at the Justice Café lived in Boone or were staying in Boone. Noah and Arnie helped people clean off their cars, while Jake and Ross shoveled the parking lot. Jake realized he needed a snow blower or even hire someone to do it. But with all the cars, shoveling was the only option.

Noah had a four-wheel-drive SUV and told Eugene and Mable to call their kids and he would bring them home. They were so worried about their kids coming back out in this weather to pick them up. Their kids lived in Ames, and the drive would be impossible. So their dilemma was solved. Their kids were also very happy they were being taken care of. Adeline sent home leftovers with them. They thought it had been the best Christmas they'd ever had.

Peggy was glad she wore her winter boots with her dress instead of her dress shoes. She was helping pack up empty dishes and left-overs and taking many trips out to the car in the snow and slush. She was not looking forward to going back to San Francisco.

There was a lot of planning to do for this trip. They had to be careful. There was a lot at stake. Nelson would be serious in trying to kill witnesses. If their statement harmed Sam and his mother, it wouldn't take long for anyone to dig a little deeper and connect Nelson. No way did they want any loose ends, and there were many if they took into consideration the Masons could also testify.

Ross and Penny wanted to come over after everything was cleaned up and people were safely on their way. Peggy was tired, and she wanted to talk to Jake about her ideas, but Penny was her sister, and she agreed to have them over. Adeline found out they were heading to Jake's, so she and Arnie went as well. Before long, Pam, Roger, Noah, and Paula were there too. The snow continued. Instead of heading home, they decided to continue the celebration no matter the weather.

Peggy felt she didn't have to offer anything to eat or drink, since she was sure everyone was stuffed from the celebration, and she didn't want to tell anyone they were traveling again.

Their friends were making themselves to home, putting their wet coats on the hooks in the small coat room off the kitchen, and sitting in the living room. Adeline made coffee and took down enough cups, found the cream and sugar. *What a wonderful day!* She looked outside and saw the snow falling in the light of the street lamp. *I'll never tire of seeing the snow so beautiful!* She thought.

"Hey, is the coffee done yet?"

"Oh, Arnie. You can carry this tray in for me."

"Not just yet." He took his wife in his arms and held her. "I thought of the first Christmases we'd had after we got married. We always had a good time and made the best of not having children, and now I think of all the family or all the friends we've made over the past year. Things are so different now. Everyone is getting married. You retired from the library, and your good friend Pam, is your replacement." Her hair smelled of gardenias, the same as it did fifty years ago.

"Who do you think will have children first, Penny or Peggy?"

"I think Roger and Pam."

"Oh, Arnie." She looked up at him. "I have to serve this coffee."

He kissed her. "Coffee or me?"

"You, always you." She kissed him back.

"You two should get a room."

Startled, they looked over and saw Roger. "I'll serve the coffee, and you two can continue what you were doing."

"I'll help you."

"No, she won't. She's busy with her main squeeze."

"Ick," said Roger. "Now for sure you need a room." He took the tray and brought the cups, cream, and sugar to the living room and set it on the coffee table. He took the coffee pot while Arnie and Adeline were still kissing. "If you don't stop that, the party will be in here."

Roger really didn't mind seeing them so in love. He'd hoped he and Gail grew old together and, over the years seeing Arnie and Adeline so in love, felt there was hope. Now he put that hope in Pam. "Hey, you two love birds. Take it outside."

Arnie couldn't help but laugh. "You're such a pest. I guess we have no choice but to join the party."

It was late when everyone left, but Jake and Peggy needed to go over their plans. Jake checked his phone earlier and noticed the text from Brad. Nelson wanted to meet with them on the twenty-seventh. They had a day to firm up their plans.

They would travel tomorrow after they called John. Jake didn't want him involved, but he felt he needed to inform him about what was happening. They were restless and couldn't sleep. When sleep didn't come, they sat on the couch under a blanket and looked at the winter wonderland outside their picture window.

Without their contact telling them what to expect, they wanted to be prepared for anything if possible. The peacefulness of the snow laden branches and virgin snow on the ground put them to sleep.

"John, how was your Christmas?"

In a shaky voice, John said, "It was the best Christmas ever." He'd been teary eyed all morning, remembering yesterday, the presents, mass, the tree, his parents, and Nell.

Jake remembered the first Christmas with his mom after they found her working in a greasy diner. That too was the best. "That's great, John." Jake hesitated, wondering if telling John was such a good idea when he was so happy, but he decided John needed to know. "Brad got a call from Lt. Jeremy Nelson, and he wants them to come to San Francisco for more questioning. They want to be able to get enough evidence to put Sam and his mom behind bars. But . . . they'd already given their statement by phone. I'm thinking they want to kill Brad and Joyce to weaken Sam's case and they can let Sam go free."

Jake continued, "Nelson has never met Brad and Joyce, so Peggy and I are going in their place."

"No! I forbid it. It's over. Whatever happens out there from now on is not our concern."

"You're right, it's not, but we're in the business of bringing justice to the guilty, to protect the innocent. In this case, your parents were the victims."

There were seconds of silence. "I want to go with you."

"They probably know who you are, in which case, it's not a good idea for you to be anywhere in San Francisco where someone could possibly recognize you."

More silence. "You're right. Okay." He continued, trying to convince himself, "You go and make sure you have a backup plan—three or four backup plans. If they meet you in a warehouse or empty building, you won't have a chance to leave, I'd be sure of it." John gave Jake the phone number of his police contact. "Tell him your every move. He can be trusted, and he's back at work now."

"We will. I'll call him as soon as I hang up. We'll be heading to the airport in a few hours. We want to get there and scope out the area."

"Good luck and give me updates every minute, and I mean that literally."

John disconnected. His parents were listening to his conversation.

"What's going on?" asked his father. John filled them in on what was happening. "As much as I love my freedom, we never intended for anyone to get hurt. If we knew someone got poisoned, and now someone might possibly get killed, we never would've left the cabin at Zephyr Cove," said John Sr.

"Dad, I can't possibly understand how you feel right now, but Jake reminded me that the Justice Team is in the business of justice, and if people continue to get by with injustice, then we haven't done our job."

"Fine," said Michelle. "Is your policeman friend trustworthy?"

"Yes, Mom, he can be trusted."

ꕤ

Jake and Peggy checked in to the hotel as Brad Hensley and Joyce Armstrong. Jake made fake ID for them both before they left Boone. They even flew in Brad's and Joyce's names. They made the decision not to go anywhere near the warehouse until the time of their meeting. They didn't want to call attention to themselves in case Nelson's thugs were there.

Mike Nash, John's policeman friend, knocked on their hotel room door an hour after they arrived at the hotel. He had on his uniform and duty belt, which was bulky with the equipment required to carry to help protect the community, and both Jake and Peggy hoped they would be protected. Nash sat in the only chair in the room, while Jake and Peggy sat on the bed.

"I don't think you should do this, it's too dangerous, but I'll help you as best I can. I know where the warehouse you're talking about is. It's been closed for three months. The owners couldn't pay their rent. It's also hard to get to, and so it makes it hard to get away from. Have either of you ever shot a gun before?"

"No," said Jake for both of them, "we haven't."

"You'll have to take something with you for protection. I can give you a gun, but if you've never shot one . . . Maybe the threat that you have one will be good enough. I'll have to think about that. I have a feeling Nelson will question you at first so it looks legitimate. Then his thugs will move in with guns drawn. Nelson won't dirty his hands with murder." He looked at Peggy. "Sorry, Peggy, I have to think realistically.

"I need to set up my guys before any of that happens. I can't promise that even if I do that, I can protect you."

"We'll take the chance." He looked at Peggy. "Right, Peg?"

"Yes, we want this over, and we want the key players behind bars so they never have the chance to do it again."

"All right. This is what's going to happen . . ."

They talked and planned for two hours, and when Nash was sure they understood their role, he left.

"I'm scared," said Peggy. "I know I always say to be positive, but our lives were never at stake before."

"We'll get through it. It might be good going in scared. We'll keep alert to what's going on, hopefully less room for error."

"Good idea. We haven't eaten since breakfast, but I don't want to go anywhere, and I'm not so sure I'm hungry either."

"Let's go through the plan one more time, just to make sure, and then we can decide if we want to eat. But we probably should to keep up our energy."

They went through the plan, devised another backup plan Nash hadn't thought of, and were content with laying the notes aside and ordering dinner.

Jake's phone beeped. It was a text from John. *Where's my update?* He showed Peggy. "If this wasn't so serious, I'd laugh." Instead of texting, Jake called, filled him in on everything that was discussed, told him the time they were meeting and the place. When John was satisfied with their plan, Jake disconnected.

They went through the motions of eating, not enjoying it or tasting it, ate only to keep up their strength. They would have one more such meal in the morning before their meeting. To keep busy, Jake went through the notes they had when they rescued the Masons just days earlier. He wondered what had happened to Abby and hoped she was safe.

"Peg, I think we should get some coffee."

"Seriously?"

"I want to try and find out about Abby."

"Are you sure we should? I don't think we need to call attention to ourselves."

"Let's go have coffee, and then we can decide what to do."

The café was less busy in the evening. A few people were paying more attention to their phones than the friends sitting across from them or who was in the coffee shop. Several people were leaving. Jake and Peggy ordered, then went to the end of the counter to wait for their drinks. The barista making the drinks looked familiar to Peggy.

"Hi," she said. "I thought you worked the noon shift."

He looked up. "I usually do. This works better for me. I only kept the noon hours because I liked one of my coworkers, but it turned out she left and didn't tell anyone. I'm counting that as a blessing. Who knows if, all of a sudden, she'd do the same thing if we were dating?"

"Do you know where she went?"

"Probably to her parent's house. They live in Reno. She couldn't have had that much money working here to get any further, but what do I know? I'm still upset about the whole thing."

"Does she have a last name?"

"Why are you interested?"

"Almost the same thing. My brother was interested in her."

"She is the type that people would get a broken heart over." He handed them their drinks. "It's Woods."

"Thanks," said Jake. "I hope you get over her in a hurry."

"Yeah, me too."

They sat at a window table and were amazed at the change in weather. The temperature was fifty degrees warmer than Iowa, no sign of snow, the sun was shining, and they felt its warmth through the window.

"Let's hope Abby is safe."

"The only way we'll find out is if we go there and see for ourselves. I would like to at least warn her somehow." He took out his phone and looked up the last name in the Reno area. There were a lot of Woods. "Her name is listed with a phone number. I'm going to call."

"Should we wait until we get back to the hotel? It's a lot more private there."

"Good idea. It's so quiet in here I thought we *were* alone."

Jake looked around and noticed a man two tables over. He had a newspaper in front of him on the table, but he didn't seem to be reading it. Jake watched him and noticed he had a routine, he took a sip of coffee, turned the page of the newspaper, looked out the window. Two minutes later, he did the same three things.

"Yeah, let's leave."

On the way to the hotel, he kept watching out his rearview mirror.

"I think we're being followed." Jake made a turn down Arguello Boulevard. It was a residential area, so he really couldn't speed up.

"We're stopping at the next hotel we see. We'll get out of the car as if we don't know we're being followed. If you still have your cardkey in your back pocket, pull it out as we walk to the entrance. It will look like we're really staying there."

"Peg, pull out that map we brought and open it." As soon as it was open, Jake pulled over to the curb and took the map. He noticed the car drove past but couldn't see the license plate. He mostly took out the map as a diversion. When a few minutes passed, he saw the same car go past in the opposite direction.

He gave the map back to Peg and pulled away from the curb. "He must've turned around to see what we were doing." Several miles later, Jake pulled into a hotel parking lot.

They got out, and as planned, Peggy pulled out her cardkey. They pushed open the front doors and walked into the lobby. Jake grabbed her hand, and they quickly walked to the back of the hotel and out the exit door.

The guy with the newspaper at the café hurried into the hotel. He didn't see them, but both elevator doors were standing open. *They must have a room on the main floor.* He walked down the hall, and no one was there. *I was right behind them. They couldn't have gotten in their room that fast.* Losing them didn't so much bother him as having to call Nelson and report that he'd lost them.

Once he felt he'd looked everywhere, he went to his car and realized the car he followed was gone. *Crap! Now I have to report they outsmarted me.* No way was he going to do that. He'll just say they were driving too fast and there was too much traffic. He hoped that would work.

ꕥ

"Abby. You've seen me in the coffee house where you worked. Before you hang up on me, hear me out. I was asking about the Masons. Sam is in jail, and so is his mother."

"What does that have to do with you or me? And why do you care? I just want to be left alone. I swear I didn't know Sam was married. He never wore a ring, and he told me he was single. And I never knew he had a son. I read all that online. I'm sick about it, and now you call."

"There is a Lieutenant Nelson asking people who know the truth to come in and give their statement. They are to meet at a warehouse so the witness is protected."

Abby was silent. "Lieutenant Nelson did call me on my cell phone and wants to meet at a warehouse in two days. How did you know?"

"He called my friends and gave them the same information. I want to tell you not to meet him. Actually, you should leave your parents' house and stay out of sight for a while."

"I don't have any money. Sam gave me money to put in my bank account, and when I left San Francisco, I went to the bank to get the money, but it was all gone."

"Is he a signer on the account?"

"No, but all he'd have to do is request a withdrawal and claim it was because a crime was committed. They all know him at the bank, so it wouldn't be that tough to get the money."

"Is it a branch bank, one that is also in Reno?"

"Yes, why? What good will that do? It's a zero balance either way."

"If you trust me with your account information, I'll wire you the money, and since he's in jail, he won't be withdrawing it."

"I don't even know you."

"You may be even more upset after I tell you this, but I'm only telling you this to let you know how serious I am about getting you out of sight. You have or had a manila envelope with information about the Masons. They were records Sam took from the precinct. You kept them under your couch."

"How do you know that? I should call the cops on *you*!"

"If you do, you'll have to explain about the envelope, and if they know you had it, you could be an accessory."

"I had that envelope for a long time and never opened it. I decided to look in there and see what was so important that Sam gave it to me to hold for him. I had already decided to move back home. When I read what had happened to the Masons, I sent it to the police. I liked the Masons. They were so nice to me, always talking to me, getting me to laugh. According to the documents, they weren't treated fairly, so I mailed the envelope and drove home. For all I know, they could be dead."

"They are safe now. Sam, his mother, and his partner have been arrested. Nelson is also guilty, and he can't afford to have his name dirtied and go to jail, so he's doing the next best thing, killing the people who can incriminate him. He just doesn't know that we know anything about him."

"I can't pay you back, I don't have a job. Once I'm working, I can send payments."

Jake was impressed with her integrity. "No need to pay me back." He wrote down her information, and first thing in the morning, he would wire the money to her. "Don't answer your phone either. We hope to take care of Nelson tomorrow. I'll keep you updated. Stay safe."

CHAPTER SEVENTEEN

Jake and Peggy put their phones on the inside of their left sock. The night before, Jake downloaded a special app that picks up sound several feet away. His phone was on record before they entered the building. Peggy set up her phone to connect to Nash live during the meeting.

There was a police car already there when they pulled up to the building. Jake assumed it was for effect. They walked into the brick warehouse. It had the smell of grain and corn. They didn't go up the stairs to the third floor as instructed. They waited where they were for twenty minutes.

"What are you doing here?" asked the man in a suit, as he walked down the stairs.

"We're here to meet Nelson. Lieutenant Nelson."

"You need to go up the stairs to the third floor."

"Can we meet right here on this floor? Joyce can't walk up the stairs. She has a leg problem."

"She's too young to have leg problems. You both need to get up the stairs. Nelson is a busy man. He needs your statements so he can get back to the department."

Peggy looked around and saw a space with overturned crates. "Let's meet over there." She limped slowly to one of the crates and sat down.

"Nelson wants you upstairs."

"Well, it seems if he's in such hurry, he could meet us down here. He has to come down here to leave anyway."

As the last resort, he offered taking the elevator. Although he was claustrophobic, he just wanted this over with. "You can take the elevator."

"I get sick on elevators."

Upset, the guy stormed up the stairs. "They won't come up here. Joyce has leg problems, and Brad gets sick in elevators."

"Just send Brad up the stairs."

"I don't think he'll come without her."

"Ah hell. I'll just go down there. What does it matter if you kill them up here or down there? You'll have to get them up here, though, once they're dead."

That's what you think. I'm getting the hell out of here immediately after I kill them. I'm not dragging anyone anywhere.

Nelson moved his heavy frame to the elevator. He had leg problems of his own and couldn't do the stairs, but the further up in the building guaranteed if they tried to escape, they would be caught by his gunman before they ran to the outside door.

He exited the elevator and saw where they were sitting. No way could he sit on one of those crates. His almost three-hundred-pound frame wouldn't allow it. He walked over to them, put on his cop face.

Jake was standing, he didn't sit down with Peggy. The heavy man held out his hand. "I'm Jeremy Nelson. Thank you for coming on such short notice. I have a few questions for you. Let's start with the day you went to Pearl's house. Tell me in detail what happened."

Jake started. "Pearl called us and told us she had more information about her neighbors. When we got there, she made tea and brought it in on a tray to the living room where Joyce and I were sitting. I noticed her tea was already poured, and she poured tea for Joyce and me.

"I realized something was wrong, and besides, Pearl didn't have any information to tell us. We left but not before Joyce drank some of her tea. I hope you lock that lady up and throw away the key. She's vicious."

"She'll be punished."

"I wonder what happened to the Masons. They were such nice people." Jake went on and on about the Masons, and after several minutes, Nelson cut in.

"I don't care about the Masons." He motioned to the guy in the suit. He came over and drew his gun.

"What's going on?" said Peggy.

"I'm sick of hearing about the Masons, Pearl, the whole damn operation. Sam screwed up, and now I have to play cleanup."

"As long as you're going to kill us, I have a few questions. What did the Masons do that was so terrible?"

"They were snooping around the storage area. They saw the drug delivery. I wanted them dead. Sam thought he could put them in protective custody but not the kind everyone thinks of. This was to punish them, not protect them. Like a fool, I let him do it. He wanted to try it out. Well, you don't try it out on witnesses to your own crimes."

"What's up with the old bat Pearl?"

"She's been working at the storage place for years. Everything her son wanted to do, according to her, was the right thing to do. What she thought behind closed doors may have been different, but she's the one who set up the drug deals and coordinated the drop-offs. But why do you care? You'll be dead, and so will Sam's mistress. She's coming here tomorrow, and she'll be dead too. Then no one is left to testify."

"How about the Masons? They could come back and testify."

"You can't fool me. They're dead. Joe here said he killed them after they escaped. He was checking up on the cabin. I didn't trust those two losers sitting in their car watching the place. He was driving down the street and almost hit the Masons running away. He chased after them and killed them."

Jake knew there wasn't anyone driving down that street when they escaped, and the Masons didn't run down the street by themselves. Joe must've told him quite a story. "What if I told you Joe was nowhere around on that night? He wasn't driving down the street, he didn't chase after the Mason's, and he didn't kill them."

"I'd say you're lying."

Peggy noticed Joe was no longer watching her but had his full attention on Jake. He was worried he was going to be ratted on. Peggy was still sitting on the crate, and now she was rubbing her right leg. Nelson was standing in front of Jake and Joe was standing closer to Peggy. Nelson had on a suit, and it was hard to tell if he had a gun. Peggy was almost certain if he did, he wasn't that quick with pulling it out and using it. But she didn't want to take any chances.

The plan was for Jake to get all the information he could out of Nelson, and they weren't supposed to do anything stupid. But Peggy was afraid Nash wouldn't intervene in time.

"I'd say *he's* lying. Why don't you ask him?"

He looked at Joe, but Joe couldn't look Nelson in the face. "Did you kill the Masons?"

"I told you I did. Why don't you believe me?"

"See," said Nelson, "he says he killed them."

"The two guys who were handcuffed to the car door didn't see Joe."

The details of the two men handcuffed to their car was kept from the media. It was for police records only. Nelson knew that for a fact. He looked at Joe and saw him sweating. *Could this get any worse?* "Joe. If you're lying to me, I'll find out, and you'll be dead. Now just shoot them so I can get back to work."

As soon as they were dead, Nelson was going to kill Joe. He was a deadbeat, and he didn't need liars working for him. He wanted honest men who had a backbone to be in his employ. He put his hand inside his jacket.

"Hold your hands in the air. Both of you!" shouted Nash.

Yes, it could get worse, thought Nelson.

Joe dropped his gun and put his hands up. Nelson made an attempt but couldn't move his arms up that far. Nash reached into Nelson's jacket and took his gun. His partner took Joe's gun off the floor. Nelson and Joe were handcuffed.

Nelson was humiliated. He'd try to get Nash fired from the department many times. He'd wanted to get someone *he* chose to work in narcotics. Nash had been in many departments before. He got things done, and not often did the guilty go free. Nelson wanted someone to turn a blind eye to the people he had on the street who were bringing in big bucks for his drug dealings.

Sam and his mother's scheme was just a few of the many deals he was into, and it paid off handsomely. He was able to eat in the best restaurants, drink expensive wine, go on exotic vacations, and had enough money to buy the fancy cars. He was living the good life.

However, his health was going to hell. He was overweight, taking medicine for high blood pressure, and had diabetes. But he had the money to hire the best doctors. What he didn't realize was the money was the reason his wife left, his children won't talk to him, and he had no friends except the ones he paid. Apparently, no one liked to hear him brag about his 'good life.'

Jake took his phone and handed it to Nash. "You should get his confession off the recorder."

"Nice work, Jake."

"What? You can't record me. You didn't have my permission. Oh! Why did you call him Jake, his name is Brad?"

"You're right, I didn't get your permission to record you," declared Nash. "So I had a civilian do it. Jake and Peggy took Brad and Joyce's place. You know the rules. Oh, silly me, you do know the rules, you just don't follow them."

Nelson looked at Jake. "Who are you, and how do you know Brad?"

Several more officers came in the room with their weapons drawn and escorted Joe and Nelson to a squad car. He never got his question answered.

"I hope you two are okay. Luckily, Joe was a little hesitant to shoot his gun." He looked at Peggy who was now standing next to Jake. "You okay, Peggy?"

"Yes, I'm fine. I was so glad to see you. I wasn't sure . . . Well, when someone has a gun pointed at me, I'm just not sure about anything."

"Understandable." He put Jake's phone in his pocket. "I'll re-record this and give you your phone back. If you have time to come down to the station, I can do it right away."

"That works," said Jake.

"By the way, I've heard great things about the two of you from John, and after you found his parents, he can't stop talking about you. I appreciated all you've done too. You have another team in Omaha I hear. They're the ones who should've been here today?"

"Yes, Joyce and Brad. They're great people."

"Tell them I appreciate them as well. Let's head down to the station. You can follow me. I promise I won't turn on my siren and race back to the precinct." He laughed.

ꟸ

The recording was rerecorded, and Jake's phone was returned to him. Now they were back at the hotel. The first call he made was to Brad. He explained what had happened, that they were safe and no one got hurt. His next call was to Abby. He told her that she should be safe now, to keep the money, and she absolutely did not have to pay him back. She was happy about the news. Then he called John.

"John."

"Why haven't you been giving me updates?" He started to pace. "Have you met with Nelson yet? Has Nash been helping?" He was rubbing his free hand through his curly hair. "I . . ."

"John, quit pacing and sit down. You might want to give those curly locks of yours a break too." After spending time with John, he knew his mannerisms. "Now listen while I fill you in."

John laughed. "Okay, I'm ready to listen."

Jake started with the trip to the coffee house, when he called Abby, being followed, and the incident at the warehouse. "Nelson was arrested and put in handcuffs. Peggy and I went to the station with Nash, and he took our statement. He thinks, along with Sam and Pearl, Nelson will be in jail a good long time."

"Do you think we can finally take a deep breath and know this is wrapped up?"

"I think we can put this behind us and move forward," said Jake. "Enjoy your parents and let us know the wedding date. Peg and I would love to come."

That touched John, to think they wanted to see him get married. Jake, Peggy, Joyce, and Brad were all considered family to him now. They helped him do something he couldn't do alone, and he would never forget it. "I'll let you know. Oh, I would like Brad and Joyce's cell numbers, their addresses too. Mom and Dad want to do something special for all of you."

Jake gave him the information. "Just remember we didn't mind at all doing this for you."

"Thanks is hardly enough, but thanks. Keep in touch. Nash has been busy since he was out sick, so no cases have come in. I'll keep you informed if you're still interested."

"We're interested. Say hi to John Sr. and Michelle. Goodbye for now."

Jake went to Peggy. "I need some Peggy time." He put his arms around her. "I think we should stay two more days, take in the sights, or never leave the hotel and have alone time."

"Never leave the hotel."

ꝏ

Dennis Coyle was back at the jail to visit Sam. He had more information on the case and hoped Sam would stop the arrogance act. If not for him, for his son. He'd visited Barry and his mom the day before, and they both seemed very nice. The wife didn't think cops were bad. Sam did bad things but never imagined he'd jeopardize his gun and badge for dealing drugs. She'd never liked her mother-in-law Pearl. She was always so negative and too nosey and never paid any attention to her grandson. She was too busy praising her own son Sam.

Barry read the news reports on his dad and didn't want to believe any of it. And yet he wondered if it *were* all true. He thought he could handle it but didn't know about his mother. She was too good, too kind, and his dad treated her like crap. He was never home, never wanted to spend time with his own kid.

He kept telling him that his badge was important to him, and it took long days and long nights to protect the community, so that's why he was never home. When he was, nothing his wife did pleased him, and yet she stuck with him.

Now Coyle would find out if Sam sang a new tune after he told him Jeremy Nelson was arrested. Then it would be Coyle's decision if he wanted to continue to represent him. He kept thinking of Barry and his mother. He didn't want to let the kid down, and yet it wasn't his nature to defend someone who knowingly committed crime after crime. He would do the best he could with the evidence and proceed from there. But he'd never done pro bono before either, so maybe it's a case for firsts.

Sam was escorted through the door and was told where to sit. He looked haggard, and his hair wasn't combed, and he had a shadow of a beard. He sat with a sigh and looked at Coyle but didn't say anything.

"Are you going to talk this time? If not, I'll never come back and you can worry about defending yourself."

"I'll talk but not to you. My family will find me the best lawyer, which isn't you."

"Your family has given up on you," Coyle lied. "Do you know Lt. Jeremy Nelson?"

"Yeah, he's a good guy. What about him?"

"He was arrested, and he ratted you out."

No, he wouldn't do that. Arrested? No one knew about him and the drugs. There must've been a leak. And my family doesn't care about me? "I don't believe anything you say. Nelson didn't do anything to get arrested for, and my family loves me."

"Do they love that you had a mistress? Or that you dealt in drugs? Or try on this one: Do they love that you kidnapped two innocent people?"

"It's not true. None of it is true."

"They think it's true. And Nelson not only has drug charges, but he's also got attempted murder hanging over his head. He claims it's your fault you let the witnesses go free, and he was only going to kill them to protect Ward, which is you, in case you couldn't put two and two together." He looked at Sam and bore his brown eyes into his. "If you don't let me help you, the only lawyer your family can afford is a public defender. Do you want that? If so, let me know and I'll walk out that door and you'll never see me again."

Sam was screwed, and he knew it, but he wasn't used to letting anyone take over his life. He was independent and made his own decisions, but he saw more and more the decisions of his life were being made for him by someone else, and it wasn't good. "Okay, you can stay."

"Start telling me what happened from the beginning."

"My mom works at the storage place, and she found drugs in one of the garages. So I came and took a look. I confiscated the drugs and brought it to the station and turned it into narcotics. The next several months, my partner and I monitored the place so it wouldn't happen again.

"One day the Masons came up to the squad car when I was staking out the place and asked that they be put into protective custody. They thought the drug dealers saw them walk by one day. I put them in protective custody. As you can see, I had nothing to do with kidnapping or dealing drugs."

Coyle knew that a cop doesn't put people in protective custody. It's a long process with lots of paperwork. There is a special set of people who take care of that. Coyle put papers in his briefcase and shut it. "I'm leaving, and when you decide to tell the truth, give me a call. This is serious, and you could be locked up for the rest of your life. If you get accessory to murder, you could be hung." Coyle walked out the door and never looked back.

Don't have to get so testy about it. As much as Sam knew he would get off and spend the rest of his days as a civilian, doing whatever he wanted, again making his own choices but there was a part of him that was scared he would spend the rest of his life behind bars. He didn't think any lawyer, no matter how good, could get him off.

Another blow to his ego was that his family couldn't afford a good lawyer. He'd paid the bills, but when he'd rented the apartment for Abby he stopped paying for anything for his family. He figured his wife was working and his kid was working too. Between the two of them, they could make it work. He shrugged. *Oh well. I'll get out of here, and then I'll show them who's boss again. I'll call Abby, and we'll take off somewhere together.* The guards escorted him back to his cell.

CHAPTER EIGHTEEN

"Jake, I know you filled me in on the trip," said John, "but have you heard anything more?"

"Barry Ward, Sam's son, is having a hard time with the whole thing. Sam's not listening to his lawyer, but that might change since he found out that Nelson was arrested and he's ratting on everyone."

"Is he?"

"No one knows, but the lawyer used it as leverage."

"Let me know if you hear anything else, and while I'm talking to you, would you be interested in taking a road trip to Minneapolis? Doc Severinsen is at Orchestra Hall for a post-Christmas concert." John laughed. "You probably don't even know who that is."

"He was the band leader on the *Tonight Show*."

John laughed again. "So you know he's good. Do you want to come? See if Brad and Joyce can get away and come too. Mom and Dad want to do something for you all for rescuing them, but they don't think that would even begin to express their thanks. If that's the case, you might be coming for concerts all year round. You can ask your friends in Boone if they want to come, especially your mom. The more the merrier as they say."

"That's great, John. I'll ask. Peggy's parents live in Minneapolis, so I'm sure they'll come. The last time I checked with Brad, they were swamped at the shelter, but I'll call again and see if they want to come."

"Perfect. I might ask my friend Max and his wife. Might as well make it a party."

"You sound happy, John. I've never heard happiness in your voice before. All those voice mails you would leave sounded so serious and sometimes sad."

"I am happy—truly happy. The three of us are going to run errands today, buy clothes. That coat you bought Mom, the one that people in Alaska wear in the darkest, coldest of weather, isn't warm enough for her. We're going to buy a down vest that fits underneath."

Jake laughed. "Once she gets used to the weather, she'll be wearing a sweatshirt and shorts."

"Not funny. That really happens here in Minnesota. We're ready to leave. Let me know as soon as possible how many are coming and we'll buy tickets." He disconnected.

Jake told Peggy about the concert, and she too knew Doc Severinsen. She made a call to her parents, and Jake called the Coles and his mom.

Jake knew his mom was at work and might not answer, but she did. "Mom, we're home. I was wondering if you could take a few days off and go on a road trip to Minneapolis." He told her the date.

"Right now, I'm on break, and when I get back, I'll ask."

"Okay. How's Sue since she retired?"

"She had a rough Christmas. Her husband died on Christmas Eve. She's thinking about coming back to work. Luckily, they haven't filled her position yet. I was filling in, but I'm fine with going back to doing what I was doing. Oh, I want to go to the funeral, so as soon as I find out when, I will let you know, and hopefully, it won't conflict with the road trip. What's in Minnesota besides the Baileys?"

"A concert." He told her the details, and his mom was thrilled about seeing Doc, as she called him.

"We used to stay up late and watch the *Late Show*, even though it was so hard to get up in the mornings and go to work." She laughed "I guess your father didn't go to work, he went to his other wife's house and probably went back to bed, explaining what a hard night at work he had." She was glad she could finally laugh about it. It probably had a lot to do with Roger. She just wanted to leave her past behind. "I would love to go. I'll let you know as soon as I can."

"Thanks, Mom. I love you."

ജ്ഞ"

"Arnie, we're back in town, and I was wondering if you and Adeline wanted to go to Minneapolis for a concert."

"Is that at Orchestra Hall?"

"Yes, how do you know about that?"

"My brother lived in Minneapolis for many years, then he died of a heart attack, and we haven't been back since. It will be good to go back after ten years, see his old house, check out the restaurants."

"So sad about your brother. I'm glad you'll be going. John and his parents live in Minneapolis, and they've invited us."

"They're probably happy you reunited them with their son. But how does Adeline and I fit into the picture?"

"Our friends are invited too."

"What concert?"

"Doc Severinsen."

"No kidding. For sure, we'll go. Adeline likes his hot-looking clothes."

"I'm assuming she means the colors and not the style."

"You're right about that. If we have something scheduled, we'll clear it. Get us two tickets."

Jake disconnected, and his phone rang. "Jake. Boss, I was wondering if I could have another week. I might need more time off later when they have the trial."

The trial. What a waste, thought Jake. "You can have all the time you need. Foxy will continue to pull double shifts."

"Good, she told me she needed the money to pay off some bills."

"How are things going?"

"Today my dad is seeing the lawyer again. If he doesn't talk this time, Coyle is dropping the case. Dad doesn't know how lucky he is to have Coyle represent him. Mom has been quiet. She goes to work every day, and when she's home, she's always on the verge of crying. I try to cheer her up, but she only thinks about Dad."

"Let me know if I can do anything, and take all the time you need."

"Oh, one more thing—if I needed you to come out here, would you come?"

Jake never expected Barry would want him to join him in San Francisco.

"For the trial, if they have one. I feel so alone out here, and like, this problem will never go away until Dad talks and works things out with the lawyer. I know you travel a lot, and you'd probably be able to get away. Adeline loves filling in while you're gone."

Jake didn't know what to say. He didn't think anyone would recognize him, but so far, this case held many surprises and made the world seem all the smaller once Barry said his dad was Sam Ward and Barry wanted to go to San Francisco because he'd been arrested. "Yes, I'll come. Let me know. Peggy would come with me, if that's all right."

"I was hoping she would. She's always so positive, and I need a dose of that right now."

"Hang in there and don't worry about work. Keep me updated."

ꕥ

This was the last time Coyle was going to the jail, he promised himself. The last time should've been the last time. Ordinarily, he would've left during the first visit and not looked back, but he kept thinking of Sam's kid. He looked so sad and wanted to believe in his dad's innocence. Then there was the mother. She looked even sadder if that were possible. She was frail and gullible. No matter what state the mother was in, he still felt he had to do the best he could to help Sam whether he was innocent or guilty.

"You'll have to wait out here. Ward's got a visitor."

ꕥ

"Mom's worried about you. She doesn't eat or sleep much. She knows you're innocent and doesn't understand why they are holding you here."

"What do you think, son? Do you think I'm innocent too?"

Barry had always been intimidated by his father. He would hang his head whenever he was around him. If Barry didn't look directly at his father, he felt he couldn't be humiliated by him. And he was always made to feel everything was his fault. He didn't want to leave his mom alone with his dad, but he couldn't handle the mental abuse anymore and took a bus to Iowa. He had many jobs, but the one at the café in Boone was the best job he'd ever had. He didn't want to lose it because he was taking too much time off, but he trusted the owners enough that if they said he could take time off, they wouldn't penalize him for it later.

He squared his shoulders and looked directly into his dad's eyes. "I think you're capable of the things they arrested you for. Are you guilty? I hope not. Are you innocent? I doubt it."

"Well, aren't you a philosopher all of a sudden. What the hell are you learning in that small hick town now that you left your mother high and dry? She'll never recover from you leaving her."

He felt his shoulders droop and his head lower. Without thinking, he corrected his shoulders and looked back into his dad's eyes. "You will no longer be able to intimidate me or humiliate me or shame me. After all, you're the one locked up, and I'm the one who's free. If you ask me, which you won't, I would listen to your lawyer. He's the only hope you have whether you're innocent or guilty.

"And I didn't leave Mom, I left you, Dad. Mom and I had a long talk before I left, and she thought the best thing to do was move out. So we're square, Mom and me. Is there anything else you want to blame me for, perhaps blame me for you being in jail, blame me for Grandma? Or I should say Pearl? Because she never once acted like my grandma. She's just like you—no feelings, always the need to be in control, and treating her family like shit."

"Stop that language," reprimanded his father. "Your grandma is the best grandma you've ever had."

"Sorry, Dad, but Grandma Helen is the best grandma. She came over and hugged me and loved me and cooked my favorite meal. I bet you don't even know what that is, do you? And you probably don't care. Tell me when was the last time Pearl came over and paid attention to me? As far as I could see, she only paid attention to you, and now you're both in jail." Barry laughed and continued until tears ran down his face. It felt so good to get it out. He wiped his eyes with his hands. "I'm going home to be with Mom. I'll be there for her. She could never say that about you. You were never there for her. Did you know she has cancer? Of course, you didn't. She didn't tell you because she thought you'd leave or, worse yet, stay and make her life more miserable."

"Don't you sass me. Why don't you get out of here and never come back? I thought you were here to support your father, not put me down. One of the commandments says to honor your father."

"But, dear old Dad, what if he doesn't honor me?" Barry walked out the door.

Sam stood, and he felt a hand push him back down into his seat. "You got another visitor. Stay right where you are."

He knew his wife didn't have cancer. She was healthy, probably healthier than him. He didn't give it another thought. The only thing he wanted to do was go back to his cot and sleep the rest of his life away. If he never woke up, it would be fine with him. Thank goodness, he was in isolation. He'd heard horror stories of how bad cops were treated in jail. Not that he was a bad cop, but his jail mates thought differently.

ꙮ

Lenny Farms had to get to the bookstore before it closed. He needed a book for his class. There were numerous verses he had to memorize. Once upon a time, one of his wives thought he would be a great minister, even though he never owned a Bible. He also thought it would be a good way to meet women. Some women were just attracted to men of the cloth. He hoped that bit of information was true. He didn't have any money to pay for the class but thought he could get student aid. So far, he was able to enroll in the first class online with no trouble.

He was in the bookstore and saw the book he needed. It was being sold for five dollars. The only time procrastination paid off, *he thought. He went to the clerk and gladly paid his money.*

"It's a little used," said the clerk. "People buy it and then bring it back within the week. There must be something wrong with it."

"Not a problem," said Lenny, not able to stop smiling at the discount.

"I don't even think the verses are right."

"There are so many versions of the Bible that I'm sure it will fit one of them."

She highly doubted it. The small print after the title, which no one read, is TAV, The Alternative Version.

He walked back to the hole in the wall he called home and started memorizing verses.

ꙮ

Jake called John and told him how many tickets to buy. John mentioned Michelle was happy with her new down vest. It helped a lot to keep warm whenever she had to go outside.

John Sr. bought a new computer, and he'd been working on it all night, checking on his neglected investments and his overseas bank account. He wanted to get some of his money to the United States so he could share it with their son. He wanted him to keep doing things for justice because if it weren't for the Justice Team, they would never be in Minnesota right now.

Sometime after midnight, John Sr. had money transferred to the account he and his wife had opened days before in Minneapolis. He'd been on the computer a lot before he and his wife were abducted, and even though he didn't miss it when they were taken, it only took several minutes and he was hooked again. Michelle came to him in the early morning and told him to go to bed.

"I'd forgotten how addicting this was." He kissed her. "Wake me at noon. I can at least have lunch with you. I got our bank accounts straightened out and rearranged our investments. I don't think I forgot anything."

"If I remember correctly, you didn't need a list to spend endless hours on that thing. But you did pay *more* attention to me than the computer, which is why I love you so much."

"We have so much to be thankful for."

"Yes, we do. Now go to bed."

He laughed. "Yes, ma'am."

John almost collided with his dad as he walked to the kitchen. "Good night, son. I'll join you for lunch. Unless you need me for something before then, you ask your mother." John Sr. laughed as he walked down the hall to his room.

"Dad hasn't changed a bit. Hey, let me make the coffee. You sit."

She did as instructed. As she watched her son, she was amazed at her thoughts. *Is this really John? Are we really free? Am I dreaming?* She knew it was all real, yet she doubted, doubted after so long of thinking that she would never see her son again and now he is right in front of her making her coffee.

"That's you, right, John?"

He turned to her and smiled. "Yep, it's me."

She'd asked the same question many times, and he never tired of answering it. For he too wondered if it were all real, wondered if they'd get snatched away from him in the middle of the night, or when they were running errands, if anyone would grab them and take them away.

John hoped that with everyone in jail, that would not happen. But *was* everyone in jail? He could only hope.

"Are you for real, John, or do I have to serve my own coffee?"

"Funny, Mom."

CHAPTER NINETEEN

The library was closed during the time of the funeral to reopen an hour after the prayer service so employees could go to the grave site. Pam didn't know much about Sue's husband, but with all the people in attendance, others certainly knew him.

She wondered what would've happened if her husband Lenny had died before she found out about his second wife. Who did he have listed as his wife in his records? Probably the other woman. He said he didn't introduce her as his wife because he didn't think it was anyone's business. Now that she thought about it, she never went to his office parties either. Did *the other wife* go, or did he even have a job?

Roger squeezed her hand, sensing her thoughts were wandering. She looked up at him and smiled. He was excited about their trip to Minneapolis the next day. Anytime he could spend time with the woman he loved was a good time. They had tried to set a date for their wedding, but whenever they came up with something, there was always something happening that weekend.

They would figure it out, he was sure of that. He wanted to put his arm around Pam and hold her close. He wanted to touch more than her hand. Since the last time they made love, they had decided to wait until they were married to do it again. He wanted to take her on a long trip to a secluded place where they could make love on the beach if they wanted to and no one would know.

His body was tight, and the thrill of anticipation was moving through him. *Stop!* he silently commanded his body. He let go of her hand, folded his arms, and focused on what was being said. Soon his thoughts were back with Pam on the beach. *I'm hopeless. Focus,* he willed himself. He moved his thoughts to their Minneapolis trip and thought of what he needed to pack. Jake was going to rent a van so they could all travel together. She would be sitting close to him, closer than she is now if it were a small van. The thought of that for a four-hour trip put his body back on alert and his thoughts were right back to the lovemaking.

"Amen," said the pastor.

Pam looked at Roger. "It was a nice service. Do you still want to go to the cemetery?"

"Yes," he whispered and not because he was in church.

"I'll have to go back to work afterward, but I'm all packed and ready to leave in the morning."

"Good thing I don't work because I haven't washed clothes in over a week. I put my duffel bag in a good place, so good I can't find it now."

"Is it still in the trunk of your car?"

Roger laughed. "You might be right. I'll look before we head to the cemetery."

The duffel bag *was* in his trunk. *One less thing to think about,* he thought. On the way, Pam talked about Sue and how hard she worked to take care of her husband and that she never once complained about the long nights and early mornings she was with him.

The conversation went to their trip and how excited they were to get out of town, but the weather in Minneapolis was anything but inviting. Twenty below was the windshield. Minneapolis had been having record-breaking temperatures and not because the temperature was too high.

ꟷ

John was excited his friends were coming to Minneapolis. Brad and Joyce were able to get away. Their assistant Julie recruited college students from the University of Nebraska to help out during the day, and several students volunteered to stay through the night, so there was someone there while the families slept. Several students volunteered to conduct classes on the basics of computers. Julie convinced Joyce that everything was under control.

Brad's son was in Minneapolis for business, and it was the perfect opportunity to visit with him, so Jake chose to make reservations at the same hotel his son was staying at. They were also looking forward to seeing the Masons again. By now, Joyce hoped they wouldn't be living in fear anymore and enjoyed being with their son. She didn't think they'd ever see John Sr. and Michelle again and was grateful for this opportunity to spend time with them.

Joyce had picked out a sexy dress to wear to the concert. She knew Brad had a black suit, so it was only right she should look good too.

ꕤ

The couples were getting ready for the concert. They were all at the same hotel as Brad and Joyce, except Jake and Peggy were invited to stay at John's house, and they gladly accepted. Noah and Paula were close enough to drive back home after the concert, but the hotel offer from Jake was sounding more and more like a good idea.

John Sr. wore a tux, and his wife Michelle wore a revealing black dress with a string of white pearls. They'd gotten their hair cut earlier in the week, and it felt good to get out and actually do something for themselves for a change. John Sr. kept a short pony tail because it tamed his wavy hair, and actually, he liked the change. It brought him back to his hippie days.

Peggy had her hair swept up and held with a diamond clip in the back. She even put on makeup. The black mascara made her eye lashes look even darker, and the gold eye shadow she used made her eyes come alive. She wore a gold slinky dress she'd found at a thrift store and couldn't believe such a nice dress was in her size.

John and Jake wore black suits. There was a knock at the door. John hurried to answer it, expecting Nell. She had on her long black coat, and he wasn't able to see what she had on underneath, but he liked the way she looked with her hair swept back with soft curls. He wanted to touch them—oh hell, he wanted to touch all of her.

"Can I come in? It's cold out here."

"Of course." He stepped aside so she could come in. "I love your hair, Nell . . ."

Before he had a chance to say more, she took off her coat. "I bet you love this more."

John gasped. She had on a tight-fitting dark purple dress with black boots. A gold chain lay on her cleavage. Her red lips invited him over for a kiss, and he did just that.

"Yum," he said in a dreamy voice. "Are you allowed to look so good out in public?"

There was a knock at the door. He took one last kiss, and Nell made sure the lipstick was off his lips before he opened the door.

"Come in, Max, Ella."

Nell hugged Ella when she came in. She whispered to Nell, "Your lipstick is smeared."

Nell laughed. "Thanks, I'll go fix it, be right back."

"John, look at you," said Max. "You look like Dr. Zorba on the *Ben Casey* show."

John laughed. "And yet the sexiest woman alive, besides Ella here, loves me and wants to have my children."

Max laughed.

Ella, with her black hair and dark Italian skin, looked slim and sexy in her winter white dress. John thought Max didn't deserve such a beautiful woman, but lately, he realized he didn't deserve such a beautiful lady as Nell. He shook his head to clear it.

"Is everyone here already?"

"So far, no one has surfaced out of their rooms. The hotel group hasn't shown up either."

"I can't wait to meet everyone. I wonder if your parents will remember me. I only went home with you once."

"Yeah, but you stayed a month."

"Oh right, I forgot that part."

"When we were dating, he wanted to live with me a week," explained Ella, "until he found an apartment. He's been living with me for the last ten years."

"But now we're married."

Nell was back in John's large kitchen with a long dining room table at one end and the cupboards and appliances on the other wall, which left a large space in the middle. Michelle and John Sr. walked into the room. Michelle went right over to Max and gave him a hug.

"My God, it's really you. You've grown up a little."

"Thanks, you're the only one who has admitted that so far. I want you to meet Ella, my wife."

Michelle gave Ella a hug, and John Sr. hugged Max. "Life's too short, I'm giving hugs instead of handshakes."

Max, not usually a hugging man, decided it felt okay to hug another person besides his wife.

There was another knock at the door, and the rest of the guests came in, were introduced, and sat at the long table. Adeline had on a navy blue dress with white pearls; she even sported dress boots as part of her accessories. Arnie had on his one and only black suit, a little worn but it still fit, and according to Adeline, he looked just as handsome as he did thirty years ago when he bought it.

Paula wore a long green skirt and white silk blouse. Her hair was short but swept back from her face. Peggy had her intense eyes and dark eyebrows. Noah had on a black suit.

John looked around at everyone. He'd never had that many people in his house. The reason he bought a bigger house was he wanted a big family someday. He liked the attention he got as an only child but wished he'd had a brother to rough around with and a sister to protect. As he got older, he thought many times of selling it because his dream wasn't coming true. He didn't date, so of course, he figured he would never have children. The relationships he'd had over the years ended after the first date. He thought of joining a dating service online, but he didn't want to work that hard to meet someone.

At his printing job, he'd called the phone company several times to get the bill straightened out, and when he'd asked for the manager every time, he was transferred to Nell. He made a casual comment about having dinner. They went out a few times, and then Nell broke it off. She was too busy at work, got a promotion, and was working long hours.

John called a year later and asked her out again, and they've been inseparable ever since. Now his parents would be able to attend his wedding. Tonight he was truly happy.

"John, was that you at the Justice Café? I think you went on a tour of the place with Jake and Peggy," said Adeline.

"Yes, that was me. How did you remember that?"

"It's that wild cat hair of yours." She laughed. "My Arnie had long hair once, now he keeps it short, but he still has all of it."

Arnie ran his hand over his hair. "Yep, all there."

Everyone laughed.

"I'll go see if Jake and Peggy are ready," said Michelle.

She walked back to the guest room and knocked gently on the door. "Jake, Peggy."

Jake opened the door. "We're ready. We started talking and forget about the time."

They followed Michelle to the kitchen. The large kitchen now looked crowded with all the people. "Yikes," said Peggy. Pam and Roger arrived while Michelle was getting Jake and Peggy. She saw her parents and walked to her mom and hugged her, then hugged her dad.

"Michelle and I want to say thank you all for coming and a special thank you to Jake and Peggy and Brad and Joyce. Without them, we would not be here." He looked at his watch. "We'd better go so we can find a parking place in the ramp.

Noah drove the second van because he knew, being from Minneapolis, where Orchestra Hall was located.

Peggy and Jake and Brad and Joyce rode with the Masons and Nell. John drove, and John Sr. was in the passenger seat. Everyone fit in the van comfortably.

John Sr. turned around. "Michelle and I want to say thank you, Jake, Peggy, Brad, and Joyce, for helping our son find us. It seemed like a cruel joke the first couple of months after we were abducted. Then we suspected the witness protection program we were in was not because the police wanted us there but because the crooks wanted us there.

"We'd devised a code, so when we said one thing, it would mean another. We suspected we were being recorded. We already knew we were being watched by the two men in the car on the street. For some reason, we were moved to a different location. Maybe the rent was too high. I wanted to leave a clue behind, but I didn't want it to be obvious because I was sure the bad guys would've come in to make sure we didn't leave anything behind.

"I knew, if you were looking for us, you would recognize my money clip, so I hid it in the wall. Lucky for me, you had Jake with you, someone who knows all about secret places in the house. Thank you to your friend, Arnie, for teaching you how to pick locks.

"And, Joyce, my God, you were poisoned for me, for us. We can never thank you or repay you."

Nell just sat and listened to their conversation. She had a lot to be thankful for this Christmas season. John and his parents had survived this horrible ordeal, and the Justice Team was the reason they were all together tonight. Yes, she would always be grateful for the reunion of family.

Jake was glad he didn't make this announcement at the house with everyone present. Only the Justice Team knew the extent of their mission. The rest would've felt betrayed by what was being said. They would've assumed it was as simple as finding Pam, and once finding out it was much more dangerous than just looking up an address or hiring a private detective to check on a few things, they would've wanted the details. It was more than just a knock on their door and taking them home.

Paula may have thought back to their trip to Hershey when her daughter had been hurt and wondered if it were just the casual vacation Peggy told her it was.

Jake looked at Peggy, the scar on her forehead barely visible.

"Taking you to the concert is our way of saying thank you to our rescuers and your friends and families. Michelle and I know there is nothing we could do that would ever repay you."

"We realized," said Michelle, "that most of your family don't know what had happened or what you do to bring justice, so we decided not to thank you at the house, but without your persistence, we would not be here. In time, though, your friends or family might need the Justice Team. Just know that we are here to help you in whatever you need or want."

"Now let's put this all behind us and enjoy the concert," said John Sr.

ꕥ

Doc Severinsen was in true form, even in his late eighties. He wore a bright sequined pink outfit. Adeline and Arnie had bet on the color before the show. Adeline won. But they knew he would change outfits at intermission, and then they would bet again.

He waltzed out to the podium, stepped up, raised his baton, and the orchestra raised their instruments in playing position. Halfway into the song, he lifted his trumpet from its holder and played like he did forty years earlier. He could still hit the high notes.

All too soon, there was an intermission. They walked through the crowd to Peavey Plaza outside and saw ice skaters on the pavilion. There was a Caribou coffee across the street, and the women decided they could get coffee and be back before intermission was over.

The inside of Orchestra Hall was renovated a year ago. The lobby was expanded and reshaped. They wanted to connect the inside directly with the outside plaza. Also, they improved access for those with physical challenges and updated the backstage area.

Arnie and Adeline were reminiscing about their first visit to Orchestra Hall soon after they were married. They'd spent some time with Arnie's brother, and he suggested going to see a concert, but they'd have to dress up, his brother stressing dress up as in really dressing up. He told Arnie just because he wore work pants on his construction job didn't mean jeans would be dressier.

They had a great time and vowed they would get back to Minneapolis to see more shows. The years passed. They visited Arnie's brother but didn't go to any more shows until now.

"I'm so glad we made it back," said Adeline. "Too bad we couldn't stay with your brother."

"God rest his soul," said Arnie, saddened by the reality. His brother never married and had his eye on Adeline every time they would visit. He was overly kind, sweet, but after several visits, Arnie realized he was that way toward everyone, not just Adeline. But his brother had confided in him that if Adeline weren't married, he would surely marry her. He turned away and wiped his eyes on his handkerchief, turned back to his wife.

Adeline didn't say anything. She knew he was sad about his brother. "What is your vote on his next outfit after intermission?"

"Whatever color he wears, he will have the bling stuff all over it."

"That's not a vote, Arnie."

"Sure it is." He smiled. "I'll say green again."

"I'll say red."

"What are you two betting on?" asked Noah.

"The color of Doc's outfit."

Noah looked at Paula. "Let's bet too. I say black."

"Black doesn't seem like a color Doc would wear," said Paula. "I bet blue."

"What do we win if we're right?" asked Noah.

"If you lose, you have to make breakfast," said Arnie. "But that's easy in a hotel. I'll just go downstairs and stack my lovely wife's plate with food and give her breakfast in bed."

Adeline laughed. "If you're in a hotel, you have to take her out to a nice restaurant for breakfast."

"Can I decide not to bet?"

"No," said Arnie and laughed. "You're stuck with black."

Pam was sharing her coffee with Roger. "I love this place. For sure, we'll have to come back here. The drive isn't that long, we can have a sleepover and be back the next day."

"I like that idea," said Roger.

John Sr. had everyone's attention by telling stories of his working days, about the guy who he was training and kept complaining about not paying his bills and then one day called and said he wasn't coming back to work. His uncle paid his bills, so he had no reason to work. John Sr. went right into another story, and soon they were laughing so hard they were holding their sides.

The trumpet sounded notifying the patrons intermission was over, and they headed back to their seats. Doc marched out for the second half of the show. He stepped on the podium with his black sequined outfit. Noah whispered to Paula, "I'll let you know what restaurant in the morning." He smiled at her and kissed her cheek then got comfortable in his seat.

While they played the introduction, the Boys Choir walked in behind the orchestra and filled the risers.

Jake's phone vibrated in his pocket. He took it out and noticed the call was from Barry Ward. He hated to miss the call but didn't want to seem rude. He decided to give his attention to Barry. Luckily, he had an aisle seat. Once in the foyer, he called Barry back.

"Barry, you called."

"I was about to leave a message. Things don't look good here."

"What's happening?"

"I think I need you to come out to San Francisco and help me and my mom."

The request Jake dreaded finally was asked. "Fill me in on what's going on."

Barry told him everything that was happening with his dad, how his mom was taking it, and how he was struggling with everything that was happening. There were times in the conversation Barry was angry. When he talked about his mom, he tried not to cry.

Jake had to go even though there was a conflict of interest. Jake told Barry he would support him, and now when that opportunity came, he needed to follow through.

"Right now I'm in Minneapolis. I'll try to fly out in the morning. I'll keep you posted."

"Thanks, boss, I mean, Jake." Barry disconnected.

Jake wasn't a drinking man but decided that a drink was exactly what he needed, but instead of giving in to the urge, he went back into the hall and sat down. Peggy took his hand, sensing he was upset. He squeezed her hand tight and kissed it. *Should Peggy go with me, or should I do this alone?* He would talk to John and his parents first.

The music was mesmerizing, the choir was excellent, and Doc was in true form. But Jake was in San Francisco trying to help his employee get through a difficult situation, a situation that could, that should, only go one way. Sam and his mother would be locked up. How could he possibly convince Barry that the evidence against his dad was all true? How could he console Barry's mother if that's what Barry wanted? He wished this whole thing was over.

He looked at the Masons so happy to be reunited, but what Jake thought would be the end of their suffering took up residence in another innocent human being, in a kid who was defenseless against his dad's crimes.

People stood, and Peggy pulled him up. He clapped with everyone else, but his mind went into overdrive thinking of all he needed to do: get plane tickets, a hotel. He only had one change of clothes and hoped that would be enough. He started to walk into the aisle, and Peggy pulled him back. Doc ran out on stage, and the orchestra played one more song.

Disappointed he couldn't leave to start planning, he reluctantly sat back down. The encore song took forever to end, and when the song did end, he was still planning in his head and didn't hear the clapping. He just assumed Doc would be playing all night long, and then Peggy whispered in his ear, "We can go now."

All of a sudden, he was jolted back to reality. The house lights seemed overly bright. He took Peggy's hand and weaved in and out of the people trying to get to the ramp.

"We have to wait for the Masons before we can get in the car." Peggy pulled him aside, away from the path of the crowd. "Tell me who called."

Jake explained the phone call from Barry, asked her if she would go with him, and before she had a chance to answer, John waved them over so they could walk to the car together. "I'll tell the Masons once we are in the car."

But John didn't lead them to the car, they went outside on the plaza. "We decided to go to Brits Pub for a drink," said Michelle.

"I would rather go to your house . . . I got a phone call from Barry, one of my employees."

"Is he Sam's son?" asked John Sr.

"Yes. He wants me to come to San Francisco. Barry is trying to hold everything together, consoling his mother, wanting his dad to get a lawyer. While I was talking to him, he was angry one minute, crying the next. If for no other reason I should go and help him through this"—he looked at his wife—"Peg, I hope you come with me."

"When do you want to leave?"

"The sooner, the better," said Jake.

"You'll need transportation to the house to pack and head to the airport." John Sr. got out his cell phone and called a taxi and talked as if he were the one needing the service. "I need a ride." He gave his address. "You need to wait until I pack because then I'll need a ride to the airport. Right now, pick me up at the corner of the Nicollet Mall and Eleventh. My wife and I will be on the curb." He disconnected. "Okay, if you need anything at all, call us."

"What do we tell everyone? That we decided to have another vacation?"

"You're sick and Peggy wanted to take you home to tuck you in," said John.

They laughed and broke some of the tension. "That will work." Jake took Peggy's hand. "But it won't explain why we're not at breakfast the next day."

"We'll think of something," said John.

"Tell one of the guys they have to drive the van back home and return it to the rental place. The paperwork is in the glove compartment."

A minute later, the taxi pulled up, and the driver helped them in the back seat.

"Those young kids are amazing," said Michelle.

"I'm lucky to have them both as my friends." John no longer referred to them as contacts. They'd gone above and beyond what anyone would consider just a contact. They'd helped find his parents, and now they were considered true friends.

They continued across the street and were able to detain Brad and Joyce before they entered the restaurant. John explained what had happened.

Joyce took out her phone and texted Peggy. *If you need Brad and me, let us know. Be careful.*

Within a minute, Peggy texted her back. *We'll keep you posted. Thanks!*

When John made his announcement about Jake and Peggy leaving, he forgot to say Jake was sick and said they were traveling instead. Immediately realizing his mistake, he stuttered to get the words out.

"In other words, they won't be with us this evening," said Michelle. She assumed everyone knew Barry from the Justice Café. "They went to help Barry with his family's situation in San Francisco, and that's the only information I know."

John felt relieved but knew he had to text Jake to tell him what everyone was told. He excused himself and went to the restroom. Jake texted back right away. *Not a problem, John.*

Relieved the situation went better than he led himself to believe, he returned to the table, and the rest of the night proved to be very enjoyable.

CHAPTER TWENTY

Peggy thought of her family and friends back home while they took a nonstop flight to San Francisco. She'd enjoyed the concert and was looking forward to the celebration afterward at the restaurant. Although she loved the barbeque sandwiches in Boone, she was looking forward to a nice steak, even though they were only going to Brit's Pub for a drink after the concert, she was hungry. Instead, she and Jake ate a hamburger at the Minneapolis airport while waiting to board the plane. Jake promised he would make it up to her.

Once they landed and got their rental, they headed straight to Barry's house. It was early in the morning, but Barry was waiting for them.

"Come in," he said as he opened the door. "I'm so glad you could come." Barry had tears in his eyes and was about to have another crying jag. *Don't cry.* He silently told himself. He just wanted to get through this, go back to Boone, Iowa, where it was quiet and beautiful and people actually cared for one another.

Growing up in San Francisco, he never had a community experience. The city was too big, too demanding, too overcrowded. His dad was always working, and when he was home, he had better things to do than to play with his only son. He knew his mom was ignored as much as he was, and now when his dad needed help, all she could do was cry.

One night they talked. His mom was angry and said some terrible things about his dad, and when she tried to apologize, Barry quietly told her those terrible things she said were all true. She didn't have the kind of friends she could confide in about her husband's imprisonment, and she didn't want to discuss it with anyone. Why would she want to tell people her husband was in jail when she didn't even know if he was guilty or not. She suspected he was guilty, and that's why all the tears. She couldn't imagine her life with people knowing she married a loser cop who broke the law and kidnapped people.

Maybe, she thought, Barry would take her back to that nice town he lived in and she could start over—*they* could start over. Being with her son is what she needed right now. She wasn't sure about the people who were coming to help, but if Barry said they were nice people, then she had to believe him.

"Mom, this is Jake and Peggy. This is my mom Marie."

Jake shook her hand. Peggy gave her a hug. "Let's sit down, and we can talk." Peggy looked at her watch. It was four o'clock. "Or Jake and I can go to the hotel, and we can talk later this morning if that works better."

"No," said Marie. "I want to do this now. Thanks so much for coming."

They sat at the kitchen table. Peggy saw the coffee pot on the counter, and instead of sitting, she walked over, opened cupboards, and found what she needed to make coffee. No one said anything, they just watched, and when she set four coffee cups on the table and sat down, Barry filled them in on the details.

"The lawyer is making some progress. Dad is listening to what he has to say, and they've gotten through a few sessions without Dad losing his temper. I talked with Coyle yesterday, and he thinks Dad is guilty."

"I think he is too," said Marie. "I've had time to think of things he's said and done or said he was doing, and I think it pertains to the case."

"Why don't you and Peggy get your coffee and go in the other room and she'll write down everything you remember?" Jake decided to pour the coffee while Peggy got out her notebook and her new recording device.

Once they were settled in the living room, Marie told Peggy everything she remembered.

"I wished I could remember in the order that it happened."

"Just do the best you can, and we'll try and put it in order once it's all down."

Marie liked Peggy. She was so kind, so soft-spoken. Barry had nothing but good things to say about his employers, but then he always was a positive kid while growing up in a dysfunctional home.

"When we got married, we loved each other so much. He was going to the academy and studied all the time. Being a policeman was his passion since grade school. He'd decided that when they had career day, and the local police department sent over an officer to talk about his profession. Sam vowed to be the best cop there was. He loved the dark blue uniform with the buttons and the badge."

Peggy listened, even though it had nothing to do with the current events that were taking place. Marie lit up as she talked about her husband in their earlier years, unlike the exhausted look she had when they arrived.

"I'm getting off track." She clutched her hands together and tightened her spine. The light was gone from her eyes. "Sam paid some attention to his son after he was born but mostly from a distance. I didn't know if he was just afraid of babies or he really didn't want children. It was a topic we'd never discussed.

"Five years passed, and he still didn't want to hold him or play with him. I found out Sam was having an affair. I confronted him on it, and he said it was over. I believed him, mostly because I didn't want our son to grow up without a father. I realized now I should've left with Barry and never looked back."

"Did he *ever* show interest in Barry?" asked Peggy. Barry is a great employee, always positive. He had a reputation for changing the mood of anyone who came into the café, who was down, or depressed, or just plain out of sorts. The patrons would actually look for Barry so they could talk to him. If it wasn't his shift, they would be disappointed and ask for his schedule. Peggy assumed he came from a happy home. This new information was disturbing, but Barry overcame the dysfunction.

"No, he didn't. I apologized to Barry, but one day he said to me that he didn't care, he enjoyed our time together, and he didn't need a dad. His grandmother was the same way, didn't want to be bothered with him. My folks more than made up for the lack of attention. They loved Barry so much, and it was hard for me to think his own dad didn't love him."

"That is so sad." Peggy touched her hand. "Let's start with the things you thought were odd or different from the norm."

"Several years ago, I looked through his mail because he wasn't home much, said he had a case at work that required him to work 24/7. There were a few hotel charges. When I asked him, he said the department would reimburse him. It was a stake out that he was required to go on. Being naïve, I believed him.

"Then he bought a new cell phone with unlimited texts. I asked if we could get on a family plan and I could get a new phone. He told me it was the departments. When he was sleeping one night, I looked at his phone. I wasn't trying to be nosy, I just had never seen a phone like that before, except people at work have them, and I just wanted to check it out.

"I turned it on, and before I swiped the bar, there was texts from someone named Abby. I swiped the bar and opened the message icon. I knew how to do this because my friend at work gave me a tutorial one day. It wasn't just one message, it was a lot of messages.

"This is Abby, remember me? Why aren't you here tonight? It's my day off tomorrow, I thought we could go on a picnic. You said you liked the outdoors. That was only a few of them. She mentioned the café where she worked because he was supposed to meet her there. I went to the café and looked for her. I wanted to see what she looked like." Marie sipped her coffee. "She was young, looked about Barry's age, in good shape, dark short hair—just the opposite of me."

Peggy noticed that Marie too was in good shape, thin, perhaps too thin. Her dark brown hair was longer, styled around her face. "Did you talk to her?"

"I ordered coffee from her. She was pleasant and kind when I didn't know what to order. She kept looking at her watch though."

"Did Sam come in while you were there?"

"Yes, but he didn't notice me sitting by the window. He went right up to the counter, Abby got her backpack and left with him. That broke my heart, but I never did anything about it. The next day he said something about his mother needing help at the storage place. That night before he left for work, I overheard him talking to his mother. He told her, when the drugs came in, to put them in storage garage 3. He would be there later. Again, I never did anything."

Marie went on to tell Peggy more incidents when she'd overheard Sam talking to his mother. Peggy wrote down what she thought was important since the recorder was recording the whole conversation.

Peggy asked more questions. "Has Dennis Coyle talked to you? Or the police?"

"No, but Coyle's talked to Barry. I haven't told Barry any of this. He hasn't talked to the police. They haven't been around to ask questions. I'm assuming, like Sam, they believe he's innocent and above reproach because he's an officer."

"Would you be willing to tell the police what you told me?"

She twisted her hands together, then fumbled for her cup, took a sip and made a face from the bitter taste of the cold coffee. "If you went with me, I would."

"Have you slept at all in the past eight hours?" Peggy noticed the darkness of the night was transitioning into day.

"Not really, but I'd like to go to the station now, or I'll never do it."

In the kitchen . . . "If my dad and grandmother were found guilty, and I go back to the café, Mom will be here all alone. I think they will be found guilty, especially now if Mom has information that adds to their guilt." He looked down at his cup, then looked at Jake. "I will give my notice now so I can stay with Mom. She needs me."

Jake didn't speak for several seconds. "I understand, Barry, but would you consider coming back to the café and bringing your mother with you? Do you think she'd like a small peaceful town to live in? I need someone to help Adeline, get to know the ropes, and give her a day off once in a while." Jake held up his hand. "Before you say no, talk it over with her first."

"I can't do that. You've already done so much for me." Barry was contemplating the offer. *Mom was born and raised in a small town and didn't like the move to San Francisco. I don't know if she'd want to move or not.* "I'll ask her. Wait! Does Adeline know about this? She seems to enjoy bossing us around." Jake laughed. "She really doesn't boss us around. Mom just might like working with Adeline. She's been burned out lately at her own job, and her coworkers are keeping their distance." Barry was about to go talk to his mother when Peggy and Marie came into the kitchen. "Sit down, Mom."

"Peggy and I are headed to the police station. I'm ready to tell the police what I know."

"You'll want to hear this first," said Barry.

Marie sat. Peggy stood behind Jake and rested her hands on his shoulders.

"Jake, well . . . wants . . ."

"What I asked earlier," said Jake, "was, if you'd want to come back to Boone, Iowa, with Barry. You can work with Adeline Cole. She's the boss when Peggy and I are traveling and even when we're there. She's busy all the time. You would learn what she does and give her a break a couple of days a week. If you need to work more days, we can fit you into the barista rotation."

Marie thought she had her emotions in check, but this brought tears to her eyes. To get out of San Francisco would be a dream she never thought would happen with her husband on the force, and she always wondered if she did move, would she find a job. Now she had a chance to do both, move *and* work without the stress of finding a place and looking for a job.

"I'll go, yes, I'll go to Boone with Barry."

"Mom!" Barry went over and hugged her. "That's wonderful."

"Right now, Peggy and I are heading to the station. When I get back, I'll start packing."

"We'll have to wait for the trial, and Dad's lawyer might need us," said Barry.

"If you want to stay, I'll stay with you, but I'm ready to leave this all behind."

"The police might want you to stay too," said Jake.

Marie looked at Jake. "I'll still pack." She got up from her chair. "The sooner we go to the police station, the sooner we find out what we need to do."

The only talking on the way to the station was Barry giving Jake directions. Marie was thinking about moving to a small town with her son, and the more she thought about it, the more she liked the idea. She hoped the authorities didn't want her to stick around for more questioning because she wanted to leave as soon as possible. She no longer wanted to be there for her husband when he went to trial, and she didn't give a damn about her mother-in-law.

Let them both rot in jail. If she weren't there for Sam, he would accuse her of being selfish, and this time she didn't care. He would also find a way of blaming her for his own actions.

Well, if she weren't here to listen to him, he could blame her all he wanted, it would fall on deaf ears, and who would believe he was innocent if he told everyone it was his wife's fault for him kidnapping two people? She hoped he got laughed at. She was done, ready to move on.

After she was settled in her son's home, she would file for divorce. Not that she ever wanted to marry again, she just wanted to be done with him. He would tell her she couldn't get anyone else because she was so unattractive, but right this minute, she didn't believe anything he had said.

She was five-seven, had shoulder-length brown hair that she sometimes kept tied back. She knew she was too thin, but that would change. She'd had compliments over the years that confirmed she was not unattractive. She sat up straighter in her seat and smiled. *Yes, today is the start of a new life. Just me and Barry.*

ꕥ

"Hello, Mrs. Ward."

"Hi." She couldn't remember his name.

"What can I do for you today? That's too bad about Sam. He'll get off, they'll see he's innocent once they find the evidence points to someone else, and how devastating for your mother-in-law." He looked at Barry. "Stay strong, Barry. Your dad and grandma will get off, and you can get back to your life."

Yeah, my life without him will finally make it normal.

He looked back at Marie. "What can I do for you?"

"I want to give the police some facts that I've been thinking about, and I think it will help the case."

"Wonderful! Sam needs your help, seems he's upset no one is coming forward to help him out and—"

"Hey, the lady wants to give her statement," said Jake. "Can she do it now?"

"Oh sorry. I am so caught up in the fact that she's here trying to help her husband."

"Like I said, call someone, and get the interview started."

"You Sam's lawyer?" He frowned at Jake but picked up the phone and made the call. "They'll be here in a couple of minutes. Like I said—"

"We'll be sitting over here," said Jake and didn't bother answering if he was a lawyer.

Well, who does he think he is? I'm the police, and I didn't hear any respect in his voice. Who cares? Sam will be back on the force soon, I'll be off desk duty, and life will be good.

Twenty minutes later, Marie and Peggy were escorted back to an interview room. The desk clerk had called Officer Fraley back and told him Marie Ward was here to give her side of the story, which will help Sam immensely prove his innocence.

"Would you like a glass of water?"

"No, thank you," they both responded.

Marie said, "I wrote everything down that I remembered." *Well, Peggy had written it down.* "Do you want me to read it, or do you want to read it for yourself?"

"I'll read it." He was glad she'd written it down, so he didn't have to take notes. As he read, he realized she was not helping her husband but had facts that would hurt him. "Are you sure these are accurate?"

"Yes, and in case you don't forward these on to the person in charge of the case, a copy is being sent right now to the commissioner."

He had every intention to take her notes. Actually, his plan was to throw them out back in the garbage once she left, but he couldn't do that now.

She took the notes back. "Now I'll read it out loud so you have it on tape. You do have your recorder turned on, don't you?"

Yes, he did have the recorder going but wanted to turn it off but didn't dare make a move to do it. "Yes, it's on."

She read every word out loud and only added to it when she felt clarification was needed. "Now if you claim that the recorder doesn't work, I've been taping our conversation."

"Why would you think you'd have to send everything to the commissioner?" He was curious.

"Because there are more people on this force who can't be trusted, and besides being married to a liar, I don't trust anyone any more. And I'd like to know if I have to stay in town. I have a trip that I really need to take before the trial."

"I'll get clearance for you. Wait here a minute." He was going to send in another officer while she waited. His partner was good at threatening people, and she'd start wavering her story, becoming unsure of the facts, which he planned to get on tape. "It won't take long."

"No, I won't wait here. I'll wait in the waiting room with my friends." She was surprised at her self-confidence. She stood, took her notes, and she and Peggy left the small conference room.

Damn! Sam's cooked for sure.

CHAPTER TWENTY-ONE

Marie Ward was given permission to leave the area but was told she'd have to come back if needed for the trial. The officer was certain the commissioner would call her back to testify. He himself was going to turn in his resignation in the morning because he was certain the trial would bring about a thorough investigation of the department. He did not want to humiliate his own family.

"You can go. You don't have to stay in the area. I'm assuming you'll be spending a few days at your parents, then come back for the trial."

That's probably what Sam told them whenever she couldn't stand it anymore and needed a safe haven to run to. But it really wasn't that peaceful at her parents. They criticized her for leaving her husband if only for the weekend. When she talked about divorcing him, her father would say she should be honored to be married to a policeman and he wouldn't tolerate her divorcing him. Her father was a police officer himself, and he was never home, but her mother was very patient with him. Marie didn't find out until last month from her mother that it was not an honor to be married to a man of the law, but it was as if she were a single parent, a widow, because he was never home, and she was always afraid he might get killed and then he would never come home, and most of all, it was lonely, especially in the evenings.

"Yes, I'm heading to San Diego to visit my parents," she lied.

He had the address of her parents and was also good friends with her father. He would ask him if his daughter talked about the case and if her facts were the same as her statement. Yes, he was feeling better, but he would still resign in the morning.

ജ്ഞ

Dennis Coyle, Sam's lawyer, was waiting for Sam to be brought to the visitor's room. He knew Sam was guilty, but so far, he never admitted his guilt. He changed the facts every time they consulted with each other.

The door opened, and Sam was escorted in. He sat heavily in his chair. "I heard my wife went to her parents' house, but she'll be back for the trial."

That's not what Barry Ward told him. Apparently, someone from the department relayed to Sam that his wife was at the station and what she'd told Fraley. It seemed the whole force was in on this one case.

"Marie *will* be here for the trial," said Sam, trying to convince himself, "and she'll change her story to the truth, that I had nothing to do with this whole mess."

"She wanted me to tell you that she didn't go to her parents' house and she would not be returning for the trial. The only way she would come back is if the commissioner himself called her back to testify."

"What? She's my wife. Doesn't she know she is required to stick by her husband, especially in times of trouble? And my son, he'll be there. Who cares about Marie? Barry will be there. He came all the way from the Midwest to be with me." He sat back smug in his chair. "My son will be there."

"Apparently, the mental abuse you dished out to both of them has finally taken its toll. I hear Marie doesn't want anything to do with you." Sam was about to speak. "Wait, I'm not finished yet. Barry left as well. He said he had to get back to work." Sam tried talking again, but Coyle wouldn't let him. "Not only are they jumping a sinking ship, but so am I. You'll have to find another lawyer."

"You can't do that. I need a lawyer, and you know the case."

"And that is the very reason I have a right to not take your case. Reason number one, and I only have one reason, is that since I started representing you, you have never told the truth."

"Now you're leaving too."

"Yes. The only person you have in the world is your mother, and she's just as guilty as you are. I hope you both rot in jail." *Not very professional, Coyle, but I need to get out of this place and never look at Sam Ward again!*

Sam sat alone in the visitor's room. He thought of Abby. She would support him. She'll come to the trial, he thought. He went back to his cell and requested to make a phone call. Abby's phone was disconnected, and there was no forwarding number. He tried her parents' house, which was also disconnected. He hung up the phone and stared into space. His life was flashing before him. He dialed Coyle's number and left a voice mail. "I'm ready to tell the truth. Please come back and see me."

Coyle was riding the elevator to his office when he listened to the message. He didn't want to delete it, but he certainly was not going back to the prison to listen to Sam, not even one more time, not even if he told the truth. He shook his head to clear it and left the elevator.

ꕥ

Barry kept looking at his mother in the plane seat next to him, each time believing more that she really was coming home with him. In his mind, he worked out a payment plan to repay Jake and Peggy for the plane tickets but had the feeling they wouldn't take the money. He'd just have to think of a more creative way to pay them back. But for now, he was so happy to have his mother with him.

Barry had heard Jake had found his own mother and brought her back to Boone. Now he was doing the same. He couldn't remember if he cleaned his apartment before he left or if it was in its usual state of disarray. Probably messy, he concluded. Nothing changes, he thought. He was a messy kid, and his habits were hard to break, but he didn't think his mom would care what the place looked like.

Marie would be in a small town, and he hoped she would love working at the café as much as he did. He already knew without a doubt she would love Adeline and Arnie. She was used to office jobs where she sat all day. She probably would like moving around more. When he was living at home, she would complain she was so stiff from sitting in a chair all day. Well, maybe she'll come to love her new job.

ഗ്ദ

Knowing his wife loved working at the café, he wasn't sure how she was feeling about a total stranger hired to help her out. She claimed she didn't need help, and yet most days she came home exhausted. Arnie tried his hand in the kitchen to help out, but mostly, he picked up food because Adeline was too tired to cook.

He was holding her as they lay in bed, resting before they started their day. "What do you think of a stranger taking over your job?"

She snuggled her back closer to him. "To tell you the truth, I was a little upset about it, but now I can't wait. If she can fill in a few days a week, then those days I can spend more time with you, and we can have a few decent meals together."

"What, you don't like the Big Macs I bring home?"

"The first night, it was good. The seventh night, not so much." She laughed.

Arnie kissed the top of her head. "I'm glad you're okay with it. I sure miss you in the evenings. Sleeping in the chair next to me does not count as being present." He kissed her again. "When is she starting?"

"Next Monday. Jake thought she'd need time to settle in."

"You'll probably need to train every day so she doesn't forget what to do. Knowing you, you've already written up your job duties and ten different things to do if anything happens." He laughed.

"Peggy encouraged me to write job descriptions for everyone. She's always writing notes about something."

"That she is." He kissed the top of her head again. "I think we should take today to stay in bed and make up for lost time."

Adeline laughed. She turned in his arms and kissed him on the lips. "I think you're right. I'll even bring you breakfast, and we can eat in bed like the olden days."

"There's nothing I would like better." He kissed her.

CHAPTER
TWENTY-TWO

A lawyer was appointed to Sam Ward, and when Sam was questioned, he did tell the truth—the truth as he saw it. His mother bought the drugs, sold the drugs, and ordered the Masons to be kidnapped. He was just an innocent bystander. When asked why he didn't arrest her, he said he was trying to convince her to turn herself in or just stop altogether. His new lawyer read the case and didn't believe a thing Ward said. He was used to clients lying to him, but he'd never heard such a denial of wrongdoing as he listened to Ward.

His mother had yet to get a lawyer. He'd heard she was telling everyone that it was her son's fault that she was in jail because he told her that she could buy and sell drugs as long as it was in certain ounces and never asked for too much money for the product being sold. As far as kidnapping, she'd never heard of the Masons, even though they lived across the street from her.

They'll both stew in jail for a long time, thought the lawyer.

ജ്ഞ

"I hope the trial doesn't drag out forever," said Joyce. She put a pair of jeans in her suitcase.

"If Pearl would've only said she was guilty, this trip wouldn't be necessary," said Brad. "Or if we had left town so we didn't get the summons that would've been better."

"Let's think of it as vacation."

"We've been traveling a lot, and none of the trips I'd consider a vacation. Promise me we'll go somewhere where there are no criminals, no wrongdoing, or for that matter, no people around—just you and me."

Joyce sat on the bed. "I know just the place, and we can go there when the trial is over—Zephyr Cove. Sure the Masons were held there, but did you notice the water, the peacefulness? And there will be no lookout cars."

Brad sat next to her and took her hand. "That's a great idea. It *was* peaceful. We'd never have to leave the cabin." He walked over to the dresser and pulled out a pair of shorts. "I have no idea what the temperature is there, but I'm going to be ready."

"Too bad, Jake and Peggy flew home already, they could join us."

"Oh, you mean I have to be alone with you? What a horror!"

Joyce laughed. "Too bad for you, pal."

He went over and pulled her to her feet and kissed her. "Keep that in mind of what we will be doing."

"I can't wait. Makes the trial seem like a piece of cake."

"I wish."

ஐஐ

There was a lot of evidence presented to prove Pearl Ward was guilty of buying and selling drugs, running the storage business with intent to store drugs and money. She'd even paid for a hotel room with her credit card for one of the drug runners who was now in jail. The police had a lead he was at the hotel, and when they found him, he'd had several bags of cocaine sitting on his bed. Of course, he claimed they weren't his and he didn't know where they came from. But once in jail, he admitted they were his, how the operation worked, and what Pearl's role was in the operation.

Pearl denied ever knowing him, complained he stole her credit card. This was day four of the trial, and Brad or Joyce hadn't been called to the stand. They were looking forward to their time alone after the trial, if only the trial would end. The judge adjourned for the day at four. He said they would reconvene in the morning at ten. Both being morning people, Brad and Joyce struggled to fill the time. They had an early breakfast at the hotel, swam for an hour, then went back to their room to shower and relax before the trial.

Brad's phone rang before he stepped into the shower. "Hello?"

"You'll be testifying this afternoon, but I would get there at ten, just in case you're called earlier. Joyce will have to testify also this afternoon."

"Once we testify, can we go home?"

"It depends on what happens. I'll keep you posted."

"Thanks."

Joyce was in the doorway. "Our turn today?"

"Yes, not until this afternoon, but we have to be there at ten."

Joyce looked at her watch. They had two more hours. "I'll get my notes and go through them again. I'll run across the street and get two strong cups of coffee and wait for you there."

Brad was already in the shower. "Make that double strong, if there is such a thing."

He let the hot water pelt down on his tired body. He was stiff from sitting all day. He stretched his neck and shoulders, did two careful squats. When he felt the stiffness leave his body, he took the soap and finished his shower. He opened the door, and steam clouded the mirror. He took the towel and wiped himself down.

He had a feeling that something was wrong but put it out of his mind. *The thought of testifying is making me nervous,* he thought. His clothes were on the bed. The door was ajar. He quickly dressed and went into the hall. No one was there.

Joyce! He took his card key off the dresser and ran down the hall to the stairs. He jaywalked across the highway to Starbucks. She was sitting at a table with her two coffees, texting on her phone. She looked up when she saw him walking toward her.

"Brad, what's the matter?"

He sat across from her. "I had a funny feeling something had happened to you. I wanted to make sure you were okay."

"I'm all right."

"I'm glad you are okay." He tried to calm his nerves. He didn't want Joyce to know he thought she was kidnapped or any of the other things going through his mind. That would add more stress to the day. "I just thought you were coming back to the hotel."

"You must not have heard me say I would wait here for you."

"No, I didn't." He leaned over and kissed her. "So glad you are all right."

She had her notes on the table. "I took your notes too. I also had a funny feeling that someone would come into the hotel room while you were showering but just shook it off, knowing I started to get paranoid ever since we landed. We might as well stay here and go through them. We've got plenty of time." She handed him his coffee and his notes.

Brad didn't want to tell her the door was ajar when he got out of the shower, but he felt she needed to know. "The door was opened a little in our room, which made me run over here to see if you were still here. I don't know if anyone else was in our room or not."

"Well, more than ever, we need to go over our notes and make sure we don't forget anything," said Joyce.

They spent the next hour going over what they had written right after the poisoning incident had happened. Now they had to make sure Pearl's lawyer didn't intimidate them to make the facts unclear and for the judge to throw out their testimony.

When they got back to their room, their clothes were all over the floor. Joyce had had it. She was more than upset, she was furious. "I'm not calling security. I'm sure that's what Sam's cop buddies want us to do. They'll make it look like we staged the break-in, and the attorney demeans our testimony. Without the attempted murder charge, Pearl gets a few years, and she's out doing the same thing."

"I agree," said Brad while he picked up his own clothes and threw them back in his suitcase. "We're lucky we had our notes with us. Who knows what they would've done with them?"

ꕥ

Sergeant Jacobson was waiting for the call from hotel security about the room being ransacked. He would ask them a lot of questions, make them go to the station where someone else would question them, and they wouldn't get to the trial on time. It was thirty minutes before the trial started and wondered if the witnesses went back to their room or just went to the trial. He needed to quickly think of what else he needed to do to scare them away or make it look like they're just paranoid about everything and the woman really didn't get poisoned. Who cares if the doctor could confirm she was poisoned? He couldn't confirm that Pearl did it.

Since they weren't calling the police or hotel security, he'd think of something else. He knew they'd gotten a blue Prius from the rental car place. He made a call and told his friend to be on the lookout for the car and make sure they never made it to the courthouse. Once that was confirmed, he sat back in his chair and put his feet on his desk. A smile came slowly to his gruff face. *Done,* he thought. *We'll be back in business soon, and now we'll know what not to do to get caught again.*

He thought of his next vacation to Hawaii. His wife and kids loved it there, and he liked it too. Paying in cash for their vacations was a lot better than always being in debt. *Yes, the good life.*

Jacobson quickly put his feet on the floor and stood up when he heard a knock at the door. The door opened, and Lieutenant Cooper walked in, "You're under arrest for aiding and abetting a drug operation and for grand larceny." The way his office was arranged, there was no way he could get by the lieutenant and run like hell. Then the lieutenant immediately read Jacobson the Miranda rights.

ꕥ

The blue Prius was spotted at the hotel parking lot. It was now ten minutes until the trial, and the car had not moved. The hit man didn't know Joyce and Brad decided to walk to the court house to walk off the stress of the break-in. So he sat and watched until eleven. He called Jacobson, but he didn't answer. He called someone who was at the trial and asked if they were there. They were. *Damn!* Jacobson would make him pay for this. He decided to head to his apartment, pack a few things, and leave town.

ꕥ

"How do you know she was poisoned?"

"I didn't know for sure, but I suspected."

"You didn't have any evidence, but you brought her to the hospital?"

Brad gave the defense attorney a look of disgust. "If you didn't have proof your mother had a broken arm and yet she couldn't move her arm and had pain, you would let her just suffer and not think to bring her to the hospital?"

"Your Honor, I'm supposed to ask the questions."

"Then don't ask stupid ones."

His face turned beet red, and he sat down. "No more questions."

The prosecutor stood and came face to face with Brad. "Tell us what happened."

Brad was glad he'd made notes and had read through them several times. He mentioned briefly their first visit to Pearl's house and then recounted the details of their second visit.

The defense attorney objected twice but was sustained.

The doctor who treated Joyce at the hospital was called next. "What kind of poisoning did you find?"

"Rat poisoning."

"No further questions."

The defense attorney was on his feet. As he walked to the witness, he asked, "Is there proof that Pearl Ward was the one that administered it?"

"You're certainly 'stuck on stupid.' You've already been warned, and if I hear one more stupid question, we adjourn for the day."

Furious, he rephrased the question. "Could it have been an accident that Joyce Armstrong ingested the poison accidentally?"

"Yes, I suppose it's possible if she decided to try it first to make sure it would work on the rats." There was laughter from the audience.

"Adjourned until tomorrow."

"Wait, Your Honor, wait . . ."

Pearl was taken away, and Joyce and Brad were the last ones to leave the courtroom. Brad spoke after twenty minutes of silence. "Let's get out of here."

They walked back to the hotel. "Do you have the car keys? I need to get the Garmin to program a restaurant that has good steak. Instead of drinking, I thought to calm my nerves with food," said Joyce.

They were standing by the front of the hotel, looking out at their rental. A woman sped into the parking lot and aimed for the empty space next to the Prius, and when she hit the back bumper, the Prius exploded into flames. Brad held Joyce against him. The heat from the bomb scorched their faces. The bell hop was thrown against the limo parked in the carport.

"Now I am calling the police. No, I'm calling an ambulance, and then I'm going to call the judge if I can get through to him. I don't want to take a chance on getting one of Sam's friends out here. Although I'm sure someone has already called the police."

Brad and Joyce went over to the bellhop and helped him sit up against the same limo that he was thrown against seconds earlier. His crooked name badge read Carlos.

"Carlos, where does it hurt?"

He pointed to his chest and his ears.

Joyce took his hand. "The ambulance should be here any minute," and she hoped it were true. Seconds later she heard the siren and hoped it *was* the ambulance and not the police.

Brad walked over to them. "The ambulance is pulling into the parking lot." He walked over and waved the driver over to where Carlos and Joyce were.

Joyce held his hand until he was on the stretcher and in the ambulance, and then waited until the ambulance pulled out onto to the street. She was oblivious to the people standing around until now when she turned around to go into the hotel. People asked her questions and she stated firmly she didn't know.

Brad pulled her aside and guided her to the pool area and was grateful no one was swimming or lounging in the chairs.

Brad made many phone calls until he was able to talk to the judge's secretary. As soon as she heard about the bombing, she connected to the judge.

"Yes, go home," the judge said after hearing Brad's story. "Be safe." There were seconds of silence. "Did you change rooms?"

"No, we still have the same room."

"I'll declare it a crime scene and get people over there to try and lift prints. You have my permission to go home, and since my secretary is so efficient, she's already typing the release." He disconnected.

Brad took Joyce's hand. They stopped at the front desk and called a cab, then went to their room. The contents of their suitcases were again strewn all over the floor. Brad asked the maid down the hall for a couple of garbage bags and helped Joyce throw all their belongings into the two bags. They left the suitcases in case there were prints. Joyce looked in the messenger bag she had with her at the courthouse to make sure their notes were still in there. A paranoid move, she thought, but with good reason.

CHAPTER TWENTY-THREE

The trial was delayed the next morning as the judge waited for the prints that were taken in the hotel room to come back. It was one o'clock, and he decided to reconvene anyway. He called both attorneys into his chambers and presented the evidence.

"Pearl wants to testify. She wants to clear her name from being associated with any wrongdoing."

Still on the stupid path, thought the judge.

Bring her up front and I'll tongue-tie her into a confession, thought the prosecutor.

Back in the courtroom, Pearl was called to the stand. Pearl confessed to the jury that she was told by her son the drug laws and all her purchases and sales did not go over that amount, so she was not at all guilty. She was abiding by the law.

It was the prosecutors turn to ask questions, but first, he faced the jury and made a statement. "Pearl talks about her son telling her the drug laws, when in 1988, she attended the antidrug 'Just Say No' to drugs at the First Interstate building in Downtown Los Angeles."

Pearl could feel the sweat running down her back.

He faced Pearl. "There were several classrooms set up, and you attended some of the sessions." He paused. "Would you like to tell us what you learned that day?"

"I don't remember. It was a long time ago."

"Let me refresh your memory. Attendees were being told how wrong drugs were. Any amount is too much. You claim your son told you a certain amount is okay when you know elementary children—schoolchildren, period—shouldn't have any amount in their systems."

"We didn't sell it to children, we sold it to adults."

"Didn't that session in '88 make an impression on you? And when your grandson was born not too long afterward, you sat down with your son and daughter-in-law and told them again about drugs in school."

"I didn't tell them that."

"And yet you listened to your son years afterward that some drugs are okay."

"I just did what I was told."

"Against your better judgment? You forgot those helpless children, thinking those drugs you were dealing would not reach young children, when you knew there was a good chance they would."

"I told you already. I did what I was told. I needed the money. I wanted a better life."

"So much so you wanted to get rid of the witnesses."

"Objection, Your Honor!"

"Go ahead with your question."

"I don't know anything about the Masons. I never met them."

"I never mentioned their name, but apparently, you knew who I was talking about." He let that sink in, and before she could debate the issue, he continued. "But you have met them. They were your neighbors. The statements I got from your other neighbors was that you knew everyone and you knew everyone's business. You could be seen perching in your upstairs window on any given day watching the neighborhood."

"I didn't see anything. I didn't see the van pick them up and take them away. I can honestly say I never saw them again."

"What kind of van was it?"

"It was one of our work . . . I don't know, I didn't see it."

"But you said you did see it."

"Leave me alone. I didn't do anything wrong. I did what I was told. I bought the drugs, I sold the drugs. Policemen, and not just my son, told me what to do and how to do it. They took the Masons."

"You're not only guilty of buying and selling drugs, trying to commit murder by poisoning, but now you've become an accessory to kidnapping."

"I have not!" she screamed. "You can't prove I tried to poison anyone. They asked for it. . . I mean, they wanted the tea. I have no idea how the poison got into their cups." She was ranting about several other things as well.

The judge pounded the gavel, but Pearl could not hear it. She was escorted out and brought back to her cell.

"We'll reconvene at ten o'clock in the morning. I want closing statements. No more witnesses."

ꕥ

"Take us to the airport," Brad said to the cab driver. Joyce was disappointed they weren't going to have a few days to themselves, but after almost getting blown up, she was anxious to get home.

When they arrived at the airport, Brad reached over the seat and handed the driver his fare and tip. Once on the curb with their bags of clothes, they walked into the terminal.

"We're not staying," whispered Brad. "I want to sit here for a while to make sure no one was following us."

Joyce didn't ask why or what Brad planned on doing after he was sure no one had followed them. She just watched everyone as he was doing. No one looked suspicious. No one lingered by them or kept passing back and forth. Sixty minutes had passed when Brad got out his phone and called Jake.

He filled him in on all that had happened so far and on their plans to take a few days to themselves.

"Are you sure you'll be safe? I'd rather you go back home."

"We've been sitting at the airport for over an hour, and no one has followed us here, at least not into the airport terminal."

"Can you change your appearance somehow, so when you walk back outside, no one would notice it's you? Just in case someone is waiting for you."

"Yeah, Joyce brought a wig with her. It's Peggy's, and she was going to give it back to her if you guys were still out here."

"Call me again once you arrive where you're going, and stay safe. Be careful."

ꕥ

Brad put on a ball cap and a pair of shorts he had in his carryon and left the restroom. He leaned against the wall and waited for Joyce. He watched everyone passing by. He couldn't remember the last time he was so paranoid, but then he'd never been poisoned or almost blown up before.

"Can you tell me where the security check is?"

He looked up and saw a woman with dark hair, lots of mascara, and blue eyeshadow.

"Ah no, I don't know where . . . Joyce?"

She snuggled up to him. "Yep, it's me."

He took her hand. "Let's get out of here. You look good, by the way."

ꕥ

Brad and Joyce were enjoying the view as they called Jake on speaker phone. "We're here and safe."

"Thank goodness. Before you called, I was reading online about Pearl's trial. Closing statements are in the morning. There was mention that four of the five cops involved have been arrested. They also showed the hotel parking lot with the two unrecognizable cars that were in the explosion. The woman who drove into your car could not be saved. I've put her family on the prayer list at church. I'm so glad you two are all right.

I think you'll be safe where you are. Keep me updated."

Peggy said, "Is there anything you need? Or something we can do at the shelter?"

"Your voice sounds wonderful," said Joyce. "Thank you, but we're good. We'll keep you both updated. Brad and I have some catching up to do"

Jake had his fingers in his ears and was humming.

Peggy laughed and disconnected.

ꕥ

Adeline and Marie were having coffee that afternoon in the loft. It was quiet there, just before the after-school rush came in. Marie was doing so well. Adeline was a little upset when Jake said she'd be having an assistant, but after Marie arrived, Adeline had been sleeping better, her appetite returned, and she had more energy.

"After we have coffee, I think we'll call it a day and go home."

Marie looked at the coffee clock on the wall. "That will give me enough time to cook Barry supper before he goes to work."

"How do you like Boone?"

"I love that I can walk or bike everywhere. One thing I would like to find is the library. I haven't been in a library in such a long time. I spent too much money buying books, but I need to start saving now."

"Our first order of business in the morning is heading to the library. I'll pick you up, although we could probably walk. I heard it's going to rain. Jake's mom works there. I'll introduce you. She walks and bikes all over town. Maybe you two can get together and go on a bike trip to Legend's Park." Adeline gave her a brief history of the park and things to do there.

"I would love that." *I truly love it here,* she thought. She rarely let Sam into her thoughts and all the trouble he was in. The trial was on the news one night, but she quickly changed the channel.

"I'll pick you up at eight. We'll go to the bakery for coffee and breakfast. I'll introduce you to Myra too. She provides us with our bakery items."

Adeline downed her coffee, threw the cup in the trash. "Let's go home."

As they left the café, Peggy was coming in. She gave them both a hug and wished them a good day.

ꕥ

Lenny arrived at his brother's house in Missouri. He didn't want to call first because he knew he would say no to the visit. He knocked, and he was face-to-face with his brother. Rick looked much younger than Lenny.

The double life he'd led for several decades was taking its toll. He wanted to settle down with one woman. The woman he chose was Pam. He wanted to see his son Jake again. He felt time was running out, and he wanted to spend the rest of his days with one good woman and his only child.

Rick opened the door, and to Lenny's surprise, he was invited in. Rick gave him a bear hug. "Where have you been?"

"Around," Lenny said, not sure of how much Rick knew about his lifestyle. "Traveling, working, hanging out. You know I never had any hobbies."

"I'm retired and loving it." He invited him in and pointed to chair for him to sit.

They talked for an hour, and Lenny asked the question he'd come for. "Have you heard from Pam and Jake? Do you know where they live?"

"I would have to say no to both of your questions." No way was Rick going to tell his sleaze of a brother where they were. "Haven't they kept in touch? I thought you two were married."

In reality, he was married to Pam. It wasn't until afterward that he married all those other women. At least in his mind he was married to Pam. "We are, but we just separated for a while." I can't believe you don't know where they are. You must be lying, thought Lenny.

"How rude of me. Let me go make coffee. You still like yours black?"

"I drink it with cream now and a lot of sugar. I've been hanging out at the coffee shops lately and like the coffee, but the added extras is what makes it special." He didn't have to tell his brother he picked up women while he was there but didn't find anyone he wanted to spend the rest of his life with, and that's when the idea of Pam and Jake came to mind. Rick walked to the kitchen.

Lenny got up and walked around, looking at his brother's living room. There was a phone stand by the door with a pile of mail. He looked through the stack and found a letter from Pam. He quickly took out his cell phone and took a picture of the return address. He put the stack of mail the way it was and sat back down on the couch.

Lenny was pretending to read one of the magazines on the coffee table when Rick came in with the coffee. "You put in your own cream and sugar."

When he added the right amount, he took one of the packaged cookies on the tray and dunked it into the creamy liquid.

CHAPTER TWENTY-FOUR

Several weeks after Pearl was found guilty by jury, she was sentenced to life in prison, with the possibility of parole, for kidnapping, attempted murder, and drug dealing. Sam was found guilty for drug dealing, kidnapping, and a few more felonies. He had yet to be sentenced. Even though there was proof of Sam's guilt, he never once admitted he did anything wrong.

ꕥ

Adeline's Creamy Cake

Mix and bake white cake mix per package instructions
When cool, poke top with fork and pour 4 oz. heavy whipping cream over top
Refrigerate for one hour
Frost with Cool Whip

Arnie likes fresh strawberries on top of the Cool Whip

Printed in the United States
By Bookmasters